THE FIRST STONE

Private Eye Felix Strange doesn't work homicide cases. He saw enough dead bodies fighting in Iran, a war that left him with a crippling disease which has neither name nor cure. So when Strange is summoned to a Manhattan hotel room to investigate the dead body of America's most-loved preacher, he'd rather not get involved. Strange has a week to find the killer, and less time to get the black-market medicine he needs to stay alive. In an America where biblical prophecy is a foreign policy, Strange knows he's being watched and that his hiring is no accident. In a race against time, Strange must face religious police and organized crime, while uncovering a conspiracy that reaches the very heart of his newly fundamentalist nation.

ELLIOTT HALL

THE FIRST STONE

Complete and Unabridged

CHARNWOOD
Leicester

First published in Great Britain in 2009 by
John Murray (Publishers)
An Hachette UK Company
London

First Charnwood Edition
published 2009
by arrangement with
John Murray (Publishers)
An Hachette UK Company
London

British Library CIP Data

Hall, Elliott, *1978* –
   The first stone.
   1. Private investigators- -New York (State)- -New
York- -Fiction. 2. Suspense fiction.
   3. Large type books.
   I. Title
   823.9′2–dc22

   ISBN 978–1–84782–918–4

Published by
F. A. Thorpe (Publishing)
Anstey, Leicestershire

Set by Words & Graphics Ltd.
Anstey, Leicestershire
Printed and bound in Great Britain by
T. J. International Ltd., Padstow, Cornwall

This book is printed on acid-free paper

For my mother and father

And early in the morning he came again into the temple, and all the people came unto him; and he sat down, and taught them.

And the scribes and Pharisees brought unto him a woman taken in adultery; and when they had set her in the midst,

They say unto him, Master, this woman was taken in adultery, in the very act.

Now Moses in the law commanded us, that such should be stoned: but what sayest thou?

This they said, tempting him, that they might have to accuse him. But Jesus stooped down, and with his finger wrote on the ground, as though he heard them not.

So when they continued asking him, he lifted up himself, and said unto them, He that is without sin among you, let him first cast a stone at her.

And again he stooped down, and wrote on the ground.

And they which heard it, being convicted by their own conscience, went out one by one, beginning at the eldest, even unto the last: and Jesus was left alone, and the woman standing in the midst.

When Jesus had lifted up himself, and saw none but the woman, he said unto her, Woman, where are those thine accusers? hath no man condemned thee?

She said, No man, Lord. And Jesus said unto her, Neither do I condemn thee: go, and sin no more.

— **The Gospel according to John viii:2-11**

Sunday

'For God so loved the world that He gave His one and only Son, that whoever believes in Him shall not perish but have eternal life,' said Brother Isaiah on TV to his dead body lying on the bed below. The men leaning over his corpse didn't hear, and if they had they would have regarded the words as prophecy, not irony. I kept my distance and let them squint.

'It looks like strangulation,' one of the men said, pointing to the faded purple bruising that ringed Isaiah's neck. He picked up Isaiah's hands for a closer look. 'No sign of defensive wounds. Nothing visible under the fingernails but we won't know for sure until forensics gets here.' The man — who was older and must have been their lieutenant — sounded like he'd actually done real police work before he took up his new career regulating women's hemlines. The younger officers clustered around him fingered their hats and listened with the respectful attention of students on a field trip.

The TV Isaiah was everything you expected from a man of God. His strong, square jaw was set against the fallen world, and his eyes managed to be both piercing and compassionate at the same time. His full, bone-white hair made him look like an Old Testament prophet after a visit to the barber. The Brother Isaiah on the bed was just a wrinkled old man in boxer shorts and long black socks who'd died in a room that was not his own.

'As you can see,' the lieutenant continued, 'there are no signs of a struggle, here or in any of the other rooms.' The room was as plush as you'd expect the executive suite at the Bingham Grand to be. TV Isaiah looked down on his own corpse from the screen that took up most of one wall, his voice manifested through surround-sound speakers. The four-poster bed his body lay on was something heavy and eighteenth-century, its twisted sheets the only sign of disorder in the room. The walls and fixtures were dark-stained oak and polished brass, so every young executive vice-president who stayed here could fancy himself one of the robber barons of old.

Not all the lieutenant's charges were behaving themselves. A few had broken away from the group and were molesting the room. They rifled drawers and picked up objects with their bare hands, smearing their fingerprints everywhere. One examined Isaiah's suits hanging in the closet, brushing away possible hair and fibres as if he were the old man's valet. Another poked around in the night table, flipping through the Gideon Bible before putting objects back in whatever place he found convenient.

A flushing sound came from another room. One of the Daveys had used the toilet of a crime scene.

'Jesus Christ,' escaped my lips.

Their heads snapped in my direction. 'Lieutenant,' said one of the officers, 'what's he doing here?'

4

The circle of faces turned in my direction. I smiled back at them, and kept holding up the wall with my shoulder.

'Somebody turn that TV off,' White said as he entered the bedroom. 'Everybody but Strange, get out.'

The lieutenant herded his charges out of the room. They were reluctant to leave such a famous corpse, and blamed me with their eyes.

It was the first time I'd seen Ezekiel White up close. His grey off-the-rack suit advertised his commitment to Protestant modesty. His dyed, thinning hair and generous pot belly did not. He had thin, humourless lips and a nose that flared wide and flat like a hammerhead shark. It was a mystery to me how he'd ever got on television, even in the more physically forgiving arena of twenty-four-hour news.

'You're better dressed than I expected,' he said.

I assumed he meant the fedora in my hand. 'I like to confound expectations, Mr White.'

'That's Dr White.' A doctor of theology, not medicine, given by an institution of questionable academic but unimpeachable political integrity.

'It's good to see you've got some people with experience,' I said, 'now that you're supposed to be actual police.'

The Elders had some old ideas about how the citizens of this country should live, and they weren't inclined to rely on the honour system to make sure people followed them. They didn't trust law enforcement, so the Elders created an entirely new parallel organization responsible for

5

the nation's moral hygiene. White got the top job as a reward for a lifetime of bootlicking on national television. I'd heard he had a nose for dirt better than any hack's and a love of blackmail that was almost sexual. He sounded more than qualified.

'All of my officers are good men,' White said. What he meant was that they were loyal to him and didn't sleep in on Sundays. The mid-level officers like the lieutenant were cops enticed away from secular forces by the promise of advancement. They had been promoted beyond their abilities, but at least their time on the job had left a residue of professionalism and common sense.

The rank and file had been filled by a type of clean-cut kid we called Daveys. They were the Elders' foot soldiers: home-schooled, God-fearing kids who haunted the corridors of power with recommendations from their pastors and a willingness to do anything for the cause. Their ignorance of the secular world was considered an asset, not a liability. Hacks who'd barely learned to shave now had the power of arrest.

'Did you take a look at the body?' White asked.

'From a distance.'

'What do you think?'

'I think one of your boys had a very good question: Why did you drag me away from a perfectly good sandwich?'

An hour ago, two of White's goons had appeared in the reflection of the Starlight's chrome counter. The badges they flashed — an eagle surmounted on a golden cross — looked like they had been won at Coney Island, but the diner went silent anyway. The name on the badge said 'Committee for Child Protection'. Everyone called them the Holy Rollers, just not to their faces.

Before I could explain the allure of the famous Starlight beef brisket on rye they had each taken an arm and dragged me away. I had decided to go along peacefully; I was curious, and the Starlight didn't deliver to Rikers Island.

White gave me a sour look. 'Do you know who this man was?'

Brother Isaiah's radio programme, *Hour of Deliverance*, was syndicated in thirty-two states. The majority of his listeners were still in the South, but fear and official patronage had pushed his message steadily north of the Mason-Dixon Line. His organization, the Crusade of Love, had been dedicated to missionary work in Africa. After what happened in Houston, he'd been offered a seat on the council of Elders and asked to bring the Crusade home. Brother Isaiah had agreed, on the condition that his organization retained complete autonomy. The Elders needed his enormous popularity and moral authority to cement their rule, so they were in no position to refuse. Somewhere over the Atlantic the Crusade went from building wells and saving souls to being shock troops for Old Testament morality.

'I never caught Brother Isaiah's radio show,' I said. 'I didn't think he appeared on television.'

'He thought all televangelists were charlatans,'

7

White said. 'That footage is from the last Day of Remembrance, re-broadcast in honour of his arrival in New York.' White's thick, unfashionable black glasses enlarged his eyes, giving an impression of increased watchfulness that didn't include heightened understanding.

'I've had a look at your file, Mr Strange. I'm one of the few people who can read it unabridged. Your service to our country in the Great Patriotic Crusade against Iran is truly remarkable, especially during the siege of the Khomeini Mosque.'

There were a lot of different names for our war with Iran. 'Great Patriotic Crusade' was a wolf-whistle between the Elders' true believers. The rest of the world used the term 'Greater Middle-Eastern War', as it was the easiest way to include all the insurrections, guerrilla wars and suicide attacks that happened in the region during the conflict. I just called it the worst three years of my life.

'You've served America before, and she needs your help again,' White continued. 'I want you to solve this murder.'

If he had seen something in my file that suggested appealing to my patriotism, then White must have been reading it upside down.

'Last time I checked you had an entire agency for that sort of thing,' I said. 'This is FBI territory, if not the secret service's.' I wasn't clear whether the secret service now guarded the real rulers of the country, or just the figurehead in the White House. 'Besides,' I said, 'I don't work murders.'

Murder's exalted status as the worst among crimes meant that they were worked by the best police, those who had proven themselves through years of putting down cases. I investigated the same things every other private eye did: infidelity, fraud, the occasional extortion or missing person to keep me awake in the afternoons. A body of this importance called for the Chief of Detectives and half the FBI. Right now I would have settled for any kind of cop, because there wasn't a single man with a real badge in the whole building.

'Look around you.'

On the night table was a framed, autographed flyer from the late President Adamson's first campaign. He was the hero of the Revivalist movement and a founder of the Council of Elders, the secret rulers of the new America. They were the ones responsible for turning Congress into the most prestigious puppet theatre in the world. The handwriting on the flyer was illegible, but it might as well have read: 'Après moi le fucking deluge'.

The rest of the table was loaded with smut. Glossies devoted to every possible kink and perversion were fanned out like coffee-table books. In the nightstand's open drawer I saw a dime bag of weed and another of what looked like cocaine, though it could just as easily have been MDMA or PCP. On the floor was a black plastic leash, white rope and two pairs of handcuffs.

'How many people do you think we want to see this?' White said.

'Somewhere south of one.'

'The Elders have told me to handle this matter. They don't trust the secular authorities.'

'And you in turn don't trust your own men.'

'Don't be ridiculous,' he said, not as offended as I'd expected him to be. 'I know the heart of every man who works for me. However, it has recently come to my attention that my agents are being shadowed.'

I let my scepticism show.

'I believe unreconstructed elements of the secular authorities, probably atheists and materialists, are trying to undermine our work. I can't risk them finding out about Brother Isaiah's death.'

'He was the spiritual counsellor for millions of people,' I said. 'You may have gelded the domestic press, but the foreign news outlets are going to start asking questions as soon as he misses a broadcast.'

'I'd throw every foreign correspondent out of the country if I could,' White said. They weren't as susceptible to his usual method of media control: promise an exclusive as compensation for killing the story (carrot) and threaten to cut the entire network's access if they didn't keep their mouths shut (stick). 'They're objectively pro-terrorist and anti-family, to a man. However, the Elders believe that would be unwise in the long term, so my hands are tied. Brother Isaiah had intended to go upstate tonight. He often retreated to fast and pray, so no one will expect him to appear until his next broadcast.'

'When's that?'

'Next Sunday, seven o'clock,' White said. 'I'll give you five thousand dollars as an advance, then twenty more when we have a conviction. I know you need the money.'

'I need the trouble less. I'll pass,' I said, and started for the door.

'Mr Strange, don't insult both our intelligences by pretending that you have a choice.'

I paused at the bedroom threshold and considered my future. They'd probably start with a complete audit of all my tax returns for the last ten years. Then they'd scrutinize every case I'd ever worked, to get at my licence. After that it would be my friends, especially anyone who might lend me money. They wouldn't hurt me; poverty would do that for them. I could try to fight them, but I'd lose, and my damn curiosity had already gotten the better of me anyway.

'I assume this room is his.' White nodded. 'Not bad for a holy man.'

'The Crusade paid for everything.'

'I'm sure it did. Is that the murder weapon?' I said, pointing to the leash.

'We don't know yet.'

'Who found him?'

'A maid. We're holding her as a material witness.'

I did another circuit of the room. Manhattan glowed through the sliding doors that led out to the balcony. A blimp hovered in the distance, one of five the NYPD had watching the city at all times. A ten-storey cross glowed from its home on top of the Empire State Building. It had been built a few years ago purely with

11

donations, old ladies sending dollars they could not spare so all of Manhattan would fall under its neon shadow.

Whoever rented the suite could admire the city's tallest peaks from his bed, imagining himself master of all he surveyed. Brother Isaiah would have seen it differently. His eyes had been attuned to the spectrum of sin, silhouettes of lust and temptation visible through the high-rise walls.

'Tell me what you see,' White said.

'The conclusion we're supposed to draw from this scene is that Brother Isaiah died in the company of a fallen woman, during or after sex, in some kind of auto-erotic asphyxiation.'

'That is a disgusting and ridiculous accusation,' White said. His eyes widened and he showed some of his bottom teeth, the beginning of the righteous indignation that had made him so popular on Sunday panel shows.

'Of course it's ridiculous. Do you know anyone who arranges their pornography this tastefully?'

White declined to answer.

The drugs were still wrapped up. There were no clothes strewn about the place or any evidence of a woman except some make-up smears on the sheets. The bedroom looked like a twelve-year-old's idea of a den of sin. 'If I hadn't seen the crime scene myself I might have been inclined to believe it. People that interested in the intimate lives of others usually have peculiar habits of their own.' I gave the room another once-over to be sure. 'This whole room is a poison pill ready to dissolve as soon as the murder becomes public; someone has constructed it to give you the finger.' I could see White didn't like my reasoning, but he couldn't argue with it. 'Do you have any suspects?'

White pulled a stack of files from his briefcase. 'These are a sample of the threats received by Brother Isaiah in the last year. The Crusade's work produces some discontent.'

'That's a surprise.' Sending in undercover agents to find unlicensed dancing, under-age drinking and anti-faith discrimination — which meant whatever they said it did — produced a lot of things. Discontent was one of them. Fear, in much greater quantities, was another.

'The Crusade arrives somewhere, makes a lot of headline-grabbing accusations, and then leaves others to clean up the mess,' White said. 'Our work — which actually drains the swamp of sin — never gets the recognition it deserves.'

It was no secret that the Crusade and the Committee for Child Protection didn't get along. The Committee was the Elders' official attack dog, with full law enforcement powers. The Crusade was really nothing more than a citizens' group, albeit a very organized and powerful one. They couldn't arrest anyone that they accused of impropriety; that was the Rollers' job. The publicity the Crusade generated meant he had to investigate their accusations. (That was what angered White so much.) His officers may have been the ones who put on the cuffs, but it was the Crusade that got all the credit.

'I'll need to look at some of those accusations. I expect the Crusade will put up a fight,' I said.

'They'll be happy to turn over something to me, but I doubt you'll find anything,' White said. He sat down on the edge of the bed and looked at the corpse. 'I'd be surprised if half a dozen people actually know why the Crusade is here. Brother Isaiah kept all the big fish to himself.'

A Crusade Mission was half old-time revival, half inquisition. The organization wasn't on an organized tour of the country; it just arrived where it knew it could cause trouble. The festivities usually began with hundreds of young women taking a purity oath — a pledge to stay unspoiled for their future husbands. There were often mass baptisms or conversions that served as a warm-up act for the main event: an address by Brother Isaiah. Every network in the country would cover it, because they knew it was during his sermon that Brother Isaiah named names.

In Cleveland, he'd destroyed the careers of six Councilmen by accusing them of atheist sympathies. He'd also dragged more than fifty people out of the closet over concern for their spiritual welfare. Those ruined lives were just the appetizer. Isaiah's centrepiece was images of the mayor with a woman much younger than his wife. The networks made sure the photos went out nationally.

'For all we know, the real cases may have died with him,' I said. Someone might be resting easier tonight, knowing that the elegant machine that had once held their secrets was now just another lump of meat.

14

'You should look at the threats first,' White said. 'I'm convinced that the only ones with both the lack of conscience and contempt for God to commit this outrage are secular nihilists.'

The murder of one of the most powerful Christian leaders in the country would of course be blamed on an unhinged atheist. The wheels of martyrdom were already spinning.

'And if he isn't an atheist?'

'Then we'll put the jihadi where he can never hurt anyone again,' White said, pointing down. He didn't have a chin so much as a piece of gristle that wobbled when he became emphatic. 'It's where he's going anyway. We'll just be giving him a six-foot head start.' He expected laughter but I'm not that polite.

'I'm sure you realize the gravity of the situation,' White said, but I could feel him warming up for a lecture anyway. 'We are besieged by enemies foreign and domestic. Islamofascists attack our heroes in the Holy Land. Atheists and their liberal tools damage the foundations of our society with terrorist-coddling and sexual licence. We must find the murderer. If we don't, when the American people hear of this atrocity, they may lose the will to fight . . . ' He trailed off, as he always did during these diatribes, to let his audience imagine whichever outcome they found most terrifying. 'A full confession, especially about the staging, would be preferable.'

'I'll see what I can do.'

'There's one more thing,' White said. 'We found this near the body.' He showed me a type of digital Dictaphone that hadn't been made in at least fifteen years.

'Is there anything on it?'

'Brother Isaiah's last sermon. The date on the file is three days ago.'

So there was no hope of hearing the killer's voice in the background then. 'Is there anything special in the sermon, anything out of the ordinary?' I asked. 'Does he mention anyone by name?'

'The themes are fairly typical for one of Brother Isaiah's sermons,' White said. 'It won't have anything to do with his death, but take a copy anyway; it might do a heathen like you some good.'

I did as I was told and copied the file to my phone.

White put an envelope of reassuring thickness in my breast pocket. 'You don't work for me. You've never met me. If I find out you've said otherwise, or you've told anyone about Brother Isaiah, I'll make you disappear.' He said the last part matter-of-factly, because that was how it was done. They probably had a standard form, just to track the expenses.

'I may not get very far without some kind of official sanction.'

Most of the other investigators I knew had been cops. They still looked like police, no matter what their tax returns said. Their walk had been refined over years of patrol, their eyes numbed to the unpleasant side of humanity. They were used to walking into a room with the full authority of the state behind them, and

16

nobody had told their body they no longer carried a badge. That demeanour had its advantages: since they talked and walked like cops, people tended to treat them like cops, which gave them a lot more gravitas than the average private dick.

I didn't have the look of authority to rely on, but that wasn't always a disadvantage. People smelled the cop on you whether you wanted them to or not. It was easier for me to become an electrician, courier, or some other working stiff people weren't inclined to take notice of. People might see the military in me if they looked hard enough, but that didn't mean much. The country was full of veterans doing everything under the sun to get by.

'You're here because I've heard that you're a very resourceful man,' White said. 'I'm sure you'll manage, and I don't want to know how.' He handed me a phone. 'You'll find a number in its memory that you can reach me on. Use that phone, and nothing else; it's encrypted. Even with these precautions, I never want to hear you say his name again.' White looked at the corpse and lapsed into silence. 'I'll expect regular updates.'

'Then you'll hear from me soon,' I said.

'Aren't you going to take the files?'

'Send them along with the others. You know where I live.'

The suite's living room was as plush as the bedroom. There was a large table for holding conferences and a crushed-velvet sofa with matching Queen Anne chairs. The Rollers loitered in a semicircle in front of the door and pretended that they hadn't been eavesdropping.

'You think we don't know what we're doing,' the lieutenant said. He was a well-built man whose greying brush cut gave him an inch on me. He would be on the Committee for Child Protection boxing team, if such a thing existed.

'If you knew what you were doing, I wouldn't be here,' I said. 'Now do you mind?'

'I heard you learned a new dance over in the Big Sandbox,' the lieutenant said. 'Why don't you show it to us? I want to see this famous 'Tehran Twitch'.' He mimed a series of spastic jerks.

The other officers laughed on cue.

'Are you going to get out of my way?'

'Not unless you've got the stones to try and make me,' said the lieutenant, leaning in. There's a fundamental flaw in the thinking of most people who fight for sport. They assume that both people have to put their hands up before anything can happen. That's why he didn't see the fingers of my left hand go from my waist into the side of his neck.

The lieutenant coughed and tried to suck in air as he fell down. The others didn't do much but stare.

'What is going on in here?' White yelled.

I let him take in the sight of me standing over one of his underlings before I started for the door.

'Tell your Daveys to stay out of my way,' I said. 'Amateur night is over.'

18

★ ★ ★

I worked out of my home or lived in my office, depending on how you looked at it. The ink-stained pine desk from which I did all my business was big enough to make me look significant. The two chairs that stood in front of it were uncomfortable enough to encourage clients to get to the point. The venetian blinds behind my desk had been purchased to slant the sunlight in forbidding ways. My office was what a private investigator's was supposed to look like, down to the block lettering on the frosted glass front door. Clients found that reassuring.

The files White had sent over covered every available surface. I'd started three hours ago on the Crusade's cases in New York; my takeout hadn't gone down well, and I wasn't ready to face the delusion and mania that made up any organization's crazy file. The Crusade had officially been in New York for less than two days, but the surveillance reports indicated that agents — their names redacted — had been laying the groundwork for months. The Crusade had put eyes and ears in every neighbourhood of every borough. The logistics required to run that many undercover operatives must have been enormous, but it was how they could arrive in a city and make a flurry of high-profile accusations immediately, a blitzkrieg in the war for souls.

The MO that emerged from the case files matched what I'd heard. Half of the operations were straight surveillance, the rest provocations. 'Cured' gay men who looked young enough to be seventeen were sent into known homosexual establishments. If anyone inside was stupid enough to make a pass, they'd say the place was aiding and abetting sexual abuse. Obnoxious people wearing prominent gold crosses were sent into restaurants and businesses to see if their behaviour elicited any comments that could be construed as insulting to their faith. Armies of good-looking youths haunted bars and night-clubs, trying to convince others to buy their oregano and baking soda. Anyone who let anyone else have too much fun would be referred to the authorities.

In practice most people ended up with nothing worse than fines and threats. Being able to go on national television and say they'd found the sinners was what was important. A few were sent away, and some even deserved it. There was nothing in the files big enough to open a press conference, certainly nothing worth assassinating an Elder over.

I streamed Brother Isaiah's last sermon from my phone to the stereo. 'Brothers and sisters, in the last few years I have travelled all over this great country spreading the news of our Lord's love and forgiveness. I have been fortunate to meet and pray with many of you; your faith is a source of great comfort and strength to me. There is a question I know many of you would like answered, because it is the one I hear most often. It is a question that the disciples asked of Jesus Himself: 'What shall be the sign of Thy coming, and of the end of the world?' '

Whatever I thought of his beliefs, Brother

Isaiah had possessed a magnificent voice. It had both gravity and warmth, the voice of an old friend telling you important news. The rest of the sermon focused on how God's plan for his children was too sublime for any human being to understand, and saying you did was the height of pride. It sounded like the usual exhortation to shut up and do as you're told, but I'd never been to Sunday school. I stopped the voice of God, and turned on the television.

'A homicide bomber attacked a coalition checkpoint west of Hebron this morning,' the TV said. They used to tell you who the bombers were, before mothers of four and grandfathers began strapping on C-4. A car burned near a line of barbed wire. The soldiers forming a cordon around the scene were watched over by a line of tanks, their turrets pointed into the desert. 'None of our heroes was hurt in the explosion, thank Jesus,' the peroxide reporter said. 'They truly are watched over by a higher power.' The camera lingered over one private's stricken face, staring at the charred body parts kept out of shot. He hadn't been in the Holy Land long enough to grow the grim mask the other men in his unit wore. That shot would probably get someone fired.

I left the TV on in case it said something useful, and opened the crazy file. It wasn't what I expected. In between the crayon rants about the second coming were pleas, of innocence and for forgiveness. Every single one of them was addressed to Brother Isaiah directly.

'Dear Brother, forgive my sin, I was trapped in

21

a loveless marriage . . . '

'We know our son made a mistake, but he has repented and come back to Jesus. With the drug possession on his record, my son will never be able to go to college. If you could find it in your heart . . . '

'Brother Isaiah, I have struggled with this terrible sickness for my whole life. I have finally received the counselling and prayer I so desperately needed. I have attached a letter from the pastor of the Colorado New Life Rehabilitation Center, pronouncing me cured. If you were to tell the proper authorities that I am now a fully recovering homosexual, I may be reinstated in my teaching job . . . '

A news segment on the Middle East always ended with a reminder of why we fight. Children played in the dust of the new settlements, obliging the camera with smiles and laughter. In the background I could see American soldiers manning the guard towers of the security wall. Orthodox Jews prayed at the Wailing Wall, tears of devotion mixing with the sweat that escaped their yarmulkes. Jesus still hung over the altar of the Church of the Holy Sepulchre. His patiently bloody face presided over the Delta soldiers who lined the church's walls. They cradled their rifles and watched everything through wraparound sunglasses, the red cross on their shoulders marking them not as healers, but guardians of that sacred place.

The Crusade had separated letters that made explicit threats into a smaller pile. The files included dossiers on every single writer and information on their families if the case officer thought it relevant. Most were easy to reject out of hand as empty threats made by angry and fearful men. Only one had the dangerous combination of rage and lucidity:

'Dear Brother Isaiah: With the support of people like you, the government sent me out into the desert to die.' I checked the handwriting to make sure it wasn't mine. 'I spent three years at the Arkangel settlement. The tour was only supposed to last a year. Most of the time we traded rifle fire with children. One morning — ' Someone had redacted the rest of that sentence, and the whole of the next two pages. 'I can't sleep. I see that morning whenever I close my eyes. You've turned my own mother against me. She's your biggest fan, never misses a broadcast. When I left for the Holy Land she was so proud that I was fulfilling God's will. I tried to tell her what it was like, what I did, but she won't listen. She just tells me to pray. I learned how to kill people because of you. I like doing it with a 30.06 rifle from far away. If you and that travelling freak show ever come to New York, I'll show you just how good a student I am.'

The author's name was Jack Small, an honourably discharged ex-marine. His tour in Israel had earned him a purple heart, a commendation, and a case of post-traumatic stress disorder. There were clues about the incident Jack had referred to, but it must have been bad to earn two pages of black. It could be ordinary bureaucratic ass-covering, or the Crusade was trying to hide something. I'd have

23

to pay them a visit tomorrow and find out.

The news ended with nothing said about Brother Isaiah. The next programme was a panel shout-fest. The topic was whether America should aid Israel in building the third temple. By aid they meant do it for them, as the Israelis didn't seem to be enthusiastic about the idea. The first step would be destroying the Dome of the Rock, and God knows what kind of new hell that would unleash. I'd seen footage of Israeli demonstrations against our presence and our plans, on foreign new channels that weren't banned as much as officially unavailable in this country. That didn't stop half the population from rigging up pirate satellite dishes, camouflaging them like the secret antennae the East Germans had set up to hear rock music on Radio Free Europe. It was worth the risk of heavy fines to get away from inane programmes like this one, and the French stations sometimes showed tits.

The panellists were stacked three to one, maybe reflecting the proportion of congregations still uneasy with the idea. I wondered how long they'd tolerate this debate, at least in the open. I turned off the TV and picked up my cell phone.

'Felix,' Benny said. 'What can I do for you?'

'Did you get those Knicks tickets?' I said, which was our code for asking if it was safe to talk.

'No one's around,' Benny said. We counted silently to three, and then activated encryption for the phone line.

24

'Why don't we use encryption all the time?' Benny said.

'Using encryption that doesn't have a back door for law enforcement is illegal, remember?'

'Not if you are law enforcement,' he said, which wouldn't do much good for me if we were caught. 'Now tell me what you want.'

'Can you meet me tomorrow?'

'You need a secure line to ask me on a date?'

'Go fuck yourself, this is important. Yes or no?'

'No. I gotta go up to Albany tomorrow and meet with some Holy Roller shitbirds. How about lunch the day after?'

'I'll see you at the Starlight.'

'What a fucking surprise,' Benny said, and hung up.

The fat envelope lay on my desk, a few hundred-dollar bills poking out. Under normal circumstances, someone like Ezekiel White would never give five thousand dollars to an independent like me. If he wanted to go outside his own organization, there were several large firms discreet enough even for his paranoid mind.

White and his people were part of a diverse group of zealots, charlatans, fantasists and thugs collectively known as the Revivalist movement. The single name made cursing them more efficient. The Revivalists had been the foot soldiers for Adamson's presidential campaign. They stuffed envelopes, knocked on doors, and maybe knocked a few other things if the stories of polling place intimidation were believed. The Elders had inherited the movement, and used it with even fewer scruples than the late President. Besides my few encounters with the Holy Rollers, I hadn't had much contact with the rest of the movement.

That went double for the Crusade of Love. I had never knowingly been within a hundred yards of its operatives or officials. We'd been swimming in the same cesspools (if these files were any indication). They might have picked up my name there. I certainly hadn't done anything lately to merit this kind of assignment, and I wasn't important enough to be made an example of. The Crusade was completely independent and never let the Elders forget it. As much its members hated White, I couldn't imagine them asking an unbeliever to investigate the murder of their household God. It wouldn't be worth it just to spite a rival in the same racket.

That left the Elders themselves. Those twenty-four men hid in plain sight, issuing orders to the President and Congress from Cabinet posts, churches and broadcast centres. Every single one was a pastor, priest, minister, or self-declared man of God. They were the only people who could give White marching orders, but I doubted that they even knew my name. I would have thought that the Elders would take the murder of one of their own more seriously, but I must be wrong. White was still in charge.

Thinking any more about it right now was pointless. All I really had was speculation, and that still wasn't admissible in a court of law. I'd just have to figure out what the angles were before I became expendable.

My watch beeped. I locked the files and the money in the safe behind my desk and went into the bathroom. There were three prescription bottles in my medicine cabinet, all from different pharmacies known to bend the rules. I shook the meagre contents of each one, let the pills fall over one another in the harsh fluorescent light.

The blue pills were called Delectra, officially prescribed to ease the nausea of Aids sufferers and those undergoing chemotherapy. The green meanies were called Evalacet, an arthritis medication I took in very small doses to treat muscle and joint pain. Those two I was supposed to take every twelve hours. I was almost out of Delectra. If I didn't get any more in the next twenty-four hours, breakfast on Tuesday would be a challenge.

The last bottle of pills I took once a day. They were red and had no brand name, their uses so specialized they didn't merit a soft-focus marketing campaign. The proper name had about sixteen letters, a third of which were 'x's. The drug had originally been developed to treat severe epilepsy and had been tested off-label on Parkinson's. They were what really kept the syndrome in check, and allowed me to function as a semi-normal human being.

I was uninsurable due to a pre-existing condition that no medical body would admit existed. Sometimes I convinced a sympathetic doctor to write me a prescription for one of the symptoms; otherwise I'd have to scare up a forged scrip. Either way I still paid for all the medication myself, out of pockets that were already empty. The five thousand White had given me was promised to someone else. Having a week to solve this case was bad enough, but I was going to be out of red pills a few days before that. The bonus White had offered was the only way to get them. I'd have to come up with results fast.

At least I finally had a real case. I spent most of my days exposing the petty deception that was the bread and butter of any private eye: insurance frauds and cheating husbands, with no more than a few grand or custody of some brat hanging in the balance. I'd wanted a big case, and you couldn't get bigger than the Isaiah murder. There were about a hundred different ways it could go sideways on me, but I didn't care. I was tired of stooping for nickels in the gutter.

Monday

If it wasn't for the giant crucifix that dominated the lobby, the Crusade's New York office might have been the headquarters of any multinational corporation. Ten feet of unpainted wood was driven into a dirt oasis cut out of the white parquet floor, its tiles reverberating under patent leather shoes and three-inch pumps. Bird sounds and soft music were piped in through speakers hidden in the walls. An olive tree stood beside the cross, a plaque beneath it reading: 'Transplanted from Bethlehem, Eretz Yisrael'. The high walls ended in skylights, to let as much of the Lord's sunlight shine down on His children as possible. If there was a waiting room in heaven it looked like this, except for the men in bullet-proof vests carrying assault rifles. They had no badges or official markings, which meant they were contractors from Stillwater Corporation's private army.

On the wall was a collage of photographs taken in Ghana. Happy baptized orphans stood in front of brand-new churches and schools, built courtesy of the Crusade of Love. The organization had drilled wells, helped with irrigation and sanitation, and spread the Word. I probably would have taken issue with a lot of the teaching in those schools, but at least the kids would be alive to make up their own minds. I couldn't remember why Brother Isaiah had

31

originally gone on his mission to Africa. It had happened before Houston. That was less than ten years ago, but anything before it felt like ancient history.

A collection of teddy bears, candles and hand-written prayers surrounded a brazier inscribed with Bible passages in Hebrew, Latin and English, an eternal flame sputtering in the centre. The destruction of Houston had eclipsed our own local tragedy. New Yorkers still lived beneath those two ghostly silhouettes, but now at least we could mourn our dead in private. It had fallen to the city of Houston to be a symbol of and justification for the strange and terrifying new world we were all imprisoned in.

Above the shrine was a large plasma-screen television showing the same Houston memorial service I'd seen in the hotel room. Brother Isaiah stood on a raised podium in the National Mall, the President at his right hand, the Vice-President on his left, and a crowd of thousands in front of them. A giant projection screen showed stock photos of Houston landmarks: San Jacinto Monument, City Hall and the Hartmann Bridge. The statue of Sam Houston had been photographed so that his finger pointed in the audience's direction.

It was the way the country wanted to remember the city. The truth was more than most could bear. Downtown Houston had been raptured up to heaven, leaving behind a crater ringed by rubble and melted steel. The mushroom cloud had loomed above for hours in the still air, the angel of death inspecting his work before the winds blew him in the direction of fresh victims all over the state. Men in spacesuits picked through the rubble, looking for evidence and remains. I had watched from a mess hall in Germany while a dozen news anchors struggled to describe the devastation without using the word perched on the tip of their tongues: Hiroshima.

I wondered if a similar memorial ceremony was ever held in Iran, an ayatollah addressing the mountains and refugee camps to which his people had been scattered. Behind him would be projections of Tehran landmarks. Like us, they would show their city as they wanted to remember it: all eight thousand marble blocks of Azadi Tower in place, a skyline of whole buildings and minarets that still reached for the sky, streets not littered with shrapnel and unexploded cluster bombs. The city itself, unlike Houston, was still standing. The weapon had left concrete and steel intact, and taken instead those who had called the city home, through swift trauma or slow poisoning by radiation.

There would be no people, in case someone recognized one of those who had disappeared or been left to die. The metropolis known as Tehran had became Ghost Town in a single, terrifying flash of light. They had always denied involvement in Houston, and almost two years later we said the same thing about Tehran. Two cities laid to waste, and no one called to account. Unless Iranians were different from ordinary human beings, they were as ignorant of our dead as we were of theirs.

I approached the front desk — shaped like an ark and big enough to be seaworthy — and was greeted with a level stare by the battle-axe behind it.

'Do you have an appointment?'

'No, ma'am,' I said. I'd nudged my voice in the direction of Kentucky before I came through the door. 'See, I've seen somethin', and — '

'You want to witness?'

'Yes, ma'am.'

'Sister Cecily,' the woman said over my shoulder.

I turned to see a young woman cradling a mug of coffee look up from a bench near the Bethlehem tree.

'Are you free?' The receptionist didn't wait for an answer. 'Escort this gentleman to the witness department.'

I watched the young woman's eyes hopscotch over the various shibboleths I'd attached to my suit. The American flag on my left lapel was practically mandatory just to walk down the street. What distinguished me from the average Joe was the Christ fish on the opposite lapel and the tie from a Christian university. She stood up, aimed a radiant smile in my direction, and motioned towards the elevator.

'I'm Frank Przowski,' I said.

'Pleased to meet you, Mr . . . ' she struggled.

I liked my fake names to be unpronounceable on the witness stand, and impossible to spell on complaint forms. 'Call me Frank.'

'Cecily Turner.'

We shook hands. The elevator arrived and

disgorged its cargo of men in double-breasted suits and women in demure ankle-length dresses. None of them was a native, as they'd point out if you gave them more than two words. They were true believers from the sprawling infill of the Sunbelt and the South, the rusted cities of the Midwest, and the old mining towns that still clung to the Appalachians. Eat a meal within earshot and you'd hear complaints about the driving, the lack of decent food in a place where the cuisine of the entire world was available, and the proud ignorance of the city they had come to save. They were an expeditionary army, here to reclaim the Devil's island for the Lord. Cecily pushed the twelfth floor.

'Ma'am, the reason I'm here — '

'It's our policy only to discuss these matters in a secure location, Frank,' she said. 'And call me Cecily.'

The mirrored walls of the elevator showed a woman in her mid-twenties, petite and much shorter than me even with the advantage of heels. A bun of auburn hair was curled tight on her head, leaving the pale neck exposed. She wore a blue pencil skirt that covered her knees with an inch or two to spare. Her jacket was of the same material, its high buttons and big shoulders almost military in appearance. I kept my observation discreet only for the sake of propriety; a woman always knows when she's being admired.

Cecily led me to an office big enough for her desk and an interviewee's single chair. The sound of manicured nails typing bled through the chipboard partitions that made up the walls. 'Please have a seat,' Cecily said. 'I'm sorry about the mess.' She put down her coffee mug and started looking through the stacks of papers that covered her desk. A conch shell paperweight rested on the edge of the desk closest to me. It was flush against a stack of manila folders, which bumped against the coffee mug. 'Ever since Brother Isaiah arrived in New York, we've been run off our feet.' Cecily handed me a thick three-ring binder. 'If you could start by telling me the types of sin you witnessed, that would be just super.'

The binder contained an alphabetical list of every crime and sexual act I'd ever heard of, and a few that were new to me. Whoever had compiled this list had led a very interesting life, or possessed the filthiest imagination I'd ever come across. Each of the transgressions listed had a number and a series of colour-coded categories, to collate precisely what kind of fiends were being brought to justice. Saying 'fuck' was just plain obscenity; 'Jesus fucking Christ' was obscenity and taking the Lord's name in vain. Prostitution was a trifecta of lust, greed and blasphemy. I would have thought that the second category contradicted the first and that the third was irrelevant, but the opinion of a non-believer didn't count for much nowadays.

We stared at each other across her desk for a few moments. 'I don't know where to start,' I said. 'I'm a little overwhelmed.'

Cecily gave me a sympathetic smile. 'Why don't you tell me what happened in your own words,' she said. 'Then I'll tell you what they did wrong. Okay?'

I nodded, and got my story ready. 'You must've heard a story start this way a thousand times, but there's this young lady. She's the receptionist for a big SoHo advertising agency. She's smart and very ambitious. The boss of the company is this big snake called Bill Watkins. The ring on his finger doesn't keep his eyes leashed, if you catch my drift.'

Cecily gave me a look that said she knew where I was going.

I paused for effect. 'He's exploiting her, Miss Turner. He's exploiting her in the most awful way.'

She began to type at high speed. While her eyes were on the screen I gave the conch shell a gentle, exploratory push. It displaced the folders, and then the coffee mug.

'Do you work for this company, Frank?'

'Not directly. I'm a driver for a limousine service that my cousin owns. He gave me the job after I finished my tour.'

'You're a veteran?'

'Yes, ma'am. I was in Iran.' I saw her eyes drift to a poster she'd tacked up on the wall. A Jesus Christ look-alike in one-hundred-watt white robes smiled down on me. His arms were draped over two actors pretending to be soldiers: a voluptuous blonde in a tight-fitting uniform and a tanned, square-jawed hero type. I couldn't tell whether he was Cecily's fantasy object, or if it was Christ himself: both were men in uniform. Written in the desert sky was the caption: 'Jesus supports our heroes in the Holy Land'. Below, in red Manichean letters, were the words: 'Do you?'.

'Thank you for your service, Frank,' Cecily said, with a smile. 'May I ask what you hope to achieve by this witness?'

'Well, I thought you could lean on Watkins, persuade him that the affair was a bad idea. He's a bad influence on her. If he wasn't around, I know she'd straighten herself out.'

Cecily gave me a look.

'Now, I can see you what you're thinking, Cecily, and it just ain't true. I'm no jealous Casanova trying to get my rival out of the way.'

Cecily wanted to be convinced, but still wasn't sure. She began to type again. I leaned forward to mask another little shove on the paperweight.

'I'm sorry, the report is confidential,' she said, so I leaned back. 'Have you said anything to this young lady?'

'Oh, I've tried. Every time I'm there, I tell her to respect herself more, that she can get ahead without wearing short skirts and flirting, but she won't listen to me.' I turned on the aw-shucks smile. 'I'm just a simple Christian man. The words don't come out right.'

'Will you tell me the woman's name?'

'Now, I don't have to go and do that, do I? I don't want to get her in trouble.'

'She's already in trouble, Frank. As a good Christian, you know staying silent isn't bringing her an inch closer to healing. Your friend has committed a grievous sin.'

'Now it ain't her fault, that man — '

'I'm not talking about the fornication, Frank,' Cecily said. 'This Watkins man has sinned badly by breaking his marriage vow, but this woman is guilty of something worse. By sleeping with him to get ahead, she is prostituting herself, violating her own flesh and showing wanton pride. She is defying God's plan for her, which we both know is suitable work until she is called to marriage and motherhood.'

'Is that every woman's destiny?'

'I believe it is.'

'But . . . The lady at the desk called you Sister Cecily.'

'We are all brothers and sisters in Christ, Frank. You thought . . . ' Cecily giggled.

'Well, I feel like a prize fool, I can tell you,' I said. 'To think, all this time I've been saying to myself: 'How did such a pretty girl become a nun?' '

The flattery lit up the freckles she'd tried to conceal with make-up. Conservative Midwestern girls always fell for a little ersatz Southern charm.

'I do apologize.'

She waved my contrition away, but didn't speak. After a while Cecily took my right hand, which I made sure obscured her view of my left. 'Frank, you're a good man with a good heart, but you can't do this alone. That's why you've come to us. If your friend is to have the wonderful life that Jesus has ordained for her, then she must step away from the dark path now.'

She really was a sweet girl. I wasn't proud of

what I would have to do to her.

'You'd just send someone to talk to her?' I said.

'That's all,' Cecily said, and she probably believed it was the truth. They wouldn't rough up a fallen woman; the Crusade was a lot more sophisticated than that. They'd just talk to her. Then they'd talk to some other people, and they might throw her out of a job or worse. It was a lucky break for my lady friend that she didn't exist.

'Maybe you're right. If someone half as stirring as Brother Isaiah had a word with her, she'd turn her life around in a second.' I radiated the appropriate level of optimism, until a cloud of doubt passed over my face. 'Cecily, forgive me for asking, but what if she won't renounce her ways?'

'We will bring her back to Jesus, Frank. Together.'

I gave the paperweight a final nudge.

The mug tumbled off the table and on to her thighs. She jumped up with a scream. 'Gosh, oh . . . !' she said, holding back the obscenities necessary to express her pain.

'Are you all right?' I said.

'Silly me, I must have knocked over the mug,' she said. 'I'll be back in a minute.' Cecily rushed out the door.

I waited until I couldn't hear her heels on the floor outside, then I went around to her workstation. She was still logged in. My report was almost complete, with the appropriate sin categories ticked and a few more besides: lying, adultery, prostitution and a little blasphemy thrown in for good measure. My tawdry, ordinary story would look damn impressive when it was buried in the stats they'd boast about on TV.

I pulled up Small's file. This version looked complete, but there was nothing worth deleting in it. He'd done three years in Arkangel, guarding mostly first-generation Russian immigrants. I didn't remember any major incidents near Jenin or Arkangel during that time, but it was difficult to keep track of who was blowing up what in the Middle East. Jack had earned a purple heart two years ago, but was back in action a month later. He had a single commendation for pulling a comrade to safety during a rocket attack, but no other incidents were reported. The Pentagon didn't like sharing information outside the family any more than other federal agencies did, so someone could have laundered the file before it even reached the Crusade.

Attached to the file were surveillance reports that the Crusade had neglected to pass along. There were pictures of Jack outside his apartment in Queens, along his route to work as a security guard in a run-down mall, and even a few snaps of him killing time in a Veterans' Administration waiting room. The place was as rough around the edges as Jack: torn furniture and mildew on the walls. The pug-faced old man behind the wire-mesh reception desk should have been running a pawn shop. The Crusade didn't officially have the power to subpoena his medical records, but one of their friends in the NYPD had tried. The VA claimed most of it was lost; only his scrip for a host of anti-depressant and anti-psychotic meds was still in the file.

I'd been in my fair share of those places. The staff had the same look wherever I went: grim, resigned eyes drained of the last of their pity by the guy in line before me. If a roadside bomb had blown my leg off, they would have given me a new plastic one. When it came to people with the syndrome, they didn't even know what part to replace. So they had pronounced me cured and kicked me out of the hospital. I shuffled from one waiting room to the next as an outpatient, reading outdated copies of *American Sportsman* until I finally got the message. Cracks were already showing in the system before the war; the Tehran boys were the deluge that broke it clean apart.

I printed out what I needed and stuffed it in my pants. I'd been alert for the sound of Cecily's heels in the corridor, but the tread I heard was flat and heavy. I took my seat and assumed a pose of innocence. The door was opened by one of the Stillwater mercenaries. Another waited outside, with a man in a dark suit. He was short and in the neighbourhood of thirty, with neat hair longer than the military trim that had become the civilian style. His face was a contrast between soft, babyish cheeks and eyes that looked at everything with detached suspicion. I'd seen that look from the old hands who had lived through Iraq, but he didn't look like a military man. His hands were soft even for a staff officer, and he didn't have the bearing that was drilled into everyone during basic training. He wore the same junk on his suit as I did, and the stick up his ass proved they were genuine.

'Come with us,' the man in the suit said.

'I'm supposed to wait for Miss Turner.'

'I won't ask you again,' the man said. The wraparound sunglasses the mercenaries wore made their faces inscrutable, but the assault rifles they cradled spoke for them. Now was not the time for passive resistance.

We met Cecily coming out of the ladies', struggling to force her hair back into its bun. 'What's going on, Mr Pyke?'

He glared at her, enraged that she'd used his name. 'He's coming with us.'

'Will you come back to my office after you're done?'

'I will try, Miss Turner,' I said. 'I will surely try.'

They led me into the elevator, a mercenary on either side. Halfway between the eighth and ninth floors, Pyke hit the stop button. 'Search him.'

One of the mercenaries patted me down. 'Do you do this just to find the ten per cent of men who enjoy it?'

In response the mercenary spun me around and slammed me against the elevator wall. Whatever they were searching for, it wasn't the .45 under my left shoulder. His wandering hands didn't find the documents I'd hidden in a sensitive area.

'He's clean,' the mercenary said, and resumed his position.

'Tell me what you're doing here,' said Pyke.

'My duty as a citizen and a Christian.'

'No Christian bears false witness, Mr Strange,' Pyke said, 'and you can drop the accent. Filing a false report with the Crusade of Love could get you in a lot of trouble.'

'Last time I checked, you weren't the police.'

'As good as, Strange. I bet you're the kind of nihilist who loves wasting good people's time with pranks and hoaxes, but that's not why you're here. Who do you work for?'

I didn't answer. Pyke stepped in and assumed what he thought was an intimidating posture. The mercenaries were probably laughing behind their sunglasses. I'm sure they'd met jumped-up little tyrants like him on the parade ground just like I had; men of limited imagination crazed by small silver bars.

'I don't know where you're from, Pyke, but this is the big city. You can't just come here and push the natives around; we have our own people for that.'

'You'd better answer the question.'

'Or what?'

Pyke tilted his head towards one of the hired gorillas.

'All the lovely mahogany in here looks like it stains easy,' I said.

'Then you'd better tell me.'

'Who said I was talking about my blood?'

'One last chance,' Pyke said. 'Who do you work for?'

'Myself.'

Pyke had made the mistake of putting his face near my left elbow. I figured I could break his nose before a rifle butt found the back of my neck. Pyke leaned in close, and then reached around me to press the resume button. He stepped back and folded his arms. The floors ticked away. I watched the mercenaries in the elevator mirrors, waiting for a movement of the shoulders or a twitch in the face that would tell me what was coming. Nobody made a sound.

The elevator beeped, and opened on the lobby. 'Leave the tie,' he said.

I pulled apart my double-Windsor and dropped the tie in his hand.

'I don't ever want to see you again.' He stared at me, his eyes blue glass cut in anger.

'Likewise, pal.' On the screen above the eternal flame, the crowds still looked at the podium, frozen for ever in their single moment of grief. Brother Isaiah raised his arms to the darkening sky and led them in prayer.

★   ★   ★

'Where are you?' White barked from the phone he'd given me.

'Queens.' The tendrils of gentrification — spreading out from the island through the midtown tunnel, searching for land to take root in — had fallen prey to market forces before they reached this part of town. Low, mean buildings held on to the sides of the street, the unlucky ones falling into ruin and becoming vacant lots for packs of wild dogs to socialize in. Neon signs advertised tattoos, gyros and pay-day loans, their tubes dark during the day.

'Why haven't you reported yet?'

'I was waiting until I had something more interesting to report than what I had for lunch.'

'Can you talk?'

'Give me a minute.' I ducked into an alley between a laundromat and a coffee shop. Only the rats nosing between garbage bags and broken syringes could overhear us. 'Go ahead.'

'Did you find something in the files?'

'Not yet, but the threats did turn up one guy capable and angry enough. The Crusade has had him under surveillance for a while.'

'I didn't see anyone like that in the files.'

'They held out on us.'

White kept to his promise not to ask me where I'd got my information.

'I'm on my way to his apartment right now.'

'What's his name?'

'First tell me what the autopsy said.'

'You're being childish, Strange.'

It would be childishly naive not to think he wanted to keep me in an alley as blind as the one I was standing in. I waited.

'Fine. The cause of death was strangulation. No DNA or prints were found in the room besides his. Toxicology was clean, and he hadn't had sex recently.'

'No surprises, then.'

'We did find something odd. There was a fine

soil on his shoes, and a little on his suit. There was too little of it to see with the naked eye unless you knew what you were looking for. We also found a few pine needles.'

How did a man found on the bed of a five-star midtown Manhattan hotel get dirt and pine needles on his suit? 'Is the dirt from the potted plants in the lobby?'

'No, and they certainly don't have anything as big as a pine tree growing down there. I had my operatives sweep the whole hotel and we found a linen cart in the basement with his skin cells inside, as well as more pine needles.'

That explained how they moved the body to the room, but gave us no clue where it came from. 'You're checking the parks?'

'Yes, as well as any green space in the area big enough to hold a pine tree. I'm not optimistic.'

The odds on my solving this case headed deeper into long shot territory.

'There's one other thing: the body of Brother Isaiah's driver has been found.'

'His driver?' I said. 'Why didn't you tell me about him?'

'I didn't know. As you said, the Crusade has been less than honest. Now that we have the body, they've been forced to acknowledge that he hadn't been seen since yesterday afternoon.'

'Was there any suggestion that he might have been involved?'

'They would only say that he was an upright Christian man chosen by Brother Isaiah for his piety. He had no criminal record.'

'He could have been involved, and then killed

47

to make sure he stayed quiet.'

'Indeed,' White said. 'The world is full of wondrous possibilities. Unfortunately I need proof.'

White's sparkling personality had made the single day I'd known him seem like a long prison sentence.

'Where was he found?'

'About an hour north, in some woods not far from the Interstate. We found him in his employer's personal car. My subordinates are bringing the body and the vehicle back. We should have a report by tomorrow.'

'I'd like to look at the body and the car myself,' I said.

'The car won't be coming into the city, and I don't think you can afford the four-hour round-trip,' White said.

'The body then,' I said, in a tone that displayed my readiness to insist.

'Fine, if you're going to make a fuss,' White said. He rattled off an address on the wrong side of the Hudson River. 'The body will be there by tomorrow morning. I'll tell them you're coming.'

'That address isn't any police morgue I recognize,' I said.

'Of course it isn't; do you think I want this body on paper yet?' White took a moment to get his irritation under control. 'I've been forthcoming with you, Mr Strange. It's time to reciprocate.'

'His name is Jack Small. He's unhappy that his three-year vacation in Arkangel didn't match the brochure, and he holds our man personally responsible. The letter he wrote to the Crusade mentioned that he'd be more than happy to demonstrate the killing prowess he'd learned in the Holy Land if our victim ever stopped by New York.'

There was a long pause at the other end. 'That sounds promising.'

It sounded like nothing, but it was the only lead I had, and therefore the best one. 'I'll let you know what I find out,' I said, and hung up.

On the laundromat's wall was an old poster from the last free election in the United States. Nine years of weather had stolen its colours and torn off the corners, but the unforgiving face of Daniel Adamson was still clearly visible. His profile had been given a hard edge to make him look resolute. The simple bold lines that had been used to draw the flag, cross and eagles in the background reminded me of those old socialist posters of the heroic proletariat driving tractors and smelting steel.

Daniel Adamson had been an obscure Georgia Congressman who had ridden a wave of fear and brimstone all the way to the White House. He had founded the Council of Elders, in secret, as a 'temporary emergency measure' they never got around to ending. He was the one the nation looked to after Houston, and he relieved us all of the pain of being free. They probably would have made him President for life if he hadn't gone to his final reward before the end of his second term. There were still elections, but all the candidates were pre-approved by the Elders. During the orientation before they shipped us out, a colonel had told us elections in Iran were done the same way. It was supposed to be another example of the superiority of the American way. It had been, once.

I fought the childish urge to deface the poster, and someone had already made a better comment than a pair of devil horns. Beside the poster in day-glo green spray paint were the words 'Matthew vii, 15: Beware of false prophets, which come to you in sheep's clothing, but inwardly are ravening wolves.' They had educated vandals for such a run-down area. I left the old bastard alone and got on my way. I had better things to do than stand in an alley wrestling with the past.

If Small's apartment building had seen better days, they were before I was born. The red brick façade had been chipped and beaten by weather, neglect and a few stray gunshots. I went up the fire-blackened stoop and wasn't surprised that Small's name wasn't on the few intact mailboxes in the lobby. The cracked glass security door had been wedged open with a broom handle to facilitate the merchants and service industries inside. The Crusade dossier had said Jack was on the fourth floor. The elevator was permanently stuck in the lobby, its doors half open. I took the stairs.

Jack's place was at the end of a narrow corridor covered in torn wallpaper and water damage. The walls were thin enough for me to hear the grunts of a man settling into his sofa, a toilet flushing, and a rhythmic thumping from the floor below that was either the sound of lovemaking or homicide. I knocked on Jack's door and waited as much to the side as the corridor allowed, in case he was the jumpy type. No answer. A cancelled credit card got me through the door. The apartment was too empty to be in disarray. A chest of drawers sat near the window, which faced the houses behind a no-man's-land of untended yards. Two unsteady wooden chairs on either side of a white plastic table and a box-spring bed took up the rest of the single room. A tiny bathroom and even smaller kitchenette rounded out the apartment. In ten years someone would buy this place, paint over all the struggle and despair that had seeped into the walls, and call it a loft. It was a pity that they couldn't renovate the residents in the same way.

Jack's lack of material possessions made searching them short work. The chest of drawers had a few army surplus T-shirts, socks and underwear, all rolled into tight balls like he was expecting another deployment. There was a toothbrush and a blunt razor in the bathroom. The single cupboard in the kitchenette had only a big jar of instant coffee.

A key turned in the lock. I had just enough time to flatten myself against the sink. The kitchenette would conceal me, unless the person coming through the door took three steps inside and turned to the left. I eased my gun out of its holster. The door closed. I heard one step, then two, rolling creaks that started when a heel hit the warped floor. I waited.

'Are we going to stand around like this all day,

51

or are you going to come out?' a male voice said.

I took the one step needed to get me into the main room, gun up. It met the gaze of another gun in Jack Small's hand. 'I'm not here to hurt you,' I said.

Jack smiled a little. His dark brown hair was greasy and long. An uneven, scraggly beard almost hid the old scars on his face. Dirty brown tennis shoes scraped uneasily against the floor as he watched me. At first glance Jack was just another of the walking wounded who lingered under overpasses and disturbed the scenery of Central Park. The stillness in the hand that held the gun and the look in his cold, grey eyes told me otherwise.

'If that's true,' Jack said, 'what's that gun doing in your hand?'

'It's keeping the one in your hand company,' I said. 'How about we put our toys away and talk like adults?'

'I don't know you from Adam, buddy,' Jack said. 'My gun stays where it is. You'd better tell me why you're here, or I'll put you through the last good window in this joint.'

'The Crusade of Love has had you under surveillance for at least a month.' There was the barest flicker of surprise in his eyes.

'May I sit down?' I said.

We pulled the chairs away from the table in tandem, keeping our guns trained on each other's hearts. I sat down, letting my automatic rest on my right knee. Jack put his chair two feet away from mine, in front of the open window. He left his gun in a similarly nonchalant position, so the two barrels nearly faced one another. My .45 had more stopping power than the snub-nosed .38 in his hand, but at this range it was academic.

'There are some pictures in my coat pocket,' I said. 'I'm going to reach for them now.'

Jack didn't respond. I took the pictures from my pocket slowly, and laid them out on his knees.

He scrutinized them with his peripheral vision, keeping his eyes and his gun on me. 'You could have taken these pictures yourself.'

'I could have shot you as soon as you came through the door.' It was then that I noticed the red dot, smaller than a dime, making its way towards his right temple.

Jack opened his mouth to make a sarcastic reply.

I'd dived at a man with a loaded gun before; this was the first time I'd done it to save his life. The .38 went off in the ceiling as the weight of our bodies shattered the chair Jack had been sitting on. The sniper's first shot cut through the space that Jack had recently occupied and tore into the wall. Jack looked at me for a fraction of a second. I could feel his gun arm twitch, trying to decide whether it should move into line with me. Two more shots, silent as cancer, sent chunks of the floor airborne. He got the picture.

We crawled towards the door. The sniper didn't fire again, even when I reached up and pulled open the door. At the other end of the hall a man was waiting. He was heavy-set, forty-five, and wore big aviator glasses. I might have had a better idea of the colour of his suit or the style of his tie if my attention hadn't been focused on the machine pistol in his hand. Coming through the door had surprised him. I used that moment to throw myself against the neighbour's front door.

The wood was rotten, like everything else in this place. The door gave around the hinges and fell in whole under my weight. I could see the holes in the wall from where the fat man had tracked my movement with his gun, the sound no more than a protracted cough. Screams filled the aftermath: a tenant seeing pieces torn out of her bedroom wall, or someone she loved. Jack threw himself into the room after me. It was empty, just bare walls and floors. Through the apartment's single window I saw a fire escape. Years of dust had sealed the window shut. I broke it while Jack fired two shots back down the corridor.

The second-storey fire escape was gone, hauled away for the metal judging by the weld marks at the end of the ladder that went to nowhere. I climbed down a storey and kicked in the window. I heard what I hoped were Jack's footsteps on the ladder behind me. I didn't have time to check before I lunged inside.

When I came out of the roll I was face to face with a child. She couldn't have been more than four, dirty blonde hair tangled around her head. She stared at me without alarm, pudgy fingers stuck into the loops of pink overalls that had seen happier times. The TV on the floor was screaming out cartoons, everything in the picture skewed slightly to the left. The mother lay against the wall. My arrival hadn't caused a stir. She had dead eyes, but moved just enough to convince me that she was still alive. She was juiced up on something, but it wasn't the home-made meth bubbling on a butane stove in the corner.

'Listen to me carefully, sweetheart,' I said to the girl. 'I want you to go under your bed and stay there, okay?'

Without a word or a nod, she ran into the next room. She'd obviously had to do it before. Jack swung in through the window feet-first.

'Is he behind us?' I said.

'No. He's probably going to try to cut us off.'

I inched the front door open. The hallway was empty. We made our way towards the stairwell, Jack covering the rear. The inhabitants of this floor had fulfilled their patriotic duty to conserve power by smashing three out of four of the light bulbs in the faux candelabra fixtures. The door nearest to the stairwell opened, and an old man in a tattered bath robe found himself staring down two barrels. He dropped the bag of garbage he was holding and put up his hands. I motioned him back inside with my gun.

I listened at the stairwell door but couldn't hear any movement. I cracked it open just enough for Jack to get a good look inside. Jack's eyes scanned the stairwell. His pupils widened. We hit the ground before the first shots from a high-calibre weapon punched through the metal door. There were two of them.

Next to the stairwell was a rusted metal baby buggy, two of its rubber wheels missing. It was piled high with broken toys, plastic bags full of aluminium cans, old clothes, mildewed paperbacks and other rubbish. It took both of us to drag it in front of the door.

'What now?' Jack said.

The elevator doors were half open, maybe enough for us to squeeze through. 'Kill the lights.' We ran back down the hallway, smashing the remaining bulbs with our pistols. I stopped Jack in front of the elevator.

He looked down the shaft, the one-storey drop to the elevator car's roof outlined in light that bled up from the floor below. 'I'm not so sure about this,' Jack said.

Someone hit the stairwell door with all their weight. The buggy fell over but held the door closed. They put a few more holes in the door.

'We don't have a lot of options,' I said. 'It's time to take a deep breath and embrace the suck.'

Jack swore under his breath and jumped. He hit the elevator hard, sending the invocation of a few saints and many curses back up my way. The two thugs were still throwing themselves against the door. I sent a few rounds down-range to discourage them, and jumped into the elevator shaft before they had a chance to answer.

Jack had opened the trapdoor and was already in the ground-floor hallway. He was limping but still mobile. I pointed towards the front door and followed behind, keeping my eyes and my gun on the stairwell door. It never opened. I hoped that meant our pursuers were stupid, and not waiting for us outside.

The street was quiet. There were a few housewives going to the market on the corner and kids running around unsupervised with mischief in their eyes. We set off at a half-jog, the most Jack was capable of. I scanned the parked cars, but didn't see anyone looking back. The sniper who'd shot at us while we were in Jack's apartment wouldn't have been able to see the street. I found it hard to believe that no one was covering the front, but maybe we were just lucky. When we reached the corner Jack flagged down a cab. In Queens. If I hadn't been so busy I would have called the Vatican and reported a miracle. Jack gave the cabbie an address in Flatbush.

The cab took us to a hole-in-the-wall masquerading as a bar. There was sawdust on the floor like a frontier saloon, useful for soaking up beer and whatever came out of the patrons.

'Are you going to tell me who those men were?' Jack said.

'I was about to ask you the same question,' I replied. Late afternoon sunlight filtered in through dirty windows and hit a floor that hadn't seen a broom in living memory. The names on the bottles behind the bar were familiar, but I'd bet the gin came from the boiler room and the whisky from a bathtub down the hall. It was the kind of place where you ordered bottled beers only, and told them to keep the cap on. 'I hope you didn't choose this place for the atmosphere,' I said.

'The owner is a friend of mine,' Jack said.

Jack indicated the short, middle-aged black

man tending bar. A thick moustache was the only hair on his head. Marine Corps tattoos were stamped on powerful arms that spread dirt on the bar with a rag. He nodded in Jack's direction, and ignored me completely.

'Safe for both of us, or just you?'

Jack ignored my question. 'Are you comfortable, at ease?'

'Reasonably.'

'Then tell me what the hell you were doing in my apartment.'

'Like I said, the Crusade has been watching you.' I reached inside my coat for the file I'd stolen. Jack didn't react except with his eyes. I got the feeling that half the barflies were watching him to see what he did, and the rest were focused on my hidden hand. 'You wrote the Crusade a letter,' I said, as I laid the printouts in front of him. 'It got someone's attention.'

'So I shot my mouth off,' Jack said. 'It was a stupid thing to do. They probably just wanted to make sure I wasn't serious.'

'You were the only one I saw in the files who was under surveillance,' I said. 'It isn't standard procedure. Did you do more than just talk?'

'I didn't go near the Crusade, or anybody who worked for it. Not knowingly, anyway. You find its agents in the most unlikely places.' Jack leaned back in his chair and took a long swig of beer, but kept his eyes on me.

I took the hint. 'The Crusade's tactics makes it a lot of enemies,' I said. 'If it plays half as rough as it did in San Francisco, it will inconvenience a lot of powerful people. My client doesn't believe in sitting back and waiting for someone to damage his interests. He's contracted me to do a little research.'

Jack laughed. 'Is that what they call digging for dirt nowadays? So you work for someone who doesn't like the Crusade,' he said. 'That lowers your potential client list to a few thousand names. You'll have to do better than that.'

'I just saved your life,' I said. 'You want me to get your cat out of a tree too?'

Jack shrugged. 'I don't know what to tell you. I can't think why the Crusade would have a beef with me.'

'Maybe it has something to do with your bedtime story,' I said, pointing to the redacted passages. 'Those can't all be dirty words.'

Jack looked at the page and its sea of black. 'It won't help you.'

'Humour me.'

Jack rapped his fingers on the uneven table.

I sipped my beer and waited.

'It was the second year of my one-year tour,' Jack said. 'Another stop-loss order had just come down, so we knew we'd be in the country for at least another six months. They'd only given us a day's notice. Some of the guys in my unit had already told their families they were coming home. God, we were angry. We were supposed to be on an airplane, and instead we were in the same shit-nowhere patch of desert we'd been babysitting for a year and a half. Have you ever been to the Holy Land?'

'They sent me to the other side of the Big Sandbox,' I said. 'Ghost Town.' I could feel a frisson pass through the drunks around me.

'You ever man one of the permanent checkpoints?'

'No, but I'm acquainted with them.' The checkpoint's perimeter was a wall of concrete blast shields to protect against car bombs and rocket-propelled grenades. People were required to leave their cars at the perimeter and enter a long and twisting line, fenced in by razor wire and watched over at all times by several machine guns. A bank of computers would scan their transit papers and compare them to the person's fingerprints. The car was subjected to the same level of scrutiny, then towed to a place where the driver could pick it up. When it worked like it was supposed to, no soldier ever got near someone trying to cross the checkpoint. If a guy wanted his virgins, he'd have to kill his own people to get them.

'They'd told us during our orientation that the Palestinians lived for jihad, that children as young as six years old dreamed of becoming martyrs. That didn't stop the settlers from hiring them to take out the trash. Anyway, it was early Saturday morning, so there wasn't much traffic. I was lucky to pull the morning shift; the heat at noon was enough to bake you inside your armour.'

'We were shooting the shit, trying to make the hours go by, when our spotter sees a single car coming up the road. There are signs in Hebrew, Arabic and English, starting at about four miles, telling motorists to slow down. Each sign tells them to reduce their speed, until by the time they reach us they're crawling.'

'I think I've seen this movie.'

'Yeah, you and everybody else who's ever watched the news. So this car — a beat-up old Ford with no windows, at least twenty years old — is barrelling towards the perimeter at twice the mandated speed. Our CO yells at it with the megaphone, tells the driver to slow down in every language he knows. The car just keeps coming. It crosses the red line, and our CO doesn't have a choice. He gives me the nod, and I open up with a minigun. The impact of all the bullets rolls the car a few times, and it stops upright. The CO's about to order someone to check for survivors when it bursts into flames. That's when we heard the screaming.' Jack finished off his beer. He stared at the bottle for a little while, and then motioned for another.

'A woman fell out of the passenger-side window. She was wearing one of those burka things, and it was on fire. She tried to stand, stumbled around a bit. We did nothing. Even my CO, who'd fought all over the Middle East, was transfixed. She screamed the whole time, until she fell over and stopped moving. We put out the fire and checked inside the car. The bodies of two young children were in the back seat, so badly burned we couldn't tell if they were boys or girls. No guns, no fugitives, no explosives.'

'When we'd cleaned up, there was a huddle with our CO. He said that this sort of thing happened, that we'd been damn lucky that it hadn't happened before, and it would probably happen again. He said checkpoints near

Jerusalem got hit so bad they'd shoot at anything that moved. We'd followed procedure and done the right thing. So our captain wrote up a report, and we forgot about it.'

'You forgot about it?' I said. I went back to the letter he'd sent the Crusade and looked it over again. 'You wrote: 'I see that morning whenever I close my eyes.' '

'The dreams didn't start until I'd been stateside for a few months,' Jack said. 'One night I slept fine, the next . . . ' Jack didn't bother to finish the sentence. 'It's the exact same day, like I'm reliving it. The same fly buzzes around my head. I know what my buddies are going to say so well I could repeat it word for word right now. I could tell you about every shadow that falls on every rock around that place. And the car, it's always the same too.'

'You always fire on it?'

'I never have a choice. I'm just watching myself do what I always do.'

I became aware of how little noise surrounded us. There was no music or television to provide white noise. Occasionally I'd hear the click of balls colliding on the pool table behind us. There were at least fifteen guys in here, and I couldn't hear a word. 'Did you ever find out why she tried to run the checkpoint?'

Jack shook his head. 'If they did, they never told us.' He swished an idea around in his mouth. 'I was on a bus from Philly this morning. Not a single passenger would meet my eye. They took one look at me and started counting the seconds until I had a flashback and lost it. It

62

didn't bother me; I'm used to it by now. I just stared out the window and didn't look at anything in particular. For some reason I started thinking about Sunday school. They'd pack us into this dingy church basement every beautiful Sunday morning and tell us God had a plan for this world. I didn't really think about it until this morning. I was just a dumb grunt, and whatever small part the Lord wanted me to play would be revealed in good time.'

'I couldn't help but think about that day. Why that one in particular? I'd had worse days out there. My conscience was clear, but I couldn't tell myself that I'd killed those people to defend anyone. It was just one more disaster in a place full of FUBARed good intentions. Then I had a, what do you call it . . . You know, that thing the Wise Men had.'

'An epiphany?'

Jack slammed the table. 'That's the one. I realized that God had tried to show me something that morning, and I'd missed it completely.'

Jack drank his beer and stopped talking. I waited, but he didn't continue.

'So what did you miss?'

'I don't know yet, but the good Lord gives me another kick at the can every time I close my eyes. I used to be terrified of sleeping,' Jack said. 'I stayed up for days, took whatever I could to keep myself awake. I wrote that letter hopped up on amphetamines and half a coffee plantation.'

'So you don't blame Brother Isaiah?'

'I don't even know him that well. I must have

heard him on the radio when I was buzzing.' He picked up his letter, read it again, and laughed. 'You wanna hear something funny? You break into my place, those thugs try to ventilate me, but today is the first day in a long time that I haven't been afraid. No matter what I see tonight, I know it has a purpose.' Jack smiled, and for a second he looked like the kid he was.

I sat back and let my eyes drift around while I thought about what he'd said. The one clean thing in the establishment was a mirror that ran the whole length of the bar. Some magic had spared it from the many fights that had carved their memories into the wooden bar with glass and furniture. I could see almost everyone in its reflection. An old drunk warmed a stool at the other end of the bar. He cradled a shot of something foul in his hands and tried to disappear inside the baseball cap on his head. There was another ageing ex-marine sitting with some others at a table near the door, the hand on his beer missing the pinkie and ring fingers. Our eyes met, and I felt someone walk over my grave.

Everybody in this joint looked or moved like someone had taught them to kill for a living. I'd spent a lot of time in vet hangouts but this place was something different. Nobody looked alive. Some had fallen in the Holy Land; the rest had come on the Great Crusade with me. They were refugees from farmsteads, strip malls and a thousand concrete stoops, men who had dreamed of something greater or run out of options, all punished the same way. None had returned. They were here, trapped between life and death, waiting for the king of kings to return and call the quick and the dead to account at last. Now that the Vatican had closed purgatory, the next best place to cool your heels was Queens.

I felt something new move through the legion of daytime drunks, something that whitened the knuckles around their glasses. Over Jack's shoulder I saw two men standing in the doorway. The fat man from the apartment building stood next to the bar, aviators still in place. His weapon was somewhere inside the trench coat that was too big even for his corpulent frame. Sweat collected on his forehead. It didn't make much sense considering the temperature outside, unless you factored in the fitness benefits of fear.

His friend was much younger, about Jack's age. Someone had bought him for his size. The muscles stuffed into a dirty T-shirt weren't from an honest day's work or a SoHo gym; prison exercise yards were less exclusive. His broad, angular face suggested a considerable reserve of stupidity. He kept a big mitt near the pocket of his bomber jacket, so everybody knew where the heat would come from.

Jack had his back to the door, but he knew what was up. Neither man moved from the doorway. Everybody in there pretended not to see the duo, but the pool game had stopped, and the bartender's hands were no longer visible. The fat man scanned the bar, but he hadn't made me yet. He was spending too much time eyeing the bottles of unsafe spirits behind the bar. I told Jack where to go with my eyes. He blinked in recognition. I walked my hand inside my coat, finger by finger, and got ready to move.

'Hey, barkeep, have you — ' The old drunk at the end of the bar finished the fat man's sentence for him, with a number three socket wrench that came from nowhere. The blow landed hard against his temple, shattering the left eye of his sunglasses. As he fell I caught a brief glimpse of an empty, porcine eye. I admit I was stunned. It was a good thing that old marine with the missing fingers was there to bring a pistol butt down on the head of the other guy.

Everybody started to breathe again. The bartender's hands came back above the bar. 'Mitch, check if they have any friends out front. You guys check out back,' he said to the pool game.

The old man and the marine were already tying the two men up.

The bartender came around the bar towards us. Jack stood up and saluted. I stood up with him; it was better to be on my feet, no matter what was going on.

'I'm sorry, Cal,' Jack said to the bartender. 'It's my fault they came here.'

Cal shrugged and spat on the floor. 'Don't sweat it, kid. We ain't exactly losing the Ritz.' He eyed me. 'Who's this?'

'I've been trying to figure that out. His ID says he's a private dick.'

'Felix Strange,' I said. 'Those two tried to punch our ticket today, along with a sniper.' I knelt by the fat man, still out cold. His half-broken sunglasses were still in place.

'A sniper?' Cal said.

'Your average criminal doesn't know his way around a high-powered rifle, and these boys are as vanilla as they come.' A small cell phone had fallen out of his breast pocket. It was a cheap, disposable model found behind the counter in any mini-mart in the country, a lot like the one White had given me.

'Subcontractors,' Cal said with disgust. 'You boys are lucky somebody's cheap.'

A sudden racket drew everyone's attention to the back of the bar. I dragged an old napkin through the pool of blood and spit leaking from the fat man's mouth. A yell from the back room assured everyone that things were fine.

Cal motioned to two of his soldiers, and they dragged the bodies away. 'We'll find out who they are when they wake up. You made any enemies lately?'

'I have enough already,' I said. 'I was only at Jack's place a few minutes, not enough time to set up an ambush like that.' My beer had survived the drama unscathed. I finished it off. 'How about your fan club?'

'You don't want to know about us,' Jack said.

'I don't,' I said. 'I just like to keep a running total of all the people who are trying to kill me.'

'They were probably after us,' Cal said. 'You'll understand if we don't explain.'

I was grateful. I had enough on my plate as it was.

'I'm sorry you got caught in the net,' he said. 'Another drink?'

'Is there anything behind that bar that won't kill me?'

'Most of those bottles are for mixing cocktails,' Cal said, in a tone that suggested I shouldn't enquire about the menu. The drinks were probably served in trucks and plain brown packages without a return address. 'One or two wouldn't hurt you, at least from the neck down.'

'The front is clear,' yelled the man Cal had called Mitch.

'Wipe everything down and then vacuum the floors,' Cal said. 'If there's so much as a hair left here, they'll find it. We need to be out of here within the hour.'

That was my cue. 'It's been fun,' I said to Jack, extending my hand. 'Let's never do it again.'

'Likewise,' Jack said, and shook my hand.

'I got one more thing to ask you,' Cal said. 'Were you really in Tehran? You look a little young.'

'I was younger then, and ten years isn't such a long time.' I was Jack's age then, barely able to get a legal drink before the rifle was in my hand.

'Who were you with?'

'Eighty-second Airborne,' I said.

Cal nodded at my answers, but the questions were just formalities. 'Forgive me, but I gotta ask: have you got it?'

'Yeah.'

Cal whistled through his teeth. 'That's rough. We were out on the *Lincoln* when it happened. A lot of good people disappeared in Ghost Town.'

It was easier for me just to nod. I was one of the lucky ones, though survival sometimes felt like a pyrrhic victory. Cal put his hand in his pocket, and everyone in the bar stopped what they were doing and did the same. I thought for a moment that they'd decided I was a loose end after all, until Cal's hand reappeared with a wad of cash.

'I can't accept that,' I said.

'We look out for our own.'

'Your pal with the socket wrench gave me all the help I need.'

'Okay,' Cal said, and stuffed the money back in his pocket. 'I got a feeling we're going to meet again anyway. Maybe then you can tell me what you're really up to.'

'Until that day,' I said, and shook his hand. 'I'd go back to Philly for a while if I were you,' I said to Jack. 'Scapegoats are in season in New York City.'

I went out the back way, through a maze of alleys and into the last of the day's sunlight. I was glad to be out of that bar, glad that I didn't have to join their vigil just yet. I walked a few blocks towards the subway, sweeping the street with my eyes in a casual way, waiting for someone in the tangle of pedestrians to be a little too eager to stay near. In a few hours the neon signs would come on and the graffiti-marked shutters would come down, ready to withstand the long siege of night.

Tuesday

White had hidden the driver's body in New Jersey, at the funeral home of Krein and Sons. It was a large Victorian house in a residential neighbourhood in Jersey City, not far from Pershing Field. The funeral director let me in the basement door so he wouldn't have to explain my presence to the wake going on upstairs.

'You're Mr Strange?' he said.

'And you're one of the Kreins.' He wasn't much older than me. Unless his toddler sons were serving canapés to the guests above us, I figured he wasn't the family patriarch.

'James,' he said, and we shook hands. 'I've got the body laid out for you.'

The house's basement was given over to preparing bodies for their final rest. The floor and walls were gleaming white tile, newly scented with disinfectant. A bank of morgue drawers took up the inner wall. A covered body was on the steel operating table. Around it were several aluminium carts full of embalming and cosmetic tools.

'Has anyone touched the body?'

'Only the coroner Mr White sent over last night. He left a copy of his report for you,' Krein said, and drifted around the room in the way people do when they look for something they're sure they just put down.

'Here it is,' Krein said, and handed me a

manila folder. I removed the sheet and skimmed the report with one eye on the body. The driver's name was Dwight Krenz, and he'd lived to the age of thirty-nine. He'd been Brother Isaiah's driver and bodyguard for the past eight years. He was a former Navy SEAL, which explained why he had been in spectacular shape for his age. He would have been more than a match for someone a decade younger. On first glance, it wasn't the body's physique that drew attention. There were three knife wounds on the body, all to the head and neck. I was glad I saw them in person, if that was the right word. The coroner's report explained where the cuts were, but it lacked the flair for language necessary to convey why they were unusual.

The first cut was a stab wound directly to the left temple. The second was a long vertical cut in the centre of the face. The third was just above the collarbone. According to the coroner, it had severed the inferior thyroid artery. Cause of death was a toss-up between brain trauma and exsanguination. The report hypothesized that the cuts had been made by a knife with a thin blade and an extremely keen edge, which described about half the sharp things in the metropolis.

'Have you ever seen this before?' Krein said, hovering at my elbow.

It did not improve my mood. 'Not exactly.'

'I hope you and Mr White catch the maniac who did this.'

'Whoever killed this man is a lot of things, but a maniac isn't one of them.' I'd had the unfortunate luck to see a fair number of stab wounds in my life. About two years ago, one of my cheating hearts cases had turned into homicide. The other woman had flipped her lid and gone after the married man with an expensive Japanese kitchen knife. I'd been staking out their love nest, trying to get something for the lawyers. In the time it took me to get across the street, she'd stabbed him thirty times. That was the work of a maniac: frenzied, jagged cuts all over the body.

These wounds were gruesome, but they were precise. It took a surprising amount of strength to cut a human body, and even more nerve to keep the knife steady. Each cut was smooth like a surgeon's incision; indication of an iron will, or the complete absence of a conscience. The killer knew where to strike, and that once he had it was just a matter of waiting for him to bleed out. If he'd hit that artery by accident, he would have stabbed Krenz a fourth time to make sure. The second cut was superficial, an afterthought between the first and third. It was practically artistic, from a professional point of view.

'Do you still have his clothes?' I asked.

Krein brought me a sealed plastic bag. Inside was a grey suit covered in blood, shoes that needed a polish, and an empty leather holster that would have rested under Krenz's left armpit.

'Did he have a gun when they brought him in?'

Krein shook his head.

It was weird from top to bottom. I looked at the report on the car, but it was a waste of time.

It didn't have a scratch on it. The wound on his neck would have ruined the leather interior if Krenz had been killed inside, but it had been cleaner than the man left in the front seat. A body dump just like Brother Isaiah. Odds were that he was killed in the line of duty, but it didn't explain why an ex-SEAL would have let anyone hostile get close enough to stab him without drawing his gun.

I'd learned all I could from Krenz, so I went on a fishing expedition. 'Mr White wanted me to have a look at another body,' I said.

Panic flashed through Krein's eyes. 'Another body?'

'An old man, they didn't tell me his name.' From the look on his face, I could tell my bluff was pointless. He didn't know what I was talking about, and it terrified him. Krein seemed like a decent person. I wondered what White had on the man, that he felt safe hiding a body here. He didn't need much to make the average working stiff's life hell. 'If he's not here, then there must have been some sort of foul-up. I'm done with him,' I said, pointing to Krenz.

Krein hastened to put the body back on ice. Upstairs the mourners came and went, the pressure of their best shoes making the ceiling creak. I wondered if White would ever bring Krenz's body back into the daylight, so his family could hold a service and share their grief in a place like this one. Maybe no one missed him, maybe he'd been detested by his wife and had no kids. Either way, he should be given the chance.

The morgue drawer closed with a click. With his fingers still on the handle Krein looked back in my direction, his eyes full of the hope that I would go.

★ ★ ★

'When did you start smoking again?' Benny asked.

'I'm not smoking,' I said, as I lit up one of his cigarettes. 'I'm saving your life, one cigarette at a time.'

Benny was a tall Brooklyn Jew with a fondness for bad haircuts. His grey eyes jumped rather than moved, and the line of his eyebrows above a slightly crooked mouth suggested an attitude of perpetual disdain for the world around him. Benny had the perfect frame for leaning against the Starlight's façade, but it made one hell of an inconvenient silhouette once snipers became involved.

We stood outside the Starlight Diner on Forty-eighth and Ninth, trading nods with our nicotine brothers and sisters across the street and breaking the current of lunchtime pedestrians. Most had left their jackets at work in defiance of the autumn weather. With nothing to do but fill my lungs, I watched the dames shimmy past. Most fell into two distinct types.

The first was a dwindling minority. Women in the latest European pantsuits, out for the exercise on the rare days they had the time. They were veterans in three-inch heels, knuckles bruised from coming out swinging during board meetings and sales reviews. They'd shattered the glass ceiling, only to watch all the king's men put it back together piece by piece. Meetings were rescheduled without their knowledge, conference calls cancelled, their names pushed down the masthead. They were kept out of sight like freaks of nature, just in case they offended the authorities with their competence. Isolated, they poured their fury into their work, kept it inside so no one would have an excuse to call them a bitch. They kept an eye on their backs, and only smiled when they were with their families.

The second type was hired as receptionists, PAs and representatives, the new faces of the image-conscious firms. They wore the very latest in haute demure to impress the religious, while the pearls around their necks drew attention to the little skin they could show for the benefit of the worldly. They'd taken courses in etiquette and deportment at the finishing schools suddenly popular in the North-east; you could put an encyclopaedia on their heads and watch it float down Eighth Avenue. The terms of employment were understood to be strictly temporary, a way to add more depth to the pool of eligible men. Once a suitable provider was found, they'd quit their jobs and move upstate, ready to make a home and a family as they'd been told.

The problem was that some had been faking it ever since college, and others were starting to have reservations — they'd breathed big city air, anything but clean: a mix of danger, sex and anonymity that gave Grandma Homestead

terrible dreams. Maybe they'd convinced themselves that they could play both sides of the
game, keep their eyes on the prize while doing
pirouettes. They were the ones who gave a
lingering sidelong glance as they drifted past, the
shadow of a smile at the corner of their mouths
to tell you they were nobody's fool but their
own.

'Makes a man glad to be alive,' Benny said.

'How's your wife?' I asked. 'When she's due
again?'

'A month and a half, fuck you very much,'
Benny said. 'All I'm sayin' is that without a ring
to constrain his enthusiasm, a man might feel the
need to do something when presented with such
a tableau.'

'These dames are way out of my league.'

'Some uptown girls like a little grit in their
soup,' Benny said.

'Maybe, but they always spit it out after
they're done chewing.' I stubbed out my
cigarette and threw it in the can.

My regular table was the best positioned
booth in the diner. It was in the back corner, and
separated from the next booth by a thin island of
fake ferns whose presence had never been
adequately explained. The ribbon of mirrors that
lined the walls gave me a pretty good view of the
street on the other side of the Starlight's
floor-to-ceiling windows, as well as half the
tables in the joint. The average diner or passer-by
would have to squint pretty hard in my direction
just to get a look at my profile, and by then their
interest would be obvious.

Lunch had arrived in our absence. Benny looked from his side of the table — a lumberjack-sized stack of pancakes, scrambled eggs, orange juice — to the single cup of coffee on mine. 'Aren't you hungry?'

'Not right now.' I was out of Delectra, which was why breakfast had come out the wrong way two hours ago. My body felt like a tuning fork struck lightly with a ball-peen hammer. It did wonders for my digestion. The vibrations weren't bad enough to make me shake, but they did make the ground undulate a little under my feet, like I could feel the city breathing. My actual appetite was unaffected; that cigarette had been to take the edge off my hunger.

I felt his eyes searching me for signs of illness. 'It's just a little indigestion, Benny. I'm fine.'

'Mrs Rose,' Benny said, 'have you seen this travesty?'

Mrs Rose Warberg was the owner of the Starlight. She was a small woman who seemed eternally in the neighbourhood of sixty without ever getting there. Rose had run the place with her husband for forty years, until he passed on a few years back. Now she was the sole proprietor. No one else would have been able to keep up.

Rose scrutinized the relative size of our meals from behind the Starlight's counter. The powerful bifocals she wore on a chain magnified her displeasure.

'You don't like my food now, Felix?' she said.

'He says it's indigestion,' Benny said.

'Well, tell him indigestion is for little dogs and women worried about their weight.'

'I've got no appetite,' I said to them both. 'Can we leave it at that please? I'm sure your customers don't want to hear about the contents of my intestines while they're trying to eat.'

'I'd better see some appetite the next time you're here,' Rose said. 'Nobody wastes away in my establishment; it's bad for business.' Her judgement passed, Rose went into the kitchen.

With no one left to appeal to, Benny accepted the explanation grudgingly and sat down. 'You shouldn't invite a man to lunch and not eat,' Benny said. 'It makes me feel self-conscious.'

'That isn't stopping you from digging in,' I said. 'And that's breakfast, not lunch.'

'Anyone who trades pancakes for a sandwich is a schmuck.'

I let him get started on his pancakes while I turned a few things over in my head. I would have kept my mouth shut about Isaiah whether I'd promised White or not. I didn't want Benny to get tangled up in this business; he had too many good things to lose.

'How was Albany?' I said.

Benny rolled his eyes. 'It was a big fat waste of my time. The only thing that made it bearable was these two state senators I met who were making the most of their expense accounts. They were kind enough to drink me under the table, and on my way down I heard some interesting things.' Benny added some syrup to the lake his pancakes were swimming in. 'Apparently, Wall Street has been expressing 'reservations' about some of the Elders' policies.'

'Which ones? Making people miserable,

spending all our money, or turning the Holy Land into a fortress?'

'They didn't go into detail,' Benny said. 'All those policies have worked out pretty good for your average corporate fat cat, so I don't know what they're crying about.'

'And the Crusade came here to bring them into line?'

Benny nodded. 'Do you hear that?' he said.

All I could hear was the sound of cutlery on plates and the murmur of general conversation.

'That's the sound of several million people trying to cover their asses simultaneously. Everyone's keeping their head down, hoping some other sap gets it first. The Crusade doesn't go anywhere unless it's got a few lambs lined up in front of the altar.'

'Any idea who the lambs are?'

'The first wave will be their usual punching bags: gays, atheists, people who drink on Sunday. Beyond that, who knows? I gotta say I'm disgusted by this collective pussying-out of my fellow New Yorkers,' he said through a mouthful of pancakes. 'It's not as if these Jesus freaks can keep an eye on everyone.'

'I used to feel the same way about Santa Claus,' I said. 'It didn't encourage me to play the odds. Why didn't they just use the Securities Exchange Commission, or you jackasses?'

'They don't trust either of us,' Benny said, 'especially the Bureau. We've still got one ball left in our nutsack. The Director has told us to stay out of the Crusade's way while it's in town; he doesn't want the Bureau to share the same fate as the CIA.'

'That doesn't sound like much of a testicle.'

'Well, it's the only one we've got, and we're holding on to it for dear life. I wish Hoover was still around; that old bastard knew how to play this game better than anyone.'

In a way J. Edgar Hoover was still around; the problem was that he'd been reborn as Ezekiel White and in this life he was playing for a different team. We kept our mouths shut while the waitress refilled my coffee.

'Our only consolation is that the Crusade pisses off the Holy Rollers even more. One of the Rollers I talked to in Albany complained that the Crusade shouldn't even be launching investigations because they weren't law enforcement officers like us. As in him and me. The chutzpah of these shmendriks is beyond me.'

It must have burned a lot of special agents to see a hack like White and his legion of Daveys be given the same powers as the Bureau.

'These Wall Street guys aren't like those poor suckers in 'Frisco and Salt Lake City. They aren't just going to roll over and whistle Dixie,' Benny said. 'Things will get ugly.'

'Ugly like that?' I said, and pointed to the TV mounted behind the counter turned to the news. Seven men in suits worth more money than I'd see all year, were doing the perp-walk, overcoats over their hands to hide the cuffs. The news headline read: 'Fortune 500 executives indicted'. The top corner of the footage was covered by the words 'Remember Houston!' emblazoned over the graphic of a flapping American flag. Below, it counted years, months and days since the city was destroyed.

'Fuck,' Benny said. 'It's started already.'

My friend didn't know the context, or he'd still be swearing. The Elders had no problem with playing rough, but they usually picked on people too weak to fight back. They needed Wall Street, and that was enough to give the people who worked there a free pass as long as they were discreet. A few whispers of discontent weren't enough to provoke this kind of extreme reaction. It could be payback for Brother Isaiah's death, which meant the Elders were already moving against anyone they thought was involved.

The image changed to a press conference being given by state prosecutor Richard Murray. The sound was off, but the subtitles said that the charge was tax evasion, with indictments for fraud in the works as well. 'They're accusing them of profiteering in supplying the troops in Israel,' I said.

Benny guffawed. 'That is rich. What did they think they've been doing the past five years?'

'It's the state that's bringing them in, not the Crusade or the Committee for Child Protection.'

'It looks better that way, more official. If the suits in Albany want to take a piss, they don't unzip their flies until they hear from the Elders. At least I can't see one of my own in that circus.' He sighed. 'The head office is probably in conniptions by now. Oy vey, it's going to be a shit week.'

'You're throwing a lot of Yiddish around lately,' I said.

'It's my new boss. The director kicked him upstairs as a suck-up to Washington.'

'A true believer, huh?' I said, sipping my coffee.

'I worked five years with Baptists, Catholics, whoever,' Benny said. 'No problems. Then this nudnik shows up and starts throwing his weight around. Suddenly we're having prayer breakfasts every week, and he ends every meeting with 'Jesus bless America' — not God, Jesus. So I'm Jewing up a little in self-defence.' He showed me his Yiddish pocket phrase book. 'If that self-righteous prick asks me if I've heard the good news just one more time, I'm going to grow ringlets and form a Klezmer band.'

I put down my coffee. If I tried to drink any more, it would come out my nose.

'Oh, you laugh now.'

'Yes, I do.'

'You're still Jewish last time I checked.'

'My mother was Jewish,' I said, 'and only near the end.' I thought about our split-level family home. A sliver of sunlight, like the crack of an open door, had found its way to me between the wall and the drawn blinds. My father and I sat still, supported silently by men and women he barely knew and I'd never met, heads covered before God.

'Good enough for us, good enough for them,' Benny said. 'Once they've convinced us flaming Jews to go to the Holy Land, you'll get the knock on the door.' He could see I wasn't convinced.

'Hey, it may not be such a bad thing. The way things have been going in the country of our birth, having an ancestral homeland to fall back on ain't nothin' to sneeze at.'

'I thought your cousin in Jerusalem hated it there.'

'Naw, he likes the place fine. It's the putzes over there that our assholes over here have put in charge. All our troops and money have gone right to their heads; he says they walk around swinging their dicks like baton twirlers on the Fourth of July.'

'Nobody seemed to mind when it started.'

'When your best friend in the world says: 'We'll defend you against your enemies and, by the way, have a shitload of money on us,' who would say no?'

The first time I met Benny was when the army was teaching us how to jump out of perfectly good planes. I was the only man in the unit who used his given name. Everyone else called him 'Profane'. When war against Iran was declared, the call to serve had been answered most by churches that organized congregation-wide enlistment. These kids arrived naive and eager to spread the good news. The rumour mill told them who the heathens were, and an attempt by one of these rookies to convert Benny was always a popcorn event. His responses became legendary throughout the battalion for the erudition of their sacrilege and the streak of curses longer than a California highway.

I let Benny finish his pancakes. 'I need a favour,' I said when his plate was gone. I showed him what I'd taken from the fat man.

'What is that?'

'It's a sample.'

'That is a napkin stained with blood and God-knows-what,' Benny said. 'What do you expect me to do with it?'

'Run it through your lab, find a name attached to the blood.'

'We usually need a reason to do these sorts of things.'

'I thought probable cause was a quaint relic nowadays.'

'I meant a reason to justify the cost. That's the only cause they care about.' Benny looked at my evidence and frowned. 'A guy saves your life a few times, and he thinks you owe him,' he said, but he wrapped the napkin in several more from the diner and stuffed it in his coat pocket. 'I'll let you know as soon as the eggheads come back with something.'

'Thanks, Benny.'

'Buy me lunch, you goldbricker, and we'll call it even.'

'I can do better than that.'

Benny looked suspiciously at the envelope I slid across to him. 'What are you trying to give me now?'

'Just what I owe you.' I hadn't borrowed the whole five grand at once: a hundred here, fifty there, just a little extra cash during those times when the world had its spells of good behaviour that put me out of work. Benny hadn't ever refused, asked questions, or asked when he'd get it back. He was maybe the only person who really understood my situation, and was better about it than any man had a right to expect. It had been easy to keep strict accounts of what I owed; the shame I felt every time I put my hand out made the figures easy to remember.

Benny opened the envelope and his eyes widened. Inside was every cent White had given me. I could see his FBI brain connecting the dots: my questions, to the bloody napkin, to more money than I'd had in a long time.

'Oy vey, Felix, what have you gotten yourself into? Wait,' he said, before I'd even opened my mouth. 'Forget I asked that question; it was a moment of temporary frickin' insanity.' Benny drummed his fingers on the envelope and shielded his face with his hands. 'I can't take this,' he said. 'Don't get me wrong; I'd love to, and Miriam would be over the moon. But then she'd ask me where it came from, and once she found out it was you . . . ' He threw up his hands.

'It's your money.'

'Miriam's sweet on you, Felix, thinks you need taking care of like an endangered species. She'll think I'm tearing the clothes off your back.'

'Then tell her you won it at the track.' He tried to give it back but I held up my hands. 'You've got a little Benny on the way, and I don't want my friendship to be such an expensive proposition.'

Benny cursed under his breath. 'If you need this to get out of whatever you've got yourself into, you'd better tell me. If you end up dead I'll never hear the end of it.'

'I'll try not to inconvenience you.'

Benny stood up and left a few crumpled notes on the table. 'Forget what I said earlier. I'm buying lunch, 'cause you sure as hell can't afford it.' He put on his hat and glanced at the television. It was still showing coverage of the Wall Street arrests.

For a moment I was afraid he would link the arrests to his suspicions about what I was doing. Benny was the opposite of stupid, but it would have taken a big leap to put the two together. I could barely believe it myself.

'Whatever you're up to, take care of yourself.'

I gave him an ironic salute, he said something unkind about my mother, and then he was gone.

I finished my coffee and let the world go by while I considered my next move. The city was already twisting in the grip of the Crusade of Love. If the Elders went on a rampage of their own, it would queer my game considerably. Their attack dog White and his Committee for Child Protection would be unleashed on half the people I'd need to talk to. They couldn't think much of White if they weren't even waiting for his investigation to finish, or they didn't care as long as someone paid.

White's phone rang. I should have known better than to invoke the devil's name.

'Where are you?' he said.

'I'm in a diner in Midtown.'

'Good, then you can meet me at the Natural History Museum in twenty minutes.' White hung up.

The man's lack of courtesy would tax a saint,

and I wasn't even close to being beatified. Benny's tip wasn't the usual amount I left as a regular. I reached into my pocket to make up the difference, and felt all the nothing inside.

★ ★ ★

Locating someone in the Natural History Museum used to be a tall order, before half the exhibits disappeared beneath scaffolding and white sheets. A renovation disease had spread to all the major museums in the last few years. It always began the same way: a 'citizens' group' no one had ever heard of suddenly appeared and started to protest. It allowed the government to claim a public mandate when they started bullying publishers, librarians and museum curators. When they came for the Museum of Modern Art, we were too busy laughing at the goatee brigade's defence of cow parts in formaldehyde to think where it might lead. By then they were already demanding that Greek statuary in the Met start showing some modesty and cover up. When they started picking fights with stuffed Neanderthals and creatures that had been dead for 65 million years, the curator closed down the entire museum rather than let the authorities treat natural history like a buffet. He was out the door the next day, along with most of the staff, replaced by a Doctor of Intelligent Design.

I found White among the wolves. A pack of North American greys stood in simulated Great Plains scrubland, preserved ears for ever pricked up at the sound of distant prey.

'Did you see the news?' he said, eyes still on the exhibit.

'I caught the highlights. Were you in on the arrests?'

'I'm as surprised as you are, Mr Strange. I'm a servant of the Council, not a member,' White said, his voice unmistakably bitter. 'Did you make any headway with this Jack Small?'

'He was a dead-end.'

'I trust you have evidence for that assertion.'

'He's a head-case who wouldn't make it past the Bingham's lobby,' I said. 'The man is so full of rage he wouldn't bother to conceal his crime by moving the body. He's more of a car bomb or grassy knoll kind of guy. He also claims to have been in Philadelphia until this morning. He's just another nut as far as I'm concerned, but check out his story if you don't believe me.'

'I'll make enquiries,' White said. 'Anything else?'

I decided not to tell him about the fat man and his partner. Something about the whole incident still bothered me, and it wasn't getting shot at. I'd managed to live long enough to get used to that. 'Are you sure no one else knows about this?'

'Every man who was in that hotel room last night is completely trustworthy,' White said. 'Apart from them, only the Elders know. We're monitoring every major channel and muckraking site. There's a lot of speculation about what's behind these indictments, but nothing even close to the mark.' The reflection of his eyes in the exhibit's glass narrowed. 'What are you getting at, Strange?'

Those two gorillas and their professional handler were still a big question mark. The sniper suggested that Jack had been the target, but I wasn't optimistic enough to explain away someone taking a shot at me on the first day I was working this case. I wanted to know if they were related to the look on Mr Pyke's face when he escorted me out of the Crusade offices. 'I'm not sure yet. Do you know a Mr Pyke? He works for the Crusade.'

'He's a prominent member, sits on the Crusade's board of governors, I believe,' White said. 'Pyke was responsible for coordinating their operations in New York, quite an honour for a man of only thirty-four. Why do you ask?'

'I met him the other day while I was following the Jack Small lead,' I said. 'He's a suspicious bird. I got the feeling he's hiding something.'

'He probably just thought you were a reporter trying to get an inside track on who they plan to expose,' White said. 'The press has been circling them like buzzards.'

I thought it was more than that, but only on my gut's say-so. The wolves' pack leader stood apart from the others. He was the only one who looked directly at us, on the lookout for the weak and the slow, his eyes as full of animal cunning as glass replicas allowed. They reminded me of Pyke's.

'You haven't given me much of a return on my investment,' White said.

'I thought the money in that envelope

belonged to the taxpayer.'

'It's fortunate for you that I want these killers found so badly I'm willing to do your job.' He held up a small flash drive inside a clear evidence bag. It was no bigger than my thumb.

'I didn't bring anything for show and tell.'

'The contents are encrypted. I've called in a few favours at the NSA, but we haven't made any progress. The encryption is as powerful as it is illegal; a case for treason could be made just for possessing it.' Not allowing law enforcement access to your personal files at any time, for any reason, was proof of disloyalty, and only a traitor would go to such lengths to hide from lawful scrutiny. Or so the thinking went.

'It was left in a lamp post on Canal Street,' White continued. 'We don't know by whom, but we do know it was intended for the Crusade.'

'How did this particular lamp post come to your attention?'

'I don't enquire about your methods, Mr Strange,' White said. 'At some point the copy we left in its place was taken, we don't know by whom.'

'Didn't you have agents watching it?'

'The crowds shielded whoever it was. We don't even know when it was taken.' White wasn't happy detailing the shortcomings of his agents. 'We're hoping whoever did will come back for another message. I want you to take over the stakeout.'

'Why me?' I said.

White waited until a group of schoolchildren were led past before he answered.

'They may be staying away because they've become aware of my men's surveillance.'

'It may have nothing to do with the case.'

'If you have a better lead, I await it with bated breath.'

I didn't reply.

'Once my people see you there, they'll withdraw. I'll tell them to expect you soon.'

★ ★ ★

Old man Song's pharmacy was in the basement of a tenement on Mulberry Street, just below Canal. The whole shop was in a single room much bigger than the exterior suggested was possible. Song stood behind the counter, chatting barely above a whisper with an old woman in Cantonese. The wall behind him was completely taken up by rows of wooden drawers, their contents marked in Chinese. There was no other furniture in the shop for the sake of feng shui, or because he was cheap.

Medical charts on the opposite wall displayed the meridians of Chinese medicine, channels circulating chi through the body rather than blood. When stimulated through acupuncture, pressure points on meridians could improve health and cure illness. If struck, those same points deadened limbs, damaged nerves and even stopped the heart. I'd never been completely sold on the curative powers of Chinese medicine, but I'd first-hand experience of using the pressure points to curb somebody's enthusiasm for violence.

Song's was the opposite of the new places that had opened on Mott Street. They had sliding glass doors, antiseptic track lighting and assistants in white coats. It was an appropriately clinical atmosphere to reassure the Westerners looking for a cheaper alternative to the extortionate costs of conventional medicine. They sought magic potions for losing weight, smoothing wrinkles and increasing prowess; the same grab-bag of human vanities people had been chasing since the days of the pharaohs. Longevity always came in a distant second.

When the old woman was gone, Song looked at me and held out his hand. I placed my arm on the counter palm up. He placed his fingers on my wrist, closed his eyes, and listened. After a while he let go of my arm. He pulled a small stepladder near the back of the shop, and took a large bottle from a drawer near the ceiling. I played a game with myself that I'd started the first time I came here: trying to guess Song's age. The evidence was contradictory. His bald head was lined deep like a freshly tilled field, and he wore large, powerful bifocals that drew your eyes to his. On the other hand, he'd had no difficulty pulling that ladder or climbing it with self-assurance. He was short, not stooped. His hands were as steady as a surgeon's, and there was a strange vitality to his presence.

He filled a small eyedrop bottle from the large one. 'Three drops in tea, twice a day,' he said, just like he had a dozen times before. He held the bottle up so the brownish liquid caught the small amount of daylight that found its way here from the street.

'Thanks, Song,' I said, but he did not offer me the bottle. Instead he stared at me from behind his bifocals, one half of me nearer, the other further away.

'You lead a life of extreme disquiet,' Song said.

I was surprised. That was the most Song had said to me in the six months I'd come to his shop.

'Perhaps you should move to a quieter place.'

'Quiet places don't need people like me,' I said. A man had to work to earn his daily bread, and afford expensive pharmaceuticals on the black market.

Song gave a slight, sad nod and handed me the bottle. He turned back to his drawers, and didn't stir when I left the money on the counter, or opened the front door.

The dead drop was around the corner on Canal. It was near an alphabet soup of subway lines: the A and C trains snaking uptown on the West side and downtown across the water, the J and E making their separate ways through Brooklyn before they joined at Jamaica Center. You could get here from anywhere in the city and disappear just as quickly.

I got a table on the second floor of a dim sum place across the street from the lamp post. If somebody did show up it would take me longer to get down there, but elevation was the only way to see the lamp post clearly through the crowds on the sidewalk. I ordered tea and some dumplings I still had no appetite for. When the waiter had gone I squeezed three drops of medicine into my teacup. It tasted like dirty rainwater. After half an hour I could keep the dumplings down, as long as I ate slowly. I ordered some more food to keep the waiter happy and kept my eyes on the lamp post.

From the second floor White's lackeys weren't difficult to spot. Every Holy Roller wore what the police called 'White Black-tie'. It was not a term of endearment. The Committee for Child Protection dress code, instituted by White himself, revolved around dark suits of a specific cut, clean hats and ties without immodest patterns that would show up badly on TV. It made every Roller look alike, and so easy to spot in a crowd they might as well have hung signs around their necks. Despite White's promise they showed no inclination to leave. I should have known he wouldn't leave that much slack in my leash.

Around ninety per cent of my job consisted of waiting for some unlucky schmuck to destroy his life in front of my eyes. I'd hidden in bushes to observe men crippled in car accidents leave wheelchairs to reach their fifth-floor walk-up apartments and women remove neck braces to do high-impact aerobics in front of bay windows in their living rooms. Hotel lobbies were always preferable — a soft chair, and the day's newspaper to hide behind — unless my mark was tight enough to choose a by-the-hour roach paradise no one could justify lingering in.

Whether it was an uptown hotel or a Bronx flophouse, men always had the same range of expressions once the deed was done. The rookies were the same bundles of conflicting impulses that had probably got them there in the first place. They tried to be nonchalant but couldn't remember how it was done, their anxious faces not yet calibrated to hide betrayal. The veterans had an identical smirk they used to tell themselves that they could get away with it for ever.

At least this time I was in a comfortable spot in one of the best places to people-watch in the country. The world had come to America, and a good part of it had settled in the Lower East Side. They came over in tight-packed holds from the Balkans, the Mediterranean, China and a dozen other countries. My ancestors had stood in line at Ellis Island while doctors checked their teeth and looked for signs of disease. Customs officials twisted vowel-free names into American shapes for easy identification. Some of those who made it disappeared into the railway's iron bloodstream, to marry and labour for people they'd never met. Others settled here, in tenement rooms without plumbing or even windows, warehoused like the boxes they'd be paid very little to move. My great-grandfather had told my mother it was worth it for one reason alone: there were no pogroms here. That was more than enough for people who had lived in fear for generations because of their religion.

About two hours in I saw a disturbance in the crowds. It wasn't enough for an accident or some other kind of commotion, just a slight pull in attention towards a part of the street that I couldn't see. A few seconds later I saw her shoe: a black heel with white highlights. It was attached to a leg that had been designed in a wind tunnel, then sheathed in black silk. It seemed to go on for ever, disappearing into the unknown that lay beneath her tan raincoat, belted tight at the waist and cut to follow the contours of its owner perfectly. Her hair was long, wavy and dark as her stockings. It was kept out the way by a jade hairclip, a sculpture of one of the immortals that bounced with each of her steps. The angle of the window made it impossible to see her face, and most of it was hidden by dark sunglasses and the upturned lapels of her coat. The crowd's interest was now clear: the men for the usual reason, the women to see what they were doing wrong.

Her stride up Canal was purposeful but unhurried. Her progress was aided by the subconscious tendency of Lower East Side hip kids and matrons with the week's groceries to make way for her. As she passed the lamp post, one of her gloved hands snatched at the space inside like a bird of prey. A strange grimace passed over her face, and then her hand was back in her pocket and the expression was gone. It happened so fast I would have missed it if I'd blinked at the wrong time. I guess that's what happened to the Rollers below, because they didn't move. It was lucky for me that she turned out to be the one I was looking for, as I hadn't been watching anyone else for the last five minutes.

I dumped more of my dwindling fortune on

the paper table-cloth and took the stairs two at a time. She was crossing Bowery by the time I got outside. The Rollers were still staring at the lamp post. I cut in front of a big family that was monopolizing the sidewalk. They screened me from White's agents until the edge of the block. I bolted across the street with another large crowd, the woman still visible half a block ahead.

At Hester she went right and down an alley. I took a peek inside and saw an Internet café squatting inside one of the ground-floor apartments. As she opened the door I caught a glimpse of a fat man in a track suit sitting behind a counter, guarding the first of a rank of computers on trestle tables. The walls were bare and discoloured and the grey carpet hadn't been cleaned since the Nixon administration. People called those places 'Holes', and not just because of the decor.

Government spy agencies had been plugged into American telecommunications since we invaded Iraq. The NSA chewed through phone calls and the Internet, looking for patterns that might detect the next terrorist attack. Some bright penny in the Revivalist administration realized that these data-mining programs could also be used to hunt for what they called 'Spiritual Terrorists'. The Committee for Child Protection was authorized to install the child-SAFE software in the servers of every Internet service provider in the country. After mergers and consolidations three companies provided almost all the Internet access in America, so it hadn't been that difficult. Now the Holy Rollers could monitor anyone viewing something they found objectionable, on the off-chance a child happened to walk by while it was on the screen.

Any eight-year-old could get around the restrictions on pornography. Everyone knew it, but like all the other obscenity laws it kept smut off the television and away from billboards, so people could pretend that it didn't exist. The illegal encryption on that thumb drive that White had shown me was another matter. Emailing that around would set off alarm bells at one of the half-dozen agencies competing to monitor all Internet traffic sooner or later. They'd smell a case to grandstand with in front of the Appropriations Committee, and come down hard on anyone they could. It was probably why this woman and her handler were playing with that lamp post in the first place.

The minute after the childSAFE went online, a lucrative market was created. Amateurs rigged up satellite feeds, while organized crime just found a technician interested in adding a few twigs to his nest egg. Both groups opened Holes like this one, where those who still valued privacy and anonymity could access foreign sites away from prying eyes.

I watched the alleyway in a store window across the street, pretending to scrutinize a modern knock-off of an art deco lamp. When she emerged from the alleyway, the woman's pace was more agitated. She went to a payphone on the corner and dialled a few different numbers. Her mouth never moved, so no one was picking up, or she was just there to listen. Whatever the tune was, she didn't like it. She slammed the phone down and headed back to Chinatown.

The woman had decided to take me on a tour. She walked up Mott for a while, then turned on to Broome, went down Mulberry, took a right on to Grand and went on to Baxter Street from there. Occasionally she'd go into one of the stores that sold every plastic object made by the human race, so many that sandals and knock-off toys spilled out on to the street. Inside narrow aisles stalked by sharp-elbowed housewives were incense, cutlery, sweet bean rolls, fake katanas, ginseng gum, mats, robes and Imperial kitsch. I didn't want to risk going inside and losing her, so I held up a lamp post until she came back outside, empty-handed.

We did another circuit. Her movements were too random for shopping, and her stride too fast and direct to be taking in the sights. Occasionally she would turn around suddenly and retrace her steps. I'd duck into an electronics store papered with Hong Kong idols or linger near a restaurant and stare at the animal parts hanging in the window. The bustle kept her away from me, and made it easy to follow when she was far enough away. I'd kept an eye out for the Rollers, but they were still nowhere to be seen. White might have belatedly kept his word, or those two mugs were still staring at the lamp post and waiting for something to happen

At Grand Street the woman did another of her sudden turnarounds. This time I was in trouble. I'd been using a group of German tourists as my cover. At the same time that the woman turned around, the group stopped to inspect cheap jade figurines arrayed in a window. I couldn't break out of their circle without drawing attention to myself. I had no choice but to let her walk right past me, separated only by a small German boy in a Statue of Liberty novelty hat. I let my eye go over her a little as it would have been suspicious, bordering on insane, for any man to pass up the chance of looking at her. Her skin was pale and clear, with very little make-up. Her chin was strong and almost pointed, the harsh edge it lent to her face magnified by the sunglasses hiding her eyes. As we drew level, the corners of our eyes met. Hers were pale grey and red-rimmed, tears still threatening to fall. The veils of cooking meat, garbage and Teutonic sweat parted long enough for me to get a hint of her perfume, something musky and alien. Chinese characters watched bemused, nesting like multicoloured birds in the tangle of signs above.

She finally sat down on a bench in Columbus Park. She stared at the ground and barely moved, mesmerized by the concrete and grass beneath her. Despite the weather, several games of Chinese chess were in progress on the tables, the players surrounded by a crowd in parkas stamping their feet to keep warm. I lingered near the pavilion, listening to the spectators argue about the games or transubstantiation for all the Mandarin I knew. I had a strong desire to sit down on that bench and comfort her. It wasn't an urge I got often, especially with a stranger.

The woman sat there for half an hour, failing to hide her grief among the park's irregular rock formations.

She stood and headed for the subway, getting on the six train uptown. I entered the next car over, and sat where I could see her through the door windows. Whatever had happened in Columbus Park was over or driven beneath her skin. She sat still and stared forward, perfectly composed. Everyone in the car stole glances in her direction, and not because she was wearing sunglasses underground. I kept an eye on her but it wasn't really necessary. I had a hunch where she was going.

The woman got off at Fifty-ninth and Lexington and headed west. It didn't take us long to reach the Bingham. The second glance the doorman gave her had nothing to do with recognition, and neither did the third. I gave her a five-second head start and then went inside. She was talking to the man behind the front desk. I hung back and took another look at the lobby. The foliage on display was desert-themed: cacti and sagebrush that fitted in with the calculated sparseness of the interior. I took a seat and picked up a newspaper. I'd let her finish charming the desk clerk, and after she'd left I'd find out if my hunch was correct.

'Strange!' The gruff voice reverberated through the lobby. The lieutenant I'd knocked down was striding towards me, red-faced and twice as mad since I'd seen him on Sunday.

The woman turned in my direction. I tried to shield my face with the newspaper but I was too slow. The outline of her face was a little softer without the glasses. It was an unconventional sort of beauty, which made it all the more striking. In those beautiful grey eyes, I saw her place me in Chinatown, calculate whether our second meeting could be a coincidence, and watched those odds grow until they reached over the horizon.

'You got me with a lucky sucker punch last time, Strange,' the lieutenant said. He stood over me with his legs spread in an intimidating posture he'd probably learned at the academy. He leaned in even further this time, trying to emphasize the greater height difference with me sitting down. I was pretending to read the front section of the *Times*, maybe ten thin sheets of paper in total. It didn't slow down my fist much when it came through in an upward arc that ended at the lieutenant's pride and joy. I heard a choking sound, deep in his throat, just before he fell over.

She smiled at me, in disbelief and provocation, and then ran out the back entrance. I ran after her, but her lead had already got her across Park Street. It was full of traffic that heralded the beginning of rush hour, family four-doors and a legion of yellow cabs fighting over tarmac wide and impassable as the sea. I saw her enter Central Park before a stampede of yellow cabs covered her retreat.

Providence had given the woman a head start, but I didn't think she was getting very far in those heels. She went north past the nature sanctuary. I was gaining on her, but every retiree and fitness freak was attracted to me by the magnetism of bad luck. The longer this chase went on, the higher the chance that one of the spectators would call the police. 'Honey, wait, I'm sorry,' I yelled after her. It might buy me some time.

The woman turned right. I went cross-country and tried to cut her off, but she reached Gapstow Bridge before I did. A large group of tourists and lovers clogged the whole span to take advantage of the photo opportunity. The mystical power she'd displayed in parting the crowds of Chinatown failed her. The woman got stuck in the middle, and no amount of shouting or elbow use would change the law of physics that stopped two things from occupying the same space at once. I got to the bridge and jumped on to the stone railing. The ledge was big enough that going over it was a reasonable proposition, unless like me you took it at a full run. A few ducks watched my progress from the pond below, anxious where exactly my hundred-and-sixty-odd pounds were going to land. I met her on the other side as she finally pushed her way through the crowd.

We didn't do much but pant and look at each other for a while. She wasn't as scared as I'd expected, but the woman looked primed to scream at any moment. I kept my hands in the open and tried to look as non-threatening as a strange man who had been chasing her could be. She stayed silent, which meant that she was as eager to get the police as I was.

'Nice footwork,' she finally said. Her voice was

local and a little nasal for my taste. 'I'm surprised you didn't end up in the drink.'

'The Lord loves a fool,' I said. 'Why don't we take a walk and discuss things?'

She took her time considering the proposal, but the bridge didn't get any wider and the crowd behind her didn't disperse. 'We stay to the public paths,' she whispered in my ear, 'or I scream my head off.'

'Fine by me,' I whispered back. 'I'm not going to hurt you.'

She didn't believe me, but she took my arm anyway. The crowd on the bridge, thinking we were lovers reunited, gave us a cheer. We waved and then perambulated north, a courting couple from a previous age.

She didn't say anything for a while and I didn't press her. I wanted to give her time to get used to me.

'Who do you work for?' she asked.

Part of my job was inventing lies and repeating them with complete sincerity, but with this woman I felt compelled to tell the truth. It wasn't that she had a trustworthy face; I just sensed that she was a better lie detector than the average dame. 'Ezekiel White.'

She stopped walking.

For some reason I had trouble meeting the disappointment and distaste in her eyes, so I looked at the skaters drifting in a circle on Wollman Rink behind her. 'It's complicated.'

'What part of you working for a power-mad hypocrite is complicated?'

'He didn't give me much of a choice, and I'm

only doing it for the money.'

'Honesty is a virtue, not a defence,' she said. 'You don't look like the type of man who would work for White.'

'That's the nicest thing anyone has said to me all week.'

'Then I'll quit while I'm ahead,' she replied. She tried to take her arm away, and found it trapped in an affectionate embrace by mine. 'Let go of my arm or every skater on that rink will hear me scream rape.'

I released her arm and she began to walk away.

'Don't you want to know who murdered Brother Isaiah?' I wasn't really talking out of school. She'd known he was dead in Chinatown, when she hadn't found what she was looking for in that lamp post.

She stopped walking, but she didn't turn back. 'I know who killed him.'

'If that was true you'd be at their door with the Crusade raising holy hell.'

That got her to turn around. 'The Crusade doesn't know I exist.'

She probably had no one in the world right now, but the upturned angle of her chin told me that wasn't enough. I didn't know how she fitted in with Brother Isaiah, but I guessed that anyone who would idolize a man like that had a strong sense of righteousness. 'If you want to see justice for Brother Isaiah in this life, you're going to need my help.'

She considered her options, and came back. 'Before I tell you anything, I need to know exactly what your relationship with White is.'

'I'm a private detective,' I said. 'White hired me to solve this case. He's convinced his own agents are under surveillance, and he probably doesn't want to be within a mile of this case if it goes wrong.'

'And you're in this for the money?'

'Not just the money,' I said. 'It'll be worth it to see the look on that tin-star finger-wagger's face when I drop the murderer in his lap. I'm sorry my motives are less than noble.'

'They'll do,' she said. She took my arm again and we resumed our stroll. 'How did you find me?'

'White found the dead drop, he didn't say how. I staked it out and waited for someone to show interest. As far as I know, the Rollers don't know you exist.'

She nodded along, but she didn't seem to be hearing me.

'You're one of the Crusade's spies.'

'We call ourselves Witnesses.'

'I've heard you do more than just watch.'

'We find the sin hidden in men's hearts; we don't create it,' she said, with surprising force.

We turned at Cat Rock and headed towards the Dairy. I backed off a little and tried something different. 'You communicated with Brother Isaiah using that lamp post?'

'His driver would leave lists of targets, and I would swap them for my reports. When the lamp post was empty this morning, I knew. I checked the fallback email and called the emergency number he'd given me just to keep myself busy.'

I expected the waterworks to start again, but

this time the valves remained closed.

'Brother Isaiah and his driver were the only ones who knew about you?'

She nodded. 'How did Brother Isaiah die?' she asked.

I filled her in on what I'd seen at the Bingham. She showed outrage and sadness in all the right places. When I got to the dirt and pine needles I hoped she would have something to add or at least react in a way that would tell me its significance, but she appeared just as dumb-founded as me. When I finished talking she was silent for a long time, so long that I began to question my new-found policy of honesty.

She didn't speak until we were on Literary Walk. It was always a bit of a relief to see Shakespeare still there; one of these days a Revivalist pastor would get around to reading one of his plays and start a petition.

'My job was to infiltrate nightspots frequented by wealthy and upper-class eighteen- to thirty-five-year-olds,' she said. 'I observed and recorded any infractions of liquor or decency laws.'

I tried to imagine her putting a ruler between dancing couples at trendy nightclubs. The vision didn't stick.

'There's a private members' club in Red Hook that I'd been trying to get into for weeks. About a week ago I met a drunk music producer at another club who was a member. He got me inside, and while I was there I met Marcus Thorpe Junior.'

A low whistle escaped me.

'You know who he is?'

'I know his father's reputation,' I said. Marcus Thorpe had created Thorpe Industries to keep track of all the government pies he had a finger in. He owned or had a controlling interest in companies that made body armour and weapons, kept the troops fed and built the bases where they slept. A grunt couldn't go to the can without making the man a nickel. Thorpe Industries' stock price had been in the upper stratosphere ever since we decided to implement God's plan for the Middle East. 'Did you know Junior would be there?'

'No, I'd never met him before. He took a liking to me.'

That was a surprise. 'What's the son like?'

She made a non-committal noise. 'Vain, self-centred, rich. He has no real malice in him, which is more than I can say for a lot of the trust-fund babies I meet. It's only a matter of time before he embarrasses his father.'

'Rich families know where to put their black sheep before they can cause any trouble,' I said. 'That's what Europe is for.'

'It's too late for that,' she said.

The Mall had been modelled on the grand boulevards of Europe, a shady area where the quality could display themselves. The American elms that lined it always reminded me of inspection during basic training, but I didn't know why. Walking between the trees put me in the role of our drill sergeant, a man as terrifying and infallible as God, and not the anxious recruit I once had been.

'What do you mean it's too late?'

'He gave me some ecstasy,' she said. 'It's hard to find nowadays, and I think he was trying to impress me.'

'How many?'

'Just a few pills. I have video of him doing it from a hidden camera. It's standard procedure for all Witnesses.'

'Isaiah must have been overjoyed,' I said.

'He was never the type to celebrate bad judgement.' That anger again, that seemed to come from nowhere. 'He told me to stay close to Junior and await further instructions.'

'And?'

'I saw Junior regularly after that, but not in the last few days.'

From the way she was looking at me, she obviously thought I was missing something. 'So the son of a prominent businessman got caught with a couple of pills. Even with the new antidrug laws that's not a big deal for a rich kid. Their parents have ways of fixing things like that.'

'You never met Brother Isaiah,' she said. 'I know your work has made you cynical, but there are still people who believe in the things they say. Do you think he spent ten years in Africa ministering to the sick and the dying to pad his résumé?'

'He didn't demur when they offered him a seat on the Council.'

'He accepted it on the condition that he would be free to do in America what he did in Africa. He was never interested in power,' she said. 'Brother Isaiah came to this city to save souls.'

'And if those souls didn't want to be saved?'

'They had to be isolated until they saw the error of their ways,' she said. 'Brother Isaiah always said that sin was contagious.'

The couples sitting on the benches along the walk stared deep into each other's eyes, but let nothing more than their hands touch in public.

'Are you saying that Thorpe had Brother Isaiah killed to protect his son?'

She nodded.

It sounded plausible only in the mirror world of the Elders' media enablers, where believers were force-fed delusions of persecution and fear. This woman could be just another head-case looking for her fifteen minutes. I didn't buy any of it. 'Do you have any proof?'

'No,' she said. 'Why do you find it so hard to believe?'

'Thorpe is a businessman. Killing one of the most powerful men in the country is all risk and no profit,' I said. 'This country has become a strange place, but it hasn't lost its mind.'

'I know I have no right to ask you to trust me, but you must,' she said. 'You didn't hear Brother Isaiah's voice after he saw my witness against Thorpe Junior. It was distant, hard, like he was preparing for war. I know Thorpe is involved somehow.'

'White has other ideas.'

'Of course he does,' she said. 'He and Thorpe are thick as thieves. Take a look at the Free Enterprise Foundation if you don't believe me. If White does find evidence against Thorpe he'll cover it up. I wouldn't even be surprised if White was involved.'

I had no good reason to believe her, but part of me did anyway. Maybe it was a desire to think even less of White than I already did. 'Can you get hold of Junior?'

'He hasn't answered his phone in a while, but I know where he hangs out. He won't be involved; Junior isn't smart or cold-blooded enough.'

'He might know if anyone has been putting the screws to his old man. We'll hit the clubs tonight and see what the prodigal son has to say for himself.' Leads weren't exactly thick on the ground at the moment, and at the very least I'd get to see how the Crusade's shadows operated.

'I can't tonight; I'm volunteering at an Office of Mercy soup kitchen in Brooklyn.' The Office of Mercy was the only part of the Revivalist government that had actually bothered to listen to what Jesus had said. They ran soup kitchens, free clinics and a nationwide network of orphanages, all on the federal dime. Most of the social safety net had been broken up and sold for scrap before the Revivalists had taken over, so people were understandably grateful. It's a shame what their bosses did with all that goodwill.

'That's dangerous to your cover,' I said. 'What happens if one of your hipster friends sees you?'

'I'll tell them I'm doing community service.'

'Tomorrow then?'

'Tomorrow.' She held out her hand and I shook it.

'I'm Felix,' I said. 'You got a name?'

'Call me Iris.'

114

I spent the night in my office digging into the life of Marcus Thorpe. Iris hadn't lied about his connection to White, who was a fellow of ten years' standing at the Free Enterprise Foundation, Thorpe's pet think tank. I found a picture of the two at the Foundation's annual retreat at Thorpe's cabin, a twelve-bedroom faux-pioneer monstrosity. It would have been built in the grounds of Versailles if Marie Antoinette had wanted to play frontier Annie instead of a provincial milkmaid. They stood with the other fellows — bunko artists and flim-flam men willing to justify whatever the chamber of commerce was doing that year — in the cool green of the Adirondacks.

The problem was that one picture didn't prove conspiracy. White had turned up to spew his worn half-truths wherever someone was willing to cut him a cheque. There was no history between Thorpe and Brother Isaiah; as far as I could tell, they'd never even met. If Thorpe's son had run into any trouble it had been kept quiet. The theory was worth a look, but I wasn't about to take the word of a woman I'd just met as gospel, no matter how well her hips cut the air when she walked. She was part of the Crusade; doctor's orders would be to take anything that came out of her mouth with a pillar of salt.

I tried to find deeper financial connections between the two, but came across another interesting fact instead. There had been a run on Thorpe Industries stock on Monday. Near the start of trading a large amount had been dumped into the market for no apparent reason, and panic pushed the price down further. By noon investors remembered that violence was the only growth industry right now and the price rallied. It ended the day's trading with ten per cent less of its value, but that loss had disappeared by this morning.

I wondered what some people on Wall Street knew about Thorpe Industries that I didn't. My attempts to find out who had dumped the stocks ended in sunny tax havens all over the world. It might have been nothing more than an anomaly if the short hadn't spiked and kept going up even after the stock price rose to its former value. That meant someone was selling the stock assuming they could buy it later at a lower price. Whoever was doing it was betting a lot of money on Thorpe's empire having a rainy day.

Somebody knocked on the front door. The silhouette looked male, and only one was visible. I opened the door a crack, the gun inside my jacket ready to shoot through the glass. The face that greeted me couldn't have been more than twenty-one. He had bright eyes, short red hair and lots of freckles. He wore a light brown suit and the accoutrements of an upstanding young man.

'Good evening, sir,' he beamed. 'I'm with the Census Bureau, and I'd like to ask you a few questions for our records.'

The rumbling in my stomach strongly encouraged me to slam the door in his face, but that could be seen as hindering his work, which now carried a fine. 'May I see some ID?'

He stuck a card in my face.

It looked kosher. 'What does the E stand for, Mr Palanov?'

'Ernest,' he said with another smile.

Of course it did. 'Come in.'

Ernest had the good breeding not to react to the state of the room inside.

'Sorry about the mess, please take a seat,' I said, and took my own behind the desk.

Ernest sat down and turned on a PDA, his stylus at the ready. 'There are a few gaps in your file that we'd like to clear up, Mr Strange. It won't take long.'

'Shoot,' I said.

'Your father was an Anabaptist and your mother was Jewish, is that correct?'

'Yes, though neither was very religious.'

'Mr Strange, are you aware that we have no record of your faith?'

Benny's prediction this morning had jinxed my luck. New York's census was notoriously unreliable, especially with regard to religion. It had probably been kept that way by a few smart, anonymous city employees who could see which way the wind was blowing. I hoped it was just bad luck that they'd found me tonight after all these years.

'If I could see any church or synagogue attendance records, we can clear this up right away,' Ernest said.

'I don't attend either.'

That lowered the wattage of Ernest's sunny disposition. This conversation was about to

117

become very awkward. 'I see. What religion should I enter then?'

'None of the above.'

'I'm afraid that's not an option.'

'This is the census, not a multiple-choice exam,' I said. 'I can say whatever I want.'

'Technically you are correct, Mr Strange,' Ernest said. 'If you want me to write that in, I will. However, I should warn you that the government will classify you as an atheist in any future interactions.'

He said it like a friendly warning, but the threat of an entire bureaucracy lay behind it. A bill probably passed in the dead of night had given responsibility for all payments from the federal government to individuals to the Office of Faith-Based Services. That meant they were the ones who sent out child benefits, social security, tax refunds and all other varieties of government cheese. In defiance of logic but not ideology, these funds were now disbursed through churches rather than sent directly, supposedly to prevent fraud and ensure the money was spent 'wisely'. Churches and synagogues, which did all right under the system, were drowning in paperwork. Temples had their cheques delayed through bureaucratic indifference, while elaborate security measures and reporting requirements meant many payments never reached mosques at all. If you were an old atheist trying to collect the social security benefits you'd earned, there was a single office in the lower Twenties for all of Manhattan, with two employees and a waiting room located precariously above the East River. No wonder most people identified themselves as Christians, whatever the case might be.

'Do you want me to lie about what I believe in?'

'Of course not,' Ernest said with a nervous smile. 'I'm trying to help you.' Ernest's fingers tapped on his PDA. 'You've never had any religious convictions at all?'

'I had a religion once,' I said. 'It was called the United States Armed Forces.'

Ernest shifted in his chair and rubbed the phantom stubble on his face. 'Would it be fair to say that you're confused?'

'Is that a valid choice?'

Ernest didn't laugh. 'What if we put you down as one of the major religions, just for now. Once you resolve your crisis of faith, we can update the records.'

'That still sounds like lying.'

'Not necessarily.' Ernest scrolled through something on his PDA. 'According to Hebrew law, your mother's Jewish heritage makes you Jewish by default.'

I hated it when Benny was right about politics, horses or women. I didn't have a name for the level of rage I felt at him being right over how they'd view my parentage.

'So if we put you down as Jewish, that is technically correct. I'll add a note saying your attendance records have been misplaced. It will take them years to notice, and by then you should have this little crisis of faith cleared up.'

'Do you really think it will work?'

'Definitely. Going with Judaism is the smart move; if you change your mind later, it's much easier to convert to Christianity than go the other way.'

The kid did have a point. 'Okay, I'm Jewish,' I said, hoping that would be enough to get this clown out the door.

'Great,' Ernest said, and began to write furiously on his screen with a stylus. 'Now, having established your Jewish faith I must at this point in the interview inform you of the United States government's voluntary resettlement assistance programme in order to comply with the President's executive order. Are you familiar with the many exciting resettlement programmes that we offer?'

'Yes,' I said.

'Well, they've gotten even better this month, so I'd better review them with you again. It says on your census records that you are self-employed. Is that still the case?'

'Yes.'

'That's a pity, Mr Strange; the matching funds being offered by patriotic American corporations are increasing every year.'

A combination of lavish tax breaks and official pressure had persuaded a lot of American companies to open branch offices in Israel, especially in the new settlements built by the government. Once the offices were open, the companies were again encouraged to transfer their Jewish employees to them. Of course the whole racket was voluntary, and with the companies matching dollar-for-dollar the large subsidies the Revivalists offered, a lot of families took the windfall and their chances in the Holy Land. For the ones who refused this generous offer, the consequences, to their careers, to the security of their jobs, were never spelled out.

'I guess it's my loss.'

'Do you have any family in the Holy Land?'

'I don't have any family, period.'

'Have you ever considered moving to Israel?'

'I'm an American,' I said. 'If I want to live in the desert, I'll move to Las Vegas.' At least there I can go to an all-you-can-eat buffet on the Shabbos.

'You may change your tune when you hear of the wonderful incentives the federal government is prepared to offer to help you fulfil your religious mandate. As an Orthodox Jew,' he said, with a wink, 'you are eligible for up to twenty thousand dollars in direct payments, and another ten in interest-free loans in order to assist in your relocation and acclimatization.'

'What determines the actual amount?' I asked, curious in spite of myself.

'We look at many factors: marital status, children, any Yeshiva education or work with Israeli organizations. I would say the one overriding criterion is the location that you settle in.'

'How much if I settled in Arkangel?' I asked. I wondered how desperate they were for people to move to Small's old posting.

He consulted his PDA. The question startled him for some reason. 'Ten thousand two hundred and forty-three dollars,' he said. 'Quite a high payout for a single person.' A number-cruncher deep in the basement of some fake think tank had probably come up with that pedantically precise valuation of looking over my shoulder for the rest of my life. 'If you decide to move to somewhere . . .' — he couldn't say safer — 'more crowded, like Tel Aviv, the compensation will be less.'

'That free ticket,' I said. 'It's one way, isn't it?'

For a man who earned his daily bread asking strangers probing questions in their own homes, Ernest didn't deal with embarrassment very well. 'Voluntary renunciation of citizenship is required,' he said, shifting uncomfortably for the umpteenth time, 'but you are free to visit the United States any time without a visa.'

I'd be free to visit my own country. How magnanimous of them. 'I'm not interested.'

'And that of course is your right,' Ernest said. 'Well, I think I've got everything I need. If you could just sign here . . .'

I stood and went around to his side of the desk to sign, figuring I would be in a better position to usher him out the door afterwards.

'Are we done?' I said, standing over him.

'The interview is concluded,' Ernest said. He signed his own name on the screen below mine. 'Why don't I leave you some brochures,' he said, hunting in his bag. 'You know, the foreign media has given people a really biased view of the settlements. When you see some of these pictures . . .'

I let him chatter on, as I clutched my desk and

tried to ride the wave of nausea passing through me. Ernest's face went out of focus, his voice leaving his body and heading down the hall. I was trying to decide whether I needed to run to the bathroom when I saw the stun gun in Ernest's hand.

I went for my pistol, but his stun gun found my hand just as it left the holster. The current was an unexpected slap in the face. I dropped the gun and he tackled me on to the desk, attempting to shove the stun gun into my neck. I held both his arms and tried to find my feet. In the struggle he sent my right arm into the overhead bulb, slicing my hand and showering us both with broken glass. One of my kicks found his shin in the new darkness. I rolled over the desk to the other side while he wasted time moaning.

The light that came through my venetian blinds showed a redacted version of Ernest, half his freckled face hidden in the darkness. The tame lightning jumping between the contacts of his stun gun gave his face a demonic glow. On my desk was a heavy black telephone from the days of rotary dialling, its guts retrofitted for the new century. A friend had given it to me because he thought I'd appreciate its heavy substance. It was about to come in handy in a way not foreseen by its creators.

I grabbed the phone as Ernest and I circled each other around the desk. I took the receiver in my right hand and stretched out the coiled black plastic cord. The only sounds in the room were a dial tone and the crackle of electricity. I leaned in a little with my right shoulder, just enough for the kid to get ideas. He lunged over the desk at my right side. I turned my body as he came, sending the base of the phone in my left hand into Ernest's face with my entire body behind it. Something in his face broke, and then something else.

I dropped the phone and went for my gun. When I straightened up, Ernest had gone. I wanted to give chase, but that zap he'd given me had taken most of my strength.

I hauled myself to the window in time to see him jump into a running brown four-door that left the scene at illegal speeds. I scribbled down the number on the back of an old grocery bill. A friend in the NYPD owed me a favour, but he was a desk jockey who wouldn't be on duty until tomorrow morning.

My hand was bleeding. In the chaos of my medicine cabinet I found disinfectant and a bandage. I wrapped the gauze around my hand, barely feeling the sting of iodine on my skin. I'd need to figure out the source of the latest attempt on my person, but I was too tired to do it tonight. One thing I already knew was that Ernest — or whatever his real name was — hadn't been trying to kill me. Anyone with deadly intentions doesn't show up with a stun gun.

Another wave of sickness, made ten times stronger by the stun and the exertion, hammered into me. I dived on top of the toilet like it was a live grenade and vomited what remained of my dinner and the dim sum, which didn't turn out to be much. After that it was just an endless series of dry heaves scratching my throat raw. When it was finally over I was too weak to stand. I cradled the toilet bowl, rested my head on the seat, and waited for the nausea to pass.

Wednesday

The New York office of Thorpe Industries was a concrete tower spitting distance from Wall Street. Its thick façade gave way to an open killing field of a lobby, with no furniture or shrubbery to hide behind. A raised, semicircular front desk commanded the whole area, flanked on either side by x-ray machines and metal detectors. Although the threat of Soviet assault was no longer imminent, the set-up was equally useful to guard against the intermittent and unfocused aggression of the working poor.

'I have something for Mr Thorpe,' I said.

The receptionist eyed the white envelope in my hand, no doubt wondering how much toxin or explosive material its small volume could contain. She pointed towards the metal detector beside her. I put the envelope in a plastic tray and watched her scrutinize it as it went through.

'I'll send it upstairs,' she said, giving me a look that suggested I wait a little further away from her. I retreated from the front desk and inspected the propaganda on the walls.

A large world map showed Thorpe Industries' involvement in twenty countries on four continents. There were pictures of Potemkin military bases built to the same design as the ones I'd haunted in Kuwait. Photogenic soldiers in mess halls held Thorpe Industries food up to the camera. They reclined in their air-conditioned barracks or socialized at the base's bowling alley. It was a parallel world where military service was a fun summer camp that lasted three years, the mortar attacks and foreign countries beyond the wire airbrushed out.

The reality in Tehran had been less photogenic. Vital supplies regularly disappeared in the labyrinth of contractors and subcontractors through which the Pentagon procured its equipment and moved it around. Almost no real soldiers were responsible for managing logistics, and the contractors who were supposed to get us what we needed operated essentially above the law. I don't know if it was fraud or run-of-the-mill incompetence, but it didn't matter when there weren't enough night-vision goggles for a midnight patrol.

I'd heard similar stories about the Holy Land. Veterans spoke of inedible food, broken appliances that were never repaired, and buildings that were one strong fart away from collapse. Outside a war zone they sounded like just inconveniences, but they got people killed. War was a business like any other, and the government got what it paid for.

A casual reading of the financial pages would tell you that Marcus Thorpe was a powerful, ruthless man. Iris had added several charges of her own, but right now all I had was her word. I didn't investigate through third parties, especially not a woman I'd met by chasing her through Central Park. I had to size up Thorpe for myself, see what he was capable of if his buttons were pushed. Iris could be lying to me, intentionally or not. With true believers, reality was always optional.

Marcus Thorpe was not the type of man you just dropped in on. In addition to an impressive roster of enemies, his time was so valuable he would delegate trips to the can if the option were available. Getting an appointment would have been difficult in the best of circumstances, and on top of that I couldn't say an honest word about my reasons for being there.

I'd considered a more indirect approach to the problem, but it wasn't the kind of joint where a stolen uniform and a fake moustache got you in the service entrance. Each of the six cameras covering the lobby had a back-up. On the other floors they would be joined by retina scanners, motion sensors and other essential accessories of the modern paranoid's corporate fortress. Stillwater was here in force as well, their mercenaries in flak jackets and wraparounds as ubiquitous as the guns they carried. Arranging an involuntary interview with Thorpe would take a lot of time and money I didn't have.

My friend in the NYPD had run the licence from last night and come up with a car stolen in Brooklyn a few hours earlier. EZ-pass had recorded them crossing the bridge about twenty minutes later. All bridges and tunnels were covered by cameras, so there might be some footage of Ernest and his driver. If the quality was good enough, he'd promised to run it through the NYPD facial recognition system. The bureaucracy meant it would take a while, but once I had a name I'd be able to see if Ernest was connected to any of the current members of my fan club.

The large black and white clock resting high on the wall ticked off twenty unlabelled minutes. One of the triad of gold elevators behind the receptionist opened, and a man stepped on to the polished floor. He was about five foot eight in expensive shoes, and his welterweight body had almost no fat on it at all. His head was shaved, not balding, and the circular gold eyeglasses that refracted his Chinese eyes looked cosmetic. The pants of his dark blue serge suit were immaculately fitted but the jacket hung loose on his shoulders to leave room for his guns. Men like him never carried just one.

None of these details was remarkable, nor would the man have been had he stood still. Every movement began at the centre of the waist and flowed outward, stimulating his perfectly relaxed limbs just enough to bring them to life. He didn't walk so much as ripple towards me, a predator at ease in territory marked as his own.

'You are Felix Strange,' he stated. The edge of his New York voice had been taken off by a few years at a good school abroad. 'I am Mr Lim. Please place your firearms and anything metallic in the tray and step through.'

I unclipped my pistol and put it in the tray, along with my phone, keys and some spare ammunition. At the last moment I remembered the punching dagger strapped to my leg and added it to the pile, placing my fedora on top.

'Quite sure that's everything?' Lim asked.

I stepped through and nothing beeped.

Lim picked up my gun. 'A 1911,' he said, turning it over in his hand. 'That's a classic rod.'

'If it ain't broke, don't fix it,' I said.

Lim inspected the pits and scratches that covered almost every inch of the pistol's surface.

'My grandfather took it to Omaha Beach, and it kept my uncle alive in Vietnam.'

'You've carried on the family military tradition,' Lim said.

I think Lim would have known about my military background even if he didn't have a file in front of him; he could see the echoes of the parade ground in the way I walked.

'It's less a military tradition than some genetic defect that makes us volunteer,' I said.

Lim hinted at a smile.

'I bet you carry a more modern pistol.'

Lim opened his jacket to reveal twin .357 revolvers. 'Like you said: if it ain't broke . . . '

At least I was right about the number of guns. 'Why bother carrying two?' I asked. 'There's no risk of jamming with a revolver, and you can't fire those two monsters at once.'

'I like to have options,' Lim said. He popped the clip out of my gun and checked the breech for a shell. 'In light of its sentimental value, I'm prepared to let you take it upstairs unloaded.'

'Don't make an exception on my account,' I said. 'I don't need a firearm to feel special.'

Lim dropped my gun back in its tray and invited me to the waiting elevator with a sweep of his hand.

The room Lim ushered me into had the

133

charm and sterility of a laboratory studying infectious diseases — there were no plants, and the crystal vases resting on the glass coffee table were filled with multicoloured stones. Thorpe's assistant watched me survey the room, and didn't say hello.

'Have a seat,' Lim said, indicating a grey curvilinear sofa the colour of ash. 'Once we've verified your credentials, Mr Thorpe will ring for you.'

I hid my surprise. The letter I'd sent up was signed by a man named Greg Knight, the CEO of the third largest bank in the country. It said: 'I have full faith and confidence in Felix Strange.' I'd helped the man out of an awkward situation in Las Vegas a few years ago, involving a vintage Aston Martin, a pre-op transsexual and a traffic camera. If they called to verify he wouldn't hesitate to sing my praises. I still had the photographs.

'What do you do for Mr Thorpe?' I said, already knowing the answer, but the way he answered the question would be important.

Lim took a moment to reply. 'I manage risk.'

I laughed. I'm sure he managed risk away from Thorpe, out the door, down the street and into a body-bag if necessary. The worst kind of bodyguards were little more than hired thugs. They strutted around flexing and snarling, believing that their performance would intimidate any potential troublemakers instead of just getting in everybody's way. The best kind were completely unobtrusive while people had a good time, melting into the background like a sculpture not worth commenting on. Once someone got too frisky or threatened harm, everyone became aware of their capacity for unspeakable violence. Mr Lim was the latter kind. 'Does it pay well?'

'What do you think?' Lim said, and let the surroundings drive the point home. 'I don't suppose you can tell me the nature of your business here?'

'My instructions are to speak only to Mr Thorpe.' My cover was a messenger boy for a cartel of Wall Street interests looking for allies. The Crusade's arrival was the last straw. They were now angry and desperate enough to contemplate retaliatory measures. That was how the story would go, as all the plotters were figments of my imagination.

'Can I get you anything? You don't look well,' Lim said, with a wolf's concern for the health of a deer.

'I'm fine, pulled something training last night.' Song's medicine was keeping my stomach level. The drug called Evalacet stopped my muscles from aching and seizing up. I'd taken the last of it I had during my morning pharmaceutical ritual, and it wasn't a full dose. If I was lucky it would keep the pain to a dull ache, rather than creeping immolation. If I was unlucky, then my evening would not go smoothly.

'You don't strike me as the sporting type,' Lim said. 'Do you mind if I ask you a personal question?'

'Knock yourself out.'

'What's your style?'

'I'm a bit of a mongrel,' I said. 'The army tried to drill their way of fighting into me, but I found it too blunt. Wing Chun kung fu has more subtlety.'

Lim wasn't surprised by my answer and I didn't expect him to be. He'd watched me walk to the elevator just like I'd seen him leave it, observing the way I shifted my weight and how I carried myself. 'I've heard Wing Chun has many virtues, but I didn't think subtlety was one of them.'

'The brutality hides it well,' I said. 'What about you?'

'T'ai chi chu'an.'

Supreme ultimate boxing. I'd already guessed as much, considering the way he moved. People thought t'ai chi was something done by older gentlemen in parks, but it had been invented by a clan of professional bodyguards for efficiently killing anything that got in their way.

We lapsed into silence. I'd expected Lim to try the best-pal act, see if he could get anything out of me with shop talk and bullshit. Instead he sat perfectly still, looking at no point in particular on the wall. Somewhere in the building men sat in front of monitors and observed our silence, armed guards ready to charge at the first sign of trouble.

The glossy covers of complimentary magazines glowed under the institutional light. I picked one up and pretended to flip through it. Lim would be a tough customer under the best of circumstances. To attack a master of t'ai chi was picking a fight with water. He would use my

136

own force against me, flowing through it into the gaps in my defences. I would be a drowning man fighting the current: the harder I struggled, the easier it would be to drag me down. To win I'd have to be more malleable than him, and the way he moved didn't give me much cause for hope. The virtue of kung fu was explosive speed, and that might be my only way in. He'd let me get close, because t'ai chi fighters liked to mix it up at point-blank range. I'd have one chance to move faster than he could follow, no flexing of the muscles or movement of the shoulder to give the game away. Even water could be moved by a controlled explosion.

I looked up from the magazine I wasn't reading to see Lim still staring at the same point, but now with the hint of a smile. 'They built a squash court down in the basement in the eighties,' Lim said. 'No one really uses it any more. It's spacious, well lit and deserted.'

The assistant stole alternating glances at us like she was watching a tennis match. She probably had the wrong idea; the truth was much more dangerous, even in these devout times. The phone on her desk beeped. She jumped and gave Lim the nod.

'Duty calls,' I said. Lim typed in some numbers on a keypad next to the office door and then gave his fingerprints. The door clicked open, but he didn't move. 'You're not coming in to babysit?'

'You'll see that isn't necessary.' He let me put my hand on the door before he continued, in a softer voice, 'Perhaps another time, Mr Strange, when you've taken your medication.'

The room was dark for this early in the afternoon. A little sunlight evaded curtains closed against the skyline. A desk lamp showed Thorpe slumped in his chair watching stocks crawl across a monitor. The broad shoulders that had been his ticket out of the projects of East Baltimore weren't yet covered by the years of easy living that had colonized his stomach and face. The grey suit that struggled to hold him in was bespoke Savile Row. Jowls thick and rippling as vaudeville curtains framed Thorpe's face, which was more weather-beaten than usual for a boardroom warrior of his age. The folds of skin emphasized his eyes rather than drowning them, two sharp lights in a smooth dark sea. His hair had retreated to the equator of his skull, black freezing to white by the time it reached his temples.

'You'll have to forgive my bluntness Mr Strange,' Thorpe said, not looking in my direction, 'because I'm sure as hell not going to change or apologize.' The low growl he spoke in sounded like his real voice, not an affectation to fit his hardnosed image.

In his hand was the letter I'd sent up. 'You know Greg well?' he said.

He knew I wasn't the type of person that the head of a large bank invited over for dinner, and wanted to see what our connection was. I let his bait dangle on the line. 'You could say Mr Knight is an admirer of my work,' I said.

'I'm expecting a call from Hong Kong in a minute. I'll let you make your pitch while I'm waiting.' He didn't offer me a seat.

With maybe five seconds to get his attention, I had to play my trump card straight off. 'I've been sent here on a matter that concerns your son.'

Thorpe's eyes narrowed. Maybe someone had already come around sniffing for hush money. 'Close the door,' he said. 'Before you continue, Mr Strange, you should know I take an old-world view of blackmail.'

Thorpe was the kind of powerful man who always got mentioned in rumours and conspiracy theories. In my research I'd found pages dedicated to ranting about him playing the market just before Houston, providing the weapon that destroyed Tehran, plus involvement with the Freemasons and a dozen alien conspiracies. One rumour I could believe concerned an enterprising photographer. He'd recorded employees of one of Thorpe's subsidiaries buying and trading young women in Angola like baseball cards. The agreement Angola had with the United States ensured that their soldiers and contractors were above the local law, but it would have been a tremendous blow to Thorpe's reputation. There were several Christian groups who took a very dim view of human trafficking, and they could be relied on to picket his headquarters until the second coming. The photographer sent copies to Thorpe, along with a demand for a million dollars to turn over the original files. According to the story, he was currently holding up a guard tower at Camp Freedom in Uzbekistan.

'With respect, Mr Thorpe, you have it

backwards. I represent the blackmailees.'

Thorpe was surprised, but only a little less hostile. 'Have a seat,' he said.

'It would be best for both of us if you turned off all the recording devices in this room,' I said. 'I'm unarmed, and your hand is on a panic button anyway.'

The arm I could see pressed a few buttons on his computer. 'We are now completely off the record. Feel free to mix yourself a drink; I'll have a Scotch and soda.'

I didn't like being anybody's servant, but a thirty-year-old single malt was fair compensation, especially if I made it a double. I didn't normally drink on the clock, but the ache in my joints made it medicinal.

'You showing up here two days after the arrival of the Crusade isn't a coincidence.'

'I'd say it's closer to cause and effect.'

'You could be one of them, here to stir things up.'

'I guess it depends on how much you trust your golfing buddy.'

'Greg lies to his shareholders and cheats on his wife,' Thorpe said, 'but he doesn't have the balls to cross me.'

'Besides,' I said, 'it would be my word against yours, and due process still applies to a man in your tax bracket.'

'You'd be surprised.' Thorpe fixed me with a stare sharpened on the dignity of his underlings. 'What do you want, who do you work for, and what does it have to do with my son?'

Maybe Iris was on to something after all. 'I

don't usually lay all my cards on the table with no guarantee of something in return.'

'Whose office do you think this is?' Thorpe said.

I began to unroll my spiel. 'I represent a citizens' group who feel this country is heading in the wrong direction.'

'I don't have a lot of time for do-gooders,' Thorpe said.

'Like everything else that happens in this country, Mr Thorpe, enlightened self-interest plays a part. Many of the members of this group have led privileged lives that insulated them from danger until it was at their doorstep, threatening them and their families.' I put a little extra weight on the last word and made sure I had his eyes when I said it. If he was going to call Lim to throw me out, now would be the time. Thorpe didn't hit his intercom, and didn't speak. 'I've been sent here to tell you that you aren't the only one being persecuted. You are not alone.'

Thorpe finished his drink in one long swig, his eyes lingering on the glass. I'd pushed my luck as far as it could go, so I kept my mouth shut.

'You may find it surprising — I certainly do — that your words are a comfort to me. I want those bastards to have as many enemies as possible. Plans are being made to take the fight to them?'

'Yes. Nothing ostentatious, hopefully nothing public, but yesterday's outrage has some significant taxpayers feeling cornered.'

Thorpe's face darkened at the mention of what the media were now calling the Wall Street

Seven. The men Benny and I had seen arrested on television were just like Thorpe. They were members of the aristocracy of global capitalism, nearly immune from common concerns and ordinary justice. That's what I, and Thorpe, had believed until yesterday.

'They didn't call it profiteering when we signed the contracts they offered us. I've done business with all of them at one time or another. Those are good men they're crucifying.' Thorpe's voice faded into a monologue of obscenities only he could hear. He pointed at the numbers on the screen. 'You think the fit the market is having is a coincidence? People have finally caught on that this country is being run by maniacs.' Thorpe watched the numbers for a while, swearing to himself as each new figure appeared. 'The men you represent may not want my help, Mr Strange. The Elders and their lapdogs have it in for me personally.'

'Does that have something to do with it?' I said, looking at the signed picture of Thorpe standing between failed presidential primary hopeful Michael Wilkes and his running mate Lee Comey. The picture was in the top row of a case set against the back wall, among other pictures of Thorpe posing with sheikhs, movie stars, NFL players and the stars of the old government. None of the current administration was present. The other rows held college football trophies, chamber of commerce awards and three honorary degrees.

Wilkes had been the favoured primary candidate of the financial class, and that had made him a near-certainty for the nomination. The only other member of the party who had anything close to a chance was Senator Adamson, darling of the Christian Right. Millions of followers had opened their hearts to him, but Adamson couldn't find enough men in suits to do the same with their cheque books.

'I was the Wilkes/Comey campaign's chief fundraiser, and people like Adamson have long memories,' Thorpe said. What would later be called 'The Primetime Massacre' had started out as a rerun of a familiar tale. 'At first we thought Adamson would be useful; we relied on people like him to bring the faithful to the ballot box when we needed them, and keep them quiet when they were an embarrassment.'

'But he didn't play ball.'

'We thought it was just a ploy to get the vice-presidency. Adamson would go away once he ran out of money or made an ass of himself. Then the goddamn media fell in love with him.'

I had dim memories of fawning articles and softball interviews, the Beltway going gaga over a bigoted demagogue because of what they called his authenticity.

'I raised double the money they had, but it didn't matter in the end.'

At the party convention, it was supposed to end the way all political Cinderella stories did: with Adamson under a bus driven by people like Thorpe. Instead, six hours before the keynote address — to be given by Adamson as sop to the rubes — Houston disappeared. 'Forgive me, but there's one thing I've always wanted to know: did he really give that speech off-the-cuff? I always thought it was part of the myth they built around him.'

'I don't know,' Thorpe said. 'I can tell you there was no tele-prompter, and he didn't have any notes or cue cards when he stepped on to the podium. It doesn't matter anyway; no one was listening to the words. It was the sound of his voice, the look on his face . . . ' Thorpe looked at the sliver of city visible between the curtains. 'I hated the man's guts, and I still think it's the greatest political speech the country has ever seen.'

Adamson gave people the words they wanted to hear, words of redemption and revenge, Manichean certainties for 300 million confused newborns crying out in the night. In the words of his supporters, the whole country could see Adamson's heart, and they wanted him to lead them. The convention and the presidency were a foregone conclusion.

'Adamson's aides called, looking for a mutually convenient time so I could come over and kiss his ass,' Thorpe continued. 'These devout men wanted to rub our faces in the turnaround after all those years of being our tools. Every lobbyist, consultant and campaign chair got in line, but I didn't give them the satisfaction. They needed me to fight their great Middle Eastern Crusade, and they knew it.'

I looked in Thorpe's eyes and understood why he was telling me this story. He had that dogged, wistful look shared by all veterans of a lost cause.

'We convinced ourselves it was going to be

business as usual.' The mysterious 'we' Thorpe kept referring to must be Wall Street money men, the investor class, CEOs. 'After all, we'd had Holy Joes in the Oval Office during some of our best years. McKinley said: 'The business of America is business.' It's corporations that pour the cement for their megachurches, keep the lights on and the organ playing. We thought even those fire-breathing hicks would figure that out.'

I didn't remember Adamson making any promises to collectivize farms or nationalize industries during his inaugural speech, but I was here in the character of an errand boy for the rich and powerful, and intended to play the part. 'I'm sure the entertainment companies expected some trouble — '

'Hollywood and the record labels were used to that shit,' Thorpe said, his Baltimore upbringing surfacing to elongate the last word. 'No surprise that industry has the best PR in the world. They'd make some noise about tightening up their ratings system and pay a few symbolic fines. While their enemies were crowing they'd invite Congressmen down to Hollywood, introduce them to celebrities and take them backstage. Sprinkle a little stardust over the average middle-aged Congressman and he starts to moon like a teenager.' Thorpe chuckled, or swirled some phlegm, it was hard to tell.

'It didn't work that time.'

'It was a time of firsts,' Thorpe said. 'Before Houston, do you know any bookie who'd take thousand-to-one odds that a Congressman couldn't be bought?'

'Point taken.'

Thorpe leaned back in his chair. 'Pretty soon they'd branched out of entertainment and were sticking their holier-than-thou noses into every-thing. The Unborn Children Defence Act sent half the biotech industry scrambling for Europe, and the other half left after the Fairness in Teaching of the Origins of Life Act meant every potential egghead in the country had to sit through a semester of intelligent design. And don't even get me started on the Office of Mercy.'

I didn't say anything but he continued anyway.

'We worked long and hard to rid this country of socialistic ideas like welfare. We would have privatized social security too if retirees weren't churchgoers who voted like it was a sport. Now those morons have brought it all back under a different name. I don't want some federal chumps bankrupting the nation to get them-selves into heaven.'

The Office of Mercy's budget was a drop in the ocean of money Thorpe's conglomerate had siphoned off the government, most of it with no-bid contracts. He hadn't complained about the Revivalists then.

'Enough about the past,' Thorpe said, rising. 'It can't help us.' He walked over to the window and peered through the curtains like a fugitive watching for the law. 'What makes your bosses think we can negotiate with them?'

'Everyone can be negotiated with,' I said. 'The only reason the Revivalists are doing this is because they think they can get away with it.

They may be true believers, but they are hardly monks. We're the ones who fund their private jets and limousines by keeping their wives and children on the payrolls of our think tanks and associations. Turn off the tap, and their mortgages will do our work for us.'

Thorpe stared out the window. He'd been on the cover of a business magazine last year in much the same position. The title of the article, 'Street Fighter', was in big letters beside him. It was a recurring theme in the financial press's coverage of Thorpe; a lazy way of adding some colour, and a reminder to all of where he'd come from.

'Lim gave me the highlights from your file,' Thorpe said.

I was starting to wonder if there was anyone in this town who hadn't read my supposedly classified service record. Maybe I should just take out a billboard in Times Square and save everyone the trouble.

'Were the Iranians you fought religious fanatics?'

'Some were. There were a lot of patriots fighting for their homeland as well. The line blurred easily.'

'Did they have any respect for their own lives?'

'They attacked main battle tanks with AK-47s,' I said. 'I suppose it depends on your definition of bravery.'

'Considering your experience, Mr Strange,' Thorpe said, 'do you really believe we can stop these crazies by cutting their pay cheques?'

'We aren't at war with them,' I said.

Thorpe heard the hesitation in my voice as loudly as a gunshot. It was the one occasion when the role I was playing had the same time as the stopped clock of my own convictions. 'You choose your words carefully, Strange.'

'It's my business.'

Thorpe nodded, but he was lost in his own thoughts. 'If you stay in my business long enough, you begin to think everything is negotiable,' Thorpe said. 'It's the businessman's disease. Your bosses like to talk tough. They'll put thugs on the payroll overseas and look the other way, but they haven't got the stomach for a fight on their front lawns. Tell Greg to send you back to me when he's come up with a plan for grown-ups. And if you hear anything about the Crusade, anything at all, you contact Mr Lim directly. You'll find I can be a generous man if the cause is right. Are we clear?'

I nodded. 'Thanks for the drink,' I said and shook his hand, felt all the invisible grime of kickbacks and dirty plays that had accumulated under those manicured fingernails.

'If your bosses don't wake up soon, they'll be trying to sell their executioners rifles while they're standing against the wall.'

I took that as my cue to leave. As I opened the door, Thorpe yelled at the intercom which activated at the sound of his voice. 'Maureen,' he said, 'I told you to put Hong Kong through the minute they called.'

'They haven't called, sir,' the intercom said. 'Should I call them?'

When I closed the door, the question still

hung in front of his brooding face. It might just be a mistake, except mistakes didn't happen to men like him.

* * *

'Are you looking for something?' Iris asked. She wore a little black dress seeded with sequins that only showed themselves when she moved. More were hidden in her hair, pinned back according to an architect's elaborate design. I was treated to a miniature light show every time Iris reached for her drink or laughed too hard.

'I'm trying to figure out where you hide the video camera.'

'Trade secret.'

'Fair enough,' I said. Speculating was more fun anyway. 'So who are we spying on today?'

Iris didn't find the joke funny. 'If you're done, I'll tell you why we're here.' She leaned in close, which was all right with me. 'I'm here to uncover illegal drug use and sales.'

'What are they peddling here, heart medication?' The bar was on the edge of Hell's Kitchen, one of a dozen like it just down the block, safe alternatives that lived off the area's old reputation. We sat in low-backed stools in front of the bar. Behind us were some black tables and a few booths at the back, upholstered in fake green leather. Posters advertising cheap oblivion between the hours of four and six shared space on the wall with glamour shots of Hollywood royalty, unable to protest because they'd been dead long before the bar opened. The whole place was as memorable as a TV dinner. 'I would've thought a professional party boy like Junior wouldn't be caught dead in here.'

'That's why it's a perfect place to score.'

It did explain the few people I'd noticed who were out of place, cool kids who should have known better. Impatience kept their fingers drumming on tables and against drinks they barely touched, more annoyed at being forced to be here than apprehensive of whatever deal they were waiting for.

'So what is he into?'

'I saw him do prescription uppers mostly, with the occasional painkiller to smooth the ride down.'

Half the kids in the country raided their parents' medicine cabinet for pills like that. 'I expected more from a man with so much time and money to destroy himself.'

'Junior's fortune didn't make him any more creative.'

'Usually someone else takes care of that,' I said. 'Guys like him always attract friends of the bloodsucking and reptilian nature. Any of his pals fit that description?'

'No one I met. All his friends were just like him: rich, bored and not very bright.'

'From what you say he isn't smart enough to score stuff like that on his own. Does he have a regular dealer?'

Iris nodded. 'I haven't seen him around lately.'

'If we can't find Junior, his dealer might be just as good.' 'Speaking of drugs,' Iris said, 'what is that?'

I'd ordered a bottle of beer and a glass of water, which had confused the waiter and my date. She watched me put three drops of Song's mixture in the water and drink it down. 'It's a herbal medicine,' I said.

'Yeah, that's what they all say.'

I scanned the crowd while I tried to drink the medicine's bad taste out of my mouth. I'd memorized Junior's face from some society photos in preparation for tonight. No one in the room even remotely fitted the bill.

A group of five secretaries shared a booth in silence, slumped against the upholstery and staring at their mojitos with the eyes of obstinate mules.

'I paid Thorpe a visit this morning,' I said. Out of the corner of my eye I saw her jaw line tighten. 'He thinks a war is coming just like Brother Isaiah did, but it isn't the Crusade he's worried about, not after the Elders threw those Wall Street men in irons.'

'I'm trying to figure out why I'm not wearing similar jewellery,' Iris said. 'It sounds like you don't believe me.'

'Something about the man bothered me, and it wasn't just the obvious. I may have missed something,' I said. 'He's so dirty it's hard to distinguish individual crimes from the general muck. Do you know what Brother Isaiah threatened him with?'

'Brother Isaiah didn't threaten people.'

'Then Thorpe wouldn't have had a reason to kill him.'

Iris didn't respond.

151

'You must have considered the possibility that it was an inside job. Someone in the Crusade with his own ideas tired of waiting for Isaiah to be called to his final reward.'

'Intimidation, assassination; you talk about us like we're the mafia.'

I held my tongue.

'The Crusade isn't like the Committee for Child Protection. If I'm wrong about Thorpe, then White is next in line. He's capable of anything.'

'And I thought you people of faith stuck together.'

'Ezekiel White is a good Samaritan only to himself,' she said. 'He's just another opportunist using our saviour to hide his own ambition.'

'Listen, White isn't paying me enough to defend his character,' I said. 'I know everything I saw at the crime scene came through him. White and your boss may have been in a turf war, but he doesn't have the balls to do something like this on his own. The order would have to come from someone higher up.'

Iris knew the only people above White were the Council of Elders, so she changed the subject. 'Whether Junior shows up here or not, I have a job to do.'

'I'm not stopping you.'

'Yes, you are.' Iris indicated someone behind me with her eyes.

I walked over to inspect the jukebox spewing out Top Forty white noise. At a nearby table was a single bridge and tunnel man in his late thirties AWOL from his wife. He had a full head of dark

152

hair and a face that had once been handsome. He'd probably been quite popular in his youth and had fancied himself a ladies' man. It was that image he saw in the mirror every morning, not the stocky ex-college-athlete exiled for fifteen years to sales. That was the only way to explain the chutzpah to think he had a chance with Iris. His pale face was flushed but he didn't take off his coat. He just glanced at Iris's naked back, growing bolder with each look, and wiped his sweating brow. I decided to call him Mark, because it was more polite than idiot, or sucker.

I returned to the stool beside her. 'He doesn't look like a drug dealer,' I said.

'He probably isn't, but he might know one.'

'And if an attractive young woman asks him the right way, he might just tell her.'

She nodded. 'Give me half an hour.'

'I'll get out of your way.'

'No one will approach me with you lurking in the background,' she said. 'People might think we're together. Not in love of course, but maybe you're my rich sugar daddy.'

I laughed. 'Not in this suit, sweetheart. What are you suggesting?'

Iris fluttered her eyelashes. 'A messy, very public break-up.'

'Well, I suppose I could dump you,' I said. 'Be outraged that you'd dared to turn twenty-one. Then he could swoop in and catch you as you rebound off the floor.'

The fluttering stopped. 'We need it to be believable.'

'Well, we're getting there.' The secretaries were

153

still watching us through their mojitos. They hadn't touched the plate of fried God-knows-what that had arrived at their table. 'Well,' I said, turning back to Iris, 'I guess I could — '

Her drink hit me full in the face. Bubbles in the tonic water tickled my nose, the drops that found the corners of my mouth giving a lemon aftertaste to my embarrassment.

'I'm sorry,' she whispered.

'Forget about it,' I whispered back with an angry face for our audience. 'It was kind of refreshing.'

A headwind of amused and disapproving glances propelled me to the men's room. I washed my face with neon-pink soap from the dispenser. It would make me smell like a hospital floor for the rest of the evening but I didn't have much choice. I splashed some water on my face, and when I opened my eyes Mark was standing behind me.

'Hey, buddy,' he said, a shit-eating grin on his face. 'I saw you get a shower.'

'I'm glad you enjoyed the show.' The guy was a first-class blowhard, the type that frightened old women into buying burglar alarms. The charming personality didn't make it any easier for me to watch him fall into the arms of the Crusade.

'What did you do to make your lady so angry? You screwing around?'

'She's not my lady.'

'Not any more,' he said.

I couldn't decide if the smug satisfaction on his face was comical or disgusting.

'I don't know what you were thinking,

154

throwing away a body like that.' He traced an hourglass with his hands.

It made me think he must be a method actor researching a role, because no one could be that crass. 'Isn't your wife expecting you home soon?' I said. It was the only way I could warn him without blowing Iris's cover. The words might find their way through all the booze to where his conscience was hiding.

'Don't worry about her,' he said. 'What she doesn't know won't hurt her, right?' His smile tried to rope me into some big male conspiracy.

I smiled back, and like the sky after a long storm, my conscience cleared right up. 'It's your funeral,' I said, and left him grinning on his own.

Next to the bathrooms was a door that led to an alley. It had been left open for smokers. I went outside and leaned against the brick wall, giving Iris and Mark time to get acquainted while I pretended to nurse my shame. In my breast pocket was a cigarette I'd stolen from Benny when he wasn't looking. I'd never planned to smoke it; I'd been stealing them from him since our army days because it drove him nuts, and the habit was impossible to break. I lit it up from a half-burned matchbook I found among the discarded butts and let it burn between my fingers for the sake of appearances.

I'd left a message on White's phone this morning, telling him I was going dark for a while to follow up on a lead. He'd be furious, but it was the least he deserved after keeping me in the dark on so many important things. In the message I claimed that no one had shown at the dead drop, and implied it was because of the presence of his agents and their 'kick me' wardrobe. White would assume my silence was anger at his tail, and that was fine with me. It was a rare day that I got to throw a temper tantrum and put it to good use.

A busboy came out the side door and threw some bags in the dumpster. He gave me a commiserating smile.

'You saw it all too, huh?'

He shrugged a yes. Above the door was a camera that covered the alley. It gave me an idea how I could turn the jilted boyfriend act to my advantage.

'This place has cameras in the bar, doesn't it?'

He took so much time answering I thought he hadn't been here long enough to pick up any English. 'Sure.'

'Who watches them?'

'Nobody. Just a lot of TVs in a little room.'

'You suppose I could get in there?' He was wary. 'She may hate my guts, but I still worry about her.'

He doubted my sincerity, until I put twenty dollars in his hand. Whether I was concerned or just jealous didn't change the colour of my money. It wasn't a lot, but it was enough for a busboy whose papers might not be in order.

He led me to a back room with the furtive look of an amateur cat-burglar. He opened the door, mumbled something about it having nothing to do with him, and then went back to the kitchen. A camera covered the front entrance, three handled the floor and two more

156

for the bar. I'd see Junior if he showed, and I could keep an eye on Iris.

She was already at work. Mark sat on the stool I'd warmed a few minutes ago. There was no audio, but I didn't need it. I'd seen my fair share of gold-diggers and professional Jezebels working matrimonial cases. The divorce laws were punitive as hell where adultery was concerned, and they'd spawned an industry used by vengeful wives to gain the upper hand. Most of the girls were young — the whiff of stolen innocence was a deadly weapon in a lawyer's hands — and not very bright. They thought seducing a man was as simple as putting on a short skirt and leaning in. That worked for desperate and stupid men, but the hard sell was too obvious to catch anyone of intelligence.

Iris played the game on a higher level. From the look on his face she was making interesting conversation, probably keeping the discussion close to the topic that interested Mark the most: himself. Iris laughed at his jokes and smiled at lines he'd used since college. Blood was already fleeing south from his brain. Mark was so busy feeling attractive, interesting and powerful that he didn't notice her wrapping him around her finger. Twenty minutes in Iris accidentally let her fingers play across his forearm on the way to her glass, and pulled the knot tight.

I texted Iris saying I'd meet her outside. She took it as an excuse to leave. Iris waved away his protests, and he had to be content with handing her his card, the only thing they exchanged. I let her leave first on the off-chance he tried to follow her. Mark didn't stir from the bar stool, just stared at the Scotch in his glass and nursed unrealistic dreams.

'Where did you go off to?' she said when I met her on the corner.

'I was playing guardian angel with the bar's security cameras,' I said. 'Did you get what you wanted?'

Iris pursed her lips. 'He's not a righteous man, but stupidity is guarding his soul.'

'Junior may still show.'

'It's too late,' she said. 'He would have moved on by now. Let's take a break.' She could see I wasn't convinced. 'If you don't trust me to do my job, we might as well part company now.'

I thought about it. There wasn't much in it for her to lead me around if she really did believe Thorpe was responsible, unless she was working some other angle. She could see the gears moving in my head, and smiled her manipulative smile. From her eyes I could tell she didn't mean it that way; it had replaced whatever facial expressions she used to have. 'At the rate I'm doling out trust, I'll be giving you blank cheques before the weekend.'

'Big deal,' she said. 'Your cheques bounce.'

Two blocks over there was a hot dog vendor on the corner. She ordered a jumbo with everything and a soda.

'This is your break?' I asked.

'What have you got against hot dogs?'

'Nothing, I just like to sit down when I eat.'

'I guess it's not very ladylike,' Iris said.

I could tell by the delight in her eyes when the

vendor handed over her frank that she couldn't care less.

'You make it look classy,' I said. Her attitude was a nice change from everyone watching their shadows, and I had to admire it. 'I just didn't think you were the type of woman who hung out on street corners.'

Iris found that a lot funnier than I expected.

An NYPD officer stopped near us. 'Evening, folks,' he said. 'Can I see your ID cards?'

I handed mine over and he gave it back after a quick glance.

Iris showed the officer her card but hid it from my view. 'I don't want him to know my real age.'

The officer laughed, and resumed his rounds with a departing thank you.

'So what's going to happen to that guy you were twisting into balloon animals?' I said.

'You mean Stanley?'

I nodded, his name restoring a shadow of sympathy.

'Probably nothing.'

She didn't seem inclined to go on. I had no good reason to press her, but I did anyway. 'Define probably.'

Iris put down her soda and looked me in the eye before she answered. I wasn't sure what she was looking for. 'It goes in my report. Adultery is a sin, not a crime. If a case officer decides it's worth pursuing, one of our evangelists will have a quiet word with him, or his pastor. That's usually all that happens for a first offence.'

'And if he already has a record?' I said, thinking of Cecily's colour-coded books.

Iris sighed. I think my conversation choice was spoiling her snack.

'I should have known you'd defend adultery.'

'I don't know what you mean.'

'Infidelity is your primary source of income.'

'That doesn't mean I like it,' I said. 'And for the record I don't like deadbeat fathers, runaways or insurance cheats either. I deal with them because it's part of my job. People whose lives are going well don't need a private investigator.'

'I deal with them for my job too. So why are you looking down on me from that tall horse?'

'I'm just an observer. You're an agent provocateur. The difference between us comes down to a single word: entrapment.'

Iris laughed. The guy in the hot dog stand showed no desire to join the conversation.

'Entrapment is just a secular word for temptation. If a man can't resist a young paralegal with self-esteem problems, he'll have no chance against the Devil. We find those who are weak and help them before their souls are imperilled. Brother Isaiah called us his hidden angels.'

All demons were angels once. I imagined the resemblance was still strong.

'Let me tell you a story,' I said. 'About a year back, a woman came to me because she thought her husband was playing around. The Romeo in question was a hotshot young aide at City Hall. He went to the right schools, photographed well, could work a crowd and was connected up the wazoo. He was one of those guys who'd been primed for a bright political future in the womb.'

'It sounds like the only mistake he'd ever made was cheating on a woman smarter than him.'

'That's what I thought, but it turned out he was already practised in the art of ass-covering. He had a fellow gumshoe following his wife, just out of general paranoia. When the investigator reported where she'd been, he knew there could be only one reason for his wife to visit me. Of course a hint of adultery, or even worse, a divorce, would make him politically radioactive. So he cleaned up his mess before I could prove it existed.'

'He stopped cheating then?'

'You could say that. He hired men to kill his mistress and hide her body.'

'Is the asshole in prison?' Iris asked.

'He's a happily married state senator,' I said. I hadn't expected the crime to shock her, but I could see his happy ending had got to her a little. 'The point is, in an age when people minded their own business, there would have been a divorce, some haggling over alimony, and a young woman would still be alive.'

Iris drank her soda and thought about it. 'The man was obviously capable of murder. In your permissive world, he probably would have killed his wife over the alimony.'

'Either way, adultery and murder still happened,' I said. 'So why go to all that trouble of making people ashamed of themselves?'

Iris sighed. 'Can we talk about something that isn't depressing?'

'Sure.'

Iris finished her hot dog, and I tried to find a few stars through light pollution and a cloudy sky. The hot dog grill sizzled and popped, and spoke for both of us.

'Break's over,' she said, and threw away her trash.

We hailed a cab and Iris gave the driver an address in Red Hook that I recognized. I wanted to know why we were going there of all places but I stayed quiet. It was known that some cabbies, postmen and even delivery boys could make a few extra bucks keeping an eye out for the authorities. The invisible hand that was quietly strangling the country ensured that there were a lot of takers. It was supposed to be another anti-terrorism initiative, but nobody knew where the information went once it disappeared down the hole.

When we entered Battery Tunnel the cabbie's eyes and mine met in the rear-view mirror. He was Eastern European, a Catholic judging from the saint bobbing on the dashboard. The government had put on an aggressive campaign to bring more Eastern Europeans over, in part to replace the Indians and Sri Lankans who had stopped coming. People weren't always polite enough to ask about your religion before they started being afraid of you. We didn't exchange small talk, and his eyes went back to the road as we returned to the night.

We got off the Gowanus Expressway and headed to the waterfront. Down the side streets I caught glimpses of the loading cranes on the waterfront, still covered in light, towering and alone. Red Hook was the up-and-coming neighbourhood that never quite arrived. Once the port of call for almost anything entering New York, it had declined in the last century to a collection of empty warehouses and urban grit. The Brooklyn Cruise Terminal had almost changed that, until Houston strangled the flow of tourists and their dollars.

What had arrived instead was a small collection of slummers and the painfully hip. They weren't worth as much as cruise passengers, but they were enough to sustain a small underground club scene. The main attraction was the belief that they could fly under the radar in such a grim and inconvenient location, keeping officials and suburbanites alike at bay. I'd never been fashionable enough to know if it worked.

We headed into the labyrinth of warehouses near the bay. When the cab stopped I reached into my wallet but Iris was there first.

'Forget it,' she said. 'I'm sure my expense account is more generous than yours.'

We stood in a side street almost at the edge of the peninsula, less than a hundred steps from the East River. It would have been easy to see Lady Liberty — lit from below, her face turned away — if it hadn't been for all the mouldering warehouses in between.

'Come on,' she said, when I didn't move. 'Community policing or not, this isn't the kind of place to stand around.'

'Maybe we should go in separately,' I said. 'If

163

I'm going to take another gin bath, I want it to be for charity.'

'I'm here to report on gamblers and the usurers who prey on them,' she said. 'I promise there won't be any scenes this time.'

'You were right when you said no one would believe we're a couple,' I said. 'For the sake of a cover we should make the relationship professional.'

Iris got the wrong idea, but she reacted in a way I didn't expect. Most women went straight to righteous indignation when it was suggested that their company was for sale. Their faces would flush, nostrils flare with outrage, and histrionics were guaranteed unless the woman was mollified immediately. I'd seen a variant in women accused of adultery enough times to know the signs.

Instead there was a strange, weary anger in Iris's eyes, a bitterness that collected at the left corner of her mouth and twisted it. She didn't get hot or scream, and when she spoke her voice was frozen. 'Like you said, in that suit you wouldn't be able to afford me.'

'I meant I'll be your bodyguard.'

Iris wasn't convinced, but she did calm down. 'They know me here. I've never had a bodyguard before.'

'You're playing a rich, spoiled party girl, right?'

Iris nodded.

'Then tell them it's Daddy's orders. Kidnapping has become a lucrative business.'

Iris thought it over and agreed with a shrug.

A few steps below street level, an unmarked steel door was set into a warehouse that looked one bad storm away from being condemned. 'I might be recognized in here,' I said.

'Will that be bad?'

It was my turn to shrug. 'It depends.'

Iris's knock opened a slit in the door. A pair of eyes stared out with suspicion until they settled on Iris, and laugh lines encircled them like a halo. The door opened just wide enough for the man behind it to get Iris in a big hug, so it had to open all the way.

Bear got his name from his size and the woeful state of underworld vocabulary. He was a six foot four Kenyan with the muscles of a weightlifter and the skin of a newborn baby. He wore a fitted charcoal double-breasted suit, with a fedora to match. Being courteous and presentable was part of his job as the first person the customer saw. Bear was the most polite bouncer you'd ever meet, until you raised a fuss.

'How you been, girl?' he said when he released Iris.

'You know me, always getting into trouble. That's why he's here,' she said, rolling her eyes in my direction.

'Been a while, Felix,' he said.

I said hello and braved one of his handshakes.

'You two know each other?'

'We went to the same parochial school.'

Iris looked from Bear to me and realized we weren't going to say another word in front of her. She took my hat. 'I'll check our things while you boys catch up.'

'I didn't think you'd come back here,' Bear said, after she'd gone.

'That makes two of us,' I replied. 'Think he's still angry?'

Bear shrugged. 'I haven't heard your name in a while. That's a good sign, but you know how he is.' Yes, I did. 'I have to tell him you're here.'

'I know. It's good to see you, Bear.'

He gave me a friendly punch on the shoulder, which would have knocked me over if I hadn't been ready for it. 'You take care,' he said, and went back to his post at the door.

Iris was already inside, but I had to make a stop at the weapons locker. I gave up my guns to a bored, skinny kid who shouldn't be out this late on a school night. Most nightspots and public buildings had started to check guns after the federal concealed-carry laws. Now anyone over eighteen with no criminal record could carry a gun if he promised to be nice. It had shot one of the only perks of being a private detective all to hell.

The Waterfront was a glass tortoise of a bar that hid inside the shell of an old warehouse. The building had been strengthened just enough to prevent it from being condemned, while the interior was left untouched. The bar had been built inside what was once the main loading area. Glass walls kept the heat in and the vermin who now owned the place out. It was gritty ambience at the perfect remove.

The interior was a Hollywood re-creation of an illegal speakeasy. The barmen and waitresses maintained a strict gangsters and molls dress code. All the furniture had been expensively designed to look like it had been made out of shipping crates. A big band fronted by a black chanteuse in a strapless dress played 'It Ain't Necessarily So'. In the crowded New York nightlife it was unique, but novelty alone hadn't kept it going. The Waterfront's enduring popularity really rested in what went on downstairs.

Iris made the rounds of the staff. She was on a first-name basis with everyone, right down to the busboys, and she even knew the names of their wives and children. I was impressed and confused at the same time, since for all her knowledge she didn't seem to know who ran the place. I played my role as silent bodyguard, scanning the tables for any sign of Junior and keeping an eye on the wrought-iron spiral staircase in the corner of the bar guarded by two bouncers. The VIP rooms and offices were upstairs, the private club downstairs. When trouble came, it would be from above.

Charlie, the manager, came over to our corner of the bar and accepted a hug from a woman half his age. When he saw me the gossip he was about to spill died on his lips. The gold horn-rimmed glasses he wore couldn't hide the fear in his eyes.

'You okay Charlie?' Iris asked.

'Sure,' he mumbled. 'Who did you say you were looking for?'

'Junior. No one has seen him around.'

'He hasn't been here in a while.' Charlie couldn't keep his eyes off me.

'He's always here.'

'Maybe he went on vacation.'

The way Charlie said the last word made me uneasy. His mouth formed the word 'vacation', but his voice said 'hell'. Before Iris could ask him another question he mumbled an excuse and vanished.

'I'm glad I have you around to put people at ease,' Iris said.

'I told you I might be recognized.'

'I couldn't tell if Charlie was afraid of you, or what might happen to you.'

I looked up to the private rooms, their one-way windows keeping out my undesirable gaze. 'If I'm cramping your style again — '

Iris waved away the rest of the sentence. She handed me one of the complimentary drinks that had started to proliferate around her, and pointed to a table that one of the waitresses was keeping free.

'You're a popular girl,' I said.

Iris shrugged her bare shoulders.

'You're not going to let any of these generous men incriminate themselves?' There were about a dozen hungry-eyed men watching her every move. Most wore the designer uniforms of trust fund babies playing at rebellion. They looked harmless enough, but their ogling had a sense of entitlement that got on my nerves.

'I told you, I'm interested in usurers, and they reveal themselves.'

A voice at the upper range of human hearing shouted her name. It belonged to a rail-thin woman about Iris's age, a sparkling blonde with green eyes glazed by drink and years of idle living. She hugged Iris close and the pair were surrounded by the woman's entourage. They were all slightly different models of her that had come from the same factory, each one showing more leg than sense. I got out of the way of the air-kissing.

'Who's this?' the woman asked.

'My bodyguard.'

'He looks dangerous,' she cooed.

Iris ruffled my hair. 'He's a puppy dog,' she said. 'You haven't seen Marcus, have you?'

'Not for ages, darling,' the woman said. 'But I will tell you who I have seen . . . '

I let them get on with gossiping. Iris played along but I could see the boredom she was trying to hide. It was strange, seeing her standing side by side with the kind of person she was pretending to be. As good an actress as Iris was, I didn't see how anyone could mistake one for the other. The gaggle around her were mercenaries in three-inch heels, unapologetically hunting for a man whose centre of mass was in his wallet and not his head. The Crusade's big book of sin didn't have a word for their behaviour, because it wasn't called prostitution if a ring was involved.

'Anything useful?' I asked when the bright young things had wandered off to torment a group of men by the bar.

Iris shook her head. 'Something's wrong. Junior always made sure the world knew what he was up to. He wasn't the shy type.' Iris's eyes widened a little when she realized she was already talking about him in the past tense.

169

'He's skipped town to avoid whatever the Crusade had planned for him,' I said. 'It isn't hard to disappear quietly when your father owns his own jet.' By now I'd figured out that the way she was tilting her head indicated scepticism. 'Well, wherever he is, Junior isn't here,' I said. 'Why don't we call it a night?'

'I've still got work to do.'

'Not here you don't.' I might as well have waved a red flag in front of her. I moved in close and got a hold of her arm before she could leave. 'For someone who knows the name of every busboy's maiden aunt, you're pretty ignorant of who actually runs this joint.'

'I've heard rumours.'

'Then you should know to leave downstairs alone.'

'I'm not intimidated by people like him.'

'Good for you. What about the people you implicate?'

Iris didn't look at me, but she didn't struggle either. Instead she smiled at someone near the bar I couldn't see.

'I can guarantee you that within a week of your big press conference, some of those chumps will disappear, and the others will get the message.'

The smile began to fail.

'That's assuming they don't figure out what you're up to and kill you first.'

'I'm going downstairs,' she said. 'You can follow, or you can go home. If you get in my way, I'll have you removed.'

I let her go.

'Are you coming?'

I took the Lord's name in vain, but I followed her. The bouncers sized us up as we approached, but Iris's open-sesame of a smile moved them aside.

The club downstairs, unlike the bar above, was actually part of the warehouse. It was a small basement relative to the size of the building, with trapdoors for moving goods between floors. It had been used during Prohibition to store liquor brought down the river from Canada and immigrants branded as undesirable after the Immigration Act of 1924. Hundreds of people had been packed in here like cattle, their hopes and fears animal sounds to the neighbours who didn't speak their language.

It was still packed, but dilettantes had replaced the huddled masses. There were dozens of gullible young things upstairs looking for someone to part them from their money, but they never got down here. Their money wasn't worth the trouble their loose lips would bring, and the place depended on a combination of snobbery and jaded bloodlust to maintain its cachet.

Around a boxing ring were rows of aluminium bleachers that screeched along with their occupants during the entertainment. They were filled with every rung of society, as long as it was encrusted with gold. Three Congressmen had been given ringside seats by the lobbyists beside them. There were rappers smoking big cigars with their entourages of women and sycophants. A row of capos from different families, grown fat on the blood of others, talked business while their girlfriends chatted among themselves. The crowd was rounded out by courtiers, hangers-on, society girls on the make and the undistinguished filthy rich.

The wall opposite the staircase had a bar and a few tables. Seated at most of them were the capos' soldiers, playing cards or reading the paper. In deference to its owner, the club was one of the few places left in the five boroughs not under the thumb of a single family, neutral territory that made the odd spectacle of so many families sitting together possible. The card players were protection for their bosses, and the men reading the newspaper were here to do business.

'Anyone looking for money to make a bet has already paid them a visit,' I said, following Iris's eyes to the tables. 'Wait until after the fight, when the losers crawl over.' Between the bleachers and the ring, connected bookies scribbled down the bets yelled at them from the stands. The fighters were doing light warm-ups in their corners so potential gamblers could look them over. In the red trunks was a twenty-year-old Dominican, a few inches taller and at least twenty pounds heavier than his opponent in the blue trunks, a black kid who couldn't have been more than seventeen.

The odds favoured Red with his size and weight advantage. Everyone was too busy looking at Red's arms pounding on the trainer's pads to see Blue's legs. He was lighter on his feet, loose and fast as hell. He danced in hypnotic patterns, hitting the pads quickly and with precision.

The roll in my pocket had shrunk to about fifty dollars and change. I'd need more just to cover the usual investigative overheads: taxicabs, black coffee and bribes. Only the desperate and the stupid wagered money they couldn't lose, but I was at least one of those things. I went to the front and asked the nearest bookie what the odds were.

'Five to one for the guy in red,' he said, out of a moustache that covered most of his face.

'On blue,' I said, putting the roll in his hand.

'Sure thing, pal,' he replied, his tone saying I was the sucker of the minute.

I joined Iris in the stands.

She gave me a disapproving look. 'I thought you were smarter.'

'When it comes to my expense account, I have to improvise.'

An emcee howled the names of the fighters into a suspended microphone, but feedback drowned out half the syllables. Their business done, the bookies sat down and stopped blocking the view. The bell rang. Red came out swinging.

'Are you going to report me?' I asked.

'I report everyone,' she said. 'Brother Isaiah made the decisions.'

He wasn't issuing any orders from the unmarked morgue drawer White had stuck him in, safe from curious eyes. Blue was doing what I expected him to: dodge, feint, and let Red tire himself out hitting air.

'He wouldn't have considered Stanley or me worth the effort,' I said. 'Not much potential for headlines.'

'Do you think gambling is harmless?'

'Only if I win,' I said. 'It's victimless, as I have only myself to blame.'

'Victimless.' Iris's voice was bitter, not the contempt I'd expect from a moral scold. 'They always say that about gambling and drugs, even prostitution. If you hurt yourself, you will hurt others. Brother Isaiah taught me that tolerating small sins only encouraged larger ones.'

I'd heard versions of this theory before; if people dropped litter in the street, pretty soon they'd be fornicating there too.

'You need to believe that everyone's got a racket, but the only thing Brother Isaiah was interested in was saving souls.'

Two minutes of shadow-boxing had made the natives restless. They'd come to see young men beat each other senseless, and the few jabs that had connected so far weren't enough. When Blue misread Red's shoulders and caught a left in the face, they cheered. Red followed up with a quick left jab, and then a powerful right hook. Blue stumbled back and Red piled on. For a second I thought the kid in blue was going to fall, and take the last of my money with him. He backed into the ropes and went into his shell. Red closed the distance and started to pound on him.

'Your boy looks like he's in trouble,' Iris said.

'Looks like it,' I said.

None of Red's punches was getting past Blue's arms. Each punch sent shivers through the ropes that Blue leaned against. That's where all Red's fury was going, through and away. The bell sounded. Red sat down in his corner panting heavily. Blue was bruised all along his arms, but didn't seem to mind.

When the second round started, Red wasn't quite as eager to get out of his corner. Blue came out the same way he did before: light and fast. The big difference was that now he was on the offensive. He let Red swing with those big arms, and then moved around them, hitting out with a flurry of jabs. Red threw a blind hook. Blue stepped to the side and hit Red with one of his own. The crowd was starting to divide against itself, a few people defecting to join the underdog.

'A valuable lesson on the evils of gambling may not be forthcoming,' I said.

'Sin always catches up with you,' Iris said. 'One way or another.'

We let the rest of the round go by. Blue ground Red down, jabbing then disappearing before Red's heavier fists could follow. The crowd didn't know what to make of it. Illegal boxing tended to attract a specific kind of fighter: big dumb brutes who would whack each other until someone fell down. They weren't used to seeing a scientist in the ring.

'Does this bloodsport happen here every night?' Iris asked when the third gong sounded.

'Sometimes it's Muay Thai or wrestling. They also put dogs in there, roosters, even a pair of mountain lions if you believe the rumours. They'll showcase anything with violence and

175

gambling potential.'

'This place needs to be shut down,' Iris said. 'Why didn't you want me to come here?'

Life had stopped going Red's way. He couldn't keep up with the slighter, faster man in blue. A cut over his left eye was pouring blood into his vision and Blue used it, sticking to the left side and hitting whenever he could.

'I'm worried about collateral damage,' I said.

'I told you I can handle myself.'

'I didn't mean you. It isn't just sinners who go to loan sharks,' I said. The jobless economy had been a godsend for the loan-sharking trade. 'A lot of regular Joes show up at those tables, hat in hand. Somebody loses a job, or gets sick and can't afford the medicine, and they end up here.'

'I told you, we're after the usurers.'

'From what I've read, the Crusade doesn't distinguish between supply and demand.'

The kid in blue had his opponent on the run. With his size advantage evaporating under fatigue and abuse, Red tried to evade, but he didn't have the footwork or the intelligence.

'I combed through the Crusade's files a few days ago,' I said. 'There was a lot of pain in there. People had lost their jobs and families because of what the Crusade had done. One man blamed Brother Isaiah for sending him to the Holy Land.'

'Well, your friend is mistaken. I don't think Brother Isaiah supported the Holy Land project or the rebuilding of the temple. He never came out and said it directly,' Iris said. 'He prayed for the troops but never encouraged any members of his flock to serve.'

That was unusual. Revivalist ministers called on eligible members of their flock to go to the Holy Land at least a few times a year. 'Brother Isaiah was never shy about telling the world what he thought was wrong. Why did he keep mum about this?'

'I don't know,' Iris said. She knew what I was getting at and didn't want to face it. Brother Isaiah needed the support of the Elders in order to do his work, and they wouldn't have tolerated public defiance of their grand plan. Maybe there had been a political bone in his body after all.

'Suppose someone does what you want and gets right with Jesus. Did Brother Isaiah ever forgive anyone?'

'Of course he did,' Iris said, her answer again more heated than it needed to be. I didn't think it was just because I was questioning her idol. 'Brother Isaiah believed in forgiveness as powerfully as he believed in sin.'

I couldn't remember him forgiving anyone the same way he accused them: on national television. I needed to work with Iris, and as long as her screwball ideas didn't interfere with my work it was no business of mine. The problem was that I couldn't get what had been in those letters out of my head, and the pain in my muscles was coming back strong, starting in my ankles and migrating upwards. The combination made me indignant and cranky. 'But Brother Isaiah's judgement is still final. Is there no right

177

of appeal? People don't even get to face their accusers.'

'It isn't a court. We obey higher commandments than the law,' Iris said. The answers she gave were rote, part of some catechism that had burned into her mind past conscious thought. 'Brother Isaiah did his best to help people understand that they were sinners, and bring them closer to the only source of grace.'

'Except the punishment is in the temporal world.' Pay now and be redeemed later; the soul was on the worst layaway plan in this world.

'It is between them and God.'

My muscles hurt like hell, but they were still working. I focused on my breathing and tried to keep calm. I couldn't risk a spasm. 'Stanley's wife is involved, and her family, and their kids, and anyone on the playground who wants to call them names. Who tells them to lay off, who tells them the good news that Stanley's all straightened out?' My right leg jerked. Iris seemed intent on the fight, but I knew she wasn't interested in the way Blue was leading Red around, clocking him every time his right hand dropped. 'Isaiah was just another angry man who loved telling people when they were wrong. He was always ready to warm the tar, stack the feathers and lead the mob, but he'd be gone by the time the consequences rolled around.'

The sound of Iris's palm hitting my face was lost in the general roar as Red hit the mat. The pain in my legs was too bad for me to rise immediately. She was already at the staircase by the time I got off the bleachers. I might lose Iris

178

if I didn't go after her now. On the other hand, someone owed me money for a change, and I needed to collect if I was going to do my job.

The crowd around the bookies was thin. Most of the crowd stayed in the bleachers and yelled at the man in red, on his feet again half a minute too late. A few eyed the sharks near the bar, mouthing what might have been figures, or prayers. The bookie handed over my winnings in an untidy stack of beautiful green bills. As I folded up the cash, I happened to catch the eye of the kid in blue. He was exhausted and more hurt than he'd let on during the fight. People liked to compare boxers to modern-day gladiators, forgetting that they slaughtered each other for the amusement of others. He was just another expendable mass of blood, flesh and bone, tenderized for the amusement of the bored and self-satisfied. Whatever I told myself, there was no getting around that I had profited from his sweat and pain. As the referee lifted his arm in glory, I spoke to him with my eyes. I said congratulations. I said I was sorry.

By the time I'd dragged myself upstairs, Iris was already gone. I made for the door, pain unbalancing my gait in a way that was neither drunken weaving nor a limp.

Bear met me at the door. 'Felix, you feeling all right?' 'I'm fine,' I said, holding on to the wall. 'Where's Iris?'

'She just left, didn't even take her coat with her. She said she didn't want a cab or — hey, Felix,' Bear said to my back, 'the boss wants — '

'Later,' I said, and pushed out the door. The

street and all the buildings that hemmed it in were empty. The only sound was a pair of high heels striking concrete. I shambled after her, focusing on the sound, keeping my mouth closed in case I had another spasm. I caught sight of her on the way to Van Brunt Street. She didn't respond when I called her name. I yelled it louder.

Iris stopped, and then turned. 'You aren't the man I thought you were.'

'I'm not in the business of living up to people's expectations.' I'd had some experience being on the receiving end of female anger, mostly when I told wives things I'd been hired to find out about their husbands that they didn't want to hear. It was easy enough to shrug off, the price of being the bearer of bad news. The look on Iris's face was harder to stomach. 'Listen, I know I've never been more than runner-up for Miss Congeniality — '

'You don't understand a damn thing, you smug bastard,' Iris said.

It was the first time I'd heard her swear. She held her mouth in a tight line of pain that didn't seem to have anything to do with me. I tried to tell myself that this dame had been trouble ever since I'd met her, that I hadn't wanted to work with her in the first place. It didn't help.

'Brother Isaiah is the only reason I wasn't found with a needle in my arm,' Iris said. 'The state put me in foster care when I was eight. My foster mother treated me like an ATM, and her husband started touching me when I was twelve. I ran away when I was fourteen. I lived on the streets and became a junkie to make the world go away. I stole, sold my body, anything that would keep me high. You've heard it all before.'

I tried to picture Iris as a frightened girl huddling in her jacket on a street corner, or a young woman, eyes rimmed by cheap eyeshadow, leaning in the direction of every car that slowed down. It didn't stick any more than the vision of her as the scold with a ruler. Stories of conversion usually emphasized the sordid details to make the redemption all the more miraculous, titillating the audience along the way. I was glad she was letting me fill in the blanks. If the needle, pipe and the nights with johns in cheap hotels had left a mark, I didn't want to see it.

'I lost a few years. I was in and out of juvie and then jail. Whenever I was released a social worker would mumble something at me and push me out the door.'

'Then I met Brother Isaiah at the soup kitchen I was volunteering in last night. The Crusade ran it then, before it turned over all its charitable work to the Office of Mercy. We used to go there for a free meal, clean needles and condoms. He was on the dinner line; he liked to be near his flock. He was doling out mashed potatoes with an ice-cream scoop. Can you imagine?' The memory tugged gently at the sides of her mouth. 'When I got to his place in the line, he didn't say a word to me. He just smiled. I'd never seen so much kindness in a face before. It was like a mirror. I saw myself as I truly was, and it broke my heart. I fell to my knees and begged him to save me.'

There was a look in her eyes that dared me to contradict her, say she had edited for drama. You couldn't swing a dead cat without hitting a story of conversion these days, and the substance of her tale was no different than a dozen others. She waited for the challenge but I stayed silent, not out of tact, but because I believed her.

'Isaiah took me to a place to get clean. Not a methadone clinic or a counselling centre, but a church where I could stay. The great man with his own Church and radio show made time every day to pray with a nobody like me for two years. I told him all the horrible, degrading things I'd done, and he never got angry or disgusted. He said that had all happened in another life. All the secular world had ever done was use my body and spit in my face. Brother Isaiah was the one who told me I was loved, that I could be something different. You wanted to know if Brother Isaiah forgave anyone? Well, he forgave me.'

It didn't do either of us much good to stand on the dark street corner and freeze, but I honestly didn't know what to say.

'I don't know what I'm going to do without him,' Iris said. 'He told me that Jesus watched over me, but it was his hand that kept me on the right path. I can't start over, Felix,' she said. 'I've already done it once.'

'You'll manage,' I said. 'You're tougher than you look.' The pain had gotten worse. I was having trouble thinking straight. Everything started to blur.

Iris caught me before I met the pavement. 'Are you all right?'

'It's nothing.' My vision began to clear. I could stand again if I gritted my teeth against the pain, but Iris didn't remove her arms.

'Am I interruptin' somethin'?' said a voice behind me.

It belonged to a man I wished I didn't recognize. 'Hello, Carmine.'

Iris recognized him too, but it was the gun in his hand that had her attention.

The angry little Italian gave me a yellow smile. Beside him were two bouncers from the Waterfront. 'Much as I hate to break up this beautiful fuckin' moment, the boss wants a word with you.' He gestured back towards the Waterfront with the pistol in his hand.

Mine was still in the weapons locker at the bar. I put up my hands, and drafted in my head the angry letter I'd send to the NRA. 'Let the lady go; it's between me and him.'

'No dice, Strange,' Carmine said. 'Boss wants to see her too.'

They led us back to the Waterfront. Bear saw the gun in Carmine's hand and considered doing something stupid. I shook my head and winked to let him know the situation was under control. Bear wasn't reassured, but he let us pass.

Carmine stopped me on the threshold of the main bar and whispered in my ear. His breath reeked of onions and last night's beer. 'I know you're thinking of a way outta this, Strange, but it ain't gonna happen. I'm gonna put my gun in my pocket and we're gonna walk upstairs all

183

chummy-like. If you bring those fancy hands of yours to town, I ain't got no problem drilling you in front of all these people. You understand me?'

I nodded.

'Then after you, shitbird.'

We marched through the main bar towards the staircase. I could hear Iris breathing hard, see her eyes darting around the room in search of a friendly face. The socialites and weekend warriors didn't even notice us, too intent on their drinks and each other. The staff knew what was up. They kept out of our way, afraid to look the walking dead in the eye.

He was waiting for us upstairs in one of the VIP rooms. Three divans stood unused against the walls, with space left for champagne stands. The other wall was a window that looked down on the bar, glass tinted against the eyes of the plebians below.

'I don't believe we've met,' he said to Iris. 'They call me the Corinthian.'

The Corinthian had one of those strange ageless faces, lined by something more infernal than ordinary time. A few silver streaks in his full black hair were the only indication that he was older than me. The black pin-stripe suit that covered his slight frame was good enough to be buried in. Iris told him her name. No one sat down.

'Mr Strange,' he said, formal as always. 'I already have enough reasons to kill you, yet you seem anxious to give me more.'

'I came here to escort the lady and watch the fights,' I said.

184

Organized crime had been globalized like any other business, and the Corinthian was the end result. He was the face for a borderless, worldwide black marketplace. Depending on who you talked to, he ran drugs for the Colombians, sold Chinese guns, and transported Eastern bloc women enslaved by the Russian mafia. He didn't even look Greek.

The Corinthian looked at Iris with his dark, watchful eyes for a long time. 'The lady seems to know my employees. She is elegant and charming, I'm sure. Had she only made the mistake of associating with you, I might have let it pass. Her second fault is an unhealthy curiosity. I don't like people asking questions in my establishment, especially about drugs.'

I looked at Iris out of the corner of my eye. If I had known she was doing something as stupid as asking the help where to score, I would have carried her out of the place without another word.

'It's not what you think,' she said. The words brought another look. Iris might have been around the block a few times, and no doubt had dealt with various species of low-life, but she couldn't meet his eyes. Instead she whispered something in my ear, a simple fact that might keep us alive.

The Corinthian's men stepped forward but he stopped them. 'It's rude to whisper in front of others.'

'Someone is selling ecstasy in your club,' I said. The temperature in the room dropped by several degrees.

The new drug laws were practically medieval when it came to street drugs, with punishments on a level not seen since the sixties. It was mostly symbolic, as abuse of the traditional narcotics was at an all-time low. It wasn't because a wave of temperance had swept the country; people killed the pain of modern life with prescription intoxicants instead, and not just because they were cleaner and more reliable than street versions. A pound of heroin could get you life in prison. If you bought a supply of painkillers under false pretences, the penalties for forging a prescription were only a few months in jail, far less than what you could get for importing generic heart medication illegally.

'That is a very serious charge,' the Corinthian said.

I met his gaze and held it. I had some experience in that area that I'd earned the hard way. 'Would I lie?'

He didn't bother to answer the question. 'Why were you trying to buy illegal drugs at my place of business?' he said to Iris. 'Strange should have warned you that I don't take kindly to smears on my character.'

'I'm looking for a friend of mine, Marcus Thorpe Junior,' Iris said. Her voice was slow and steady. She hadn't known the Corinthian existed until a minute ago, but that was all it took to understand fully the value he placed on human life. 'I thought his dealer might know where he is.'

'And his dealer is a regular here?'

'He works here.' The temperature dropped

again. The Corinthian's men looked at each other, bringing an inventory of their sins up to date in their minds. 'He sold Junior a bag of pills three weeks ago, in one of these rooms.' Her finger pointed at Carmine.

There was fear on his face for a fraction of a second. Most people would have missed it, but the Corinthian's peripheral vision was fine-tuned to spot weakness and betrayal.

'I'm disappointed in you, Carmine.'

'You're gonna believe a slut and a spastic over me?' Carmine yelled.

His act impressed no one. Two of the Corinthian's men took hold of Carmine as he sputtered and shook. There was a dazed, pleading smile on his face, showing off all his piss-coloured teeth. It was the smile of a body entering rigor mortis.

'Take him to the farm.'

Carmine thrashed and screamed so much the men who had escorted us here had to help the other two take him away. Carmine begged for mercy during the entire struggle. The Corinthian's face was unperturbed, as if he were being addressed in a foreign language.

'You've done me a favour,' he said to Iris, after they'd dragged him from the room. 'In recognition, I'll repay your facts with some of my own: Thorpe's employees haven't seen the prodigal son since Monday. Their private jet is still in a hangar at LaGuardia. No missing person's report has been filed with the police.'

'Ransom demands?' Iris asked.

He shook his head. 'If he's been kidnapped,

the authorities don't know about it.'

'He could have jack-rabbited without his father's knowledge,' I said.

'Junior couldn't put on his pants in the morning without the help of a maid,' the Corinthian said. 'He wouldn't last twenty-four hours on his own.'

'You seem very interested in Junior's movements,' I said.

The Corinthian did his interpretation of a smile. 'He owes me some money. Not a large amount for a man of his resources, but significant to me as a general principle. In another time, Strange, I would have handed this matter to you.'

I felt Iris's eyes on my face. They burned. I refused to give the Corinthian the satisfaction that would come from anger or denial.

'The amount isn't worth killing the son of a prominent man over, before you ask,' the Corinthian continued. 'I simply dislike question marks in my accounts.'

'A man stupid enough to borrow money from you probably has other creditors,' I said.

'No outfit with the capital to satisfy his appetites has seen him either,' the Corinthian said. 'I've been thorough.'

He was too paranoid to come out and say it, but his implication was obvious: someone in the government had made Junior disappear. That didn't narrow down the suspect list as much as I'd like: more than one federal agency was in the bag-over-your-head business, and those were just the ones I knew about. 'I didn't think Junior would have those kinds of enemies.'

'They say every man is his father's son,' the Corinthian said. He turned to Iris. 'If you do run into Junior, I'd appreciate it if you told him to pay me a call.' His voice said he doubted it would happen in this life.

I got the feeling it was time to leave. I nudged Iris in the direction of the door before she could ask another question.

'Strange,' the Corinthian said, as I made to follow her out. 'It was a mistake to let you live the first time.'

Four of his employees were tied up dealing with Carmine. There were two bouncers working the door, three more on the ground floor and another three downstairs. None would get here fast enough to stop me from throwing the Corinthian through the tinted glass behind him. I'd never leave the Waterfront alive, but that wouldn't have mattered much if I hadn't had things to do. 'We'll chalk this one up to carelessness then,' I said. Down the stairs, through the bar and out the door, I felt the weight of his gaze resting between my shoulder blades.

Out in the street, Iris and I looked at each other for a while. The air of Brooklyn had rarely tasted so sweet.

'Do you think he was telling the truth about Junior?' she said.

'The Corinthian has his own way of doing things,' I said. 'I wouldn't exactly call it ethics. Your information was a fair trade, and he wouldn't waste time lying to us. Wherever Junior

189

is, I doubt they allow visitors.'

'It doesn't do much for my case,' Iris said.

'I'm going to suspend judgement for now.' The Corinthian was courteous even when ordering your death, but he was never so opaque. Whatever he'd heard about Junior had spooked him too much to say it out loud, and the Corinthian was not an easy man to scare. Something bad was coming, and I had the feeling I wouldn't know what it was until it was too late. 'Consider it part of the debt I owe you for what happened in there,' I said. 'If you hadn't fingered Carmine, odds are we'd be clogging up the East River by now.'

'If you want to show your gratitude, there's something I want you to listen to. I'm not trying to convert you,' she said to my rolling eyes. 'I want you to know something about the man whose death you're investigating. It's a sermon called 'My Exile'. It will be with the others on the Crusade website.'

'I'll listen to it.' The worst thing that would happen is I'd catch up on my sleep.

'When he said he'd give the matter to you,' Iris said. 'What did he mean?'

'I did some work for the Corinthian once.'

'What kind of work?'

'I found people for him.'

Judging by her face, Iris had imagined something much worse. 'That doesn't sound so bad.'

'Trust me, it was enough.' The night's activities, or a stray memory, dizzied me for a moment.

'How do you feel?' Iris asked.

I couldn't hear that question without remembering the sting of antiseptic on my nose. Every day a different VA doctor would arrive at my bed, test my reflexes, shine a flashlight in my eye, and ask me that damn question.

'Can you make it home?'

Adrenaline and fear had muted the pain. It would be enough to get me to my door. 'I'm fine,' I said, 'and I don't need your pity. I've got a lifetime supply.'

'I think you know concern when you see it,' she said. Her hands were on my shoulders again, though I was in no danger of falling. 'Will you tell me what's wrong?'

'Something happened to me in the war,' I said.

Iris waited for me to go on, but I didn't. Iris got the message. 'I'll call you tomorrow,' she said.

'Sure.'

There was nothing left to say. Iris let go, and disappeared into the fog of the early morning.

Thursday

I awoke in screaming pain. The clock said eight before I knocked it over. I rolled off the bed and hit the floor with a definite lack of finesse. My legs were useless and the spasms had contorted my hands into claws. I had enough feeling in my arms to drag myself into the bathroom on my elbows. I got up on my knees, just high enough to see the bottle of reds on top of the sink. I swatted it with my twisted hand. The bottle rolled into the office. I watched the single pill spin inside, in too much agony to follow it immediately.

The medication wouldn't do a lot for my pain, but that was the least of my medical problems. A point of empty clarity was forming in the centre of my head; the eye of a storm that would come if I didn't take that pill. I crawled into the office and found the bottle sitting against a leg of my desk. My hands were still frozen, unable to work the damn childproof top. I trapped the bottle between my wrists, twisted the cap into place with my teeth and then pulled it off like an animal. I swallowed the pill dry; coughing, exhausted and thankful.

There were some painkillers in the bathroom. They blunted the edge of my perceptions and filled my head with fog, but I didn't have much choice. I couldn't be very productive screaming in agony every five minutes. I crawled back to the bathroom and found the pills. After that all I could do was lie on the tiles and consider my situation.

Without Junior's testimony to wave in White's face, I was in trouble as far as accounting for yesterday was concerned. I thought about Iris, facts not relevant to the case: the shimmer of her black dress, the line of her legs in high heels, the tears I had seen behind the sunglasses.

I was starting to feel as close as I got to normal. I hadn't kept down much solid food in the last two days even with the help of Song's medicine. Protein shakes and multivitamins added just enough fuel to keep my body turning over, but did nothing for the dizziness. I kept images of stacked pancakes, bacon and wedges of pie out of my mind, put myself in the shower and washed off the sweat. The attack had been mild enough to handle on my own. It wouldn't be that way tomorrow.

I turned on the TV and hunted for a clean shirt. On the television was a helicopter shot of a fleet of container ships anchored just off Haifa. 'The ships have been holding position here for the last six hours,' a female voice said. 'They've made no move to dock at Haifa or unload their cargo. All ships are owned or leased by Thorpe Industries.' That got my attention. I flipped over to the BBC on the pirate satellite feed. They were showing an almost identical helicopter shot, but it changed to a montage of several Israeli airbases where cargo planes were landing. 'All container ships controlled by Thorpe Industries subsidiaries have been halted,' said a reassuringly

British voice, 'as well as those from the Cowan Group and Rice-Palmer. Air deliveries to Israeli airbases continue. Together, the three companies provide most of the logistics and supply for the American presence in Israel.' It was a shot across the bow if ever I'd seen one. The air deliveries would stop the troops from starving, but a machine as massive and hungry as the United States military required constant resupply. It could skip lunch without a headache, but no dinner would cause serious problems. 'Questions have been raised about how long the force can sustain itself without sea-borne supplies. For more we turn to our military affairs correspondent — '

I switched back to our patriotic media to see what kind of knot they'd twist themselves into to explain this. 'While initial reports have focused on terrorism,' the female voice said, 'sources now say a technical problem in new navigation software may be at fault. Engineers are being flown in to make repairs, and sources have said they expect the problem to be fixed by tomorrow.' That excuse wasn't going to last long, but the Elders didn't think it would need to. That prediction was an ultimatum. 'Share prices in Thorpe Industries have lost forty per cent, with no end to the stock's downturn in sight.' Whoever had been short selling on Monday had just made a lot of money.

The fact that the media hadn't declared open season on Thorpe yet showed the Elders wanted to play nice if they could. If they did have something to do with Junior's disappearance,

197

that wouldn't be enough to convince the boards of the Cowan Group and Rice-Palmer to take such a radical step. Detaining those Wall Street executives had put the shadow of fear in every boardroom in the country. We'd gotten used to living under that cloud, but it had never reached the penthouse before.

I looked out the window to see what weather I would have to endure. Parked on the street was a familiar brown sedan. I found my binoculars and checked the licence plate. It was Ernest's getaway car. Being an unbeliever, I had no one to thank for making my enemies this stupid. I sped up the rest of my morning dress routine: shoulder holster, gun, jacket and fedora.

My building had a back door the occupants of the car wouldn't be able to see. I went over a block and then back through an alley that opened near where the car was parked. I hid behind some garbage cans and tried to get a look at who was inside. There was a single silhouette in the driver's seat, and he was snoring loud enough for the whole block to hear. He was making this so easy I felt embarrassed on his behalf.

The back door of the sedan was unlocked. I got in the back, and slammed the door hard. The man snorted awake. His eyes widened when he saw me in his rear-view mirror with a gun pointed at the back of his head.

'What the hell are you doing, buddy?'

'I'm neighbourhood watch,' I said. 'We take a dim view of strange men sleeping in cars around

198

here. There are a lot of kiddie-fiddlers and freaks in this town.'

'Hey, I ain't no — '

'Keep your hands where I can see them,' I said. 'Now reach into your jacket with your right hand and get me your wallet. Do it slowly.'

'So this is a stick-up now, Mr Neighbourhood Watch?' he said, but did as he was told.

George Zimmermann had the misfortune of looking exactly like his driver's licence. His face, like his body, was broad, thick and badly defined; a child's drawing smeared before it had a chance to dry. The few brownish strands of hair he had left were combed tight across his skull, and his weak chin wobbled a little even when he was silent. George watched me search the wallet, his hazel eyes tiny and uncertain in the rear-view mirror. Sandwiched between some store discount cards was another, more interesting piece of photo identification.

'You don't look like a pious man, George,' I said, holding up his Crusade of Love identification card. 'Is that research?' I pointed to the girly magazine he had open in the front seat, the centrefold's modesty preserved by plastic cups and crumpled wax paper wrappers from every drive-through in the area.

'You can't do this to me, I got friends.'

'You mean Ernest?' I said. 'Have they put his face back together yet?' After what that phone did to him, all the king's horses and all the king's men better be on his HMO's approved list of doctors. 'Maybe you mean your other friend, the one who's insulted me by sending a chump like

199

you to be my shadow. You're going to tell me who he is.'

'I don't know who you're talkin' about,' George said. 'When I call the police — '

'Feel free,' I said. 'You can explain to them why an EZ-pass camera on the Brooklyn Bridge captured you chauffering the man who assaulted me.' It might not have been a lie. I hadn't heard from my NYPD friend yet.

George got a cagey look in his eye that was stupid and possibly dangerous. Mugs of this variety weren't smart enough to realize that there were certain things they shouldn't do. He might try to make a run for it, and I didn't want to plug anyone this early in the morning.

'Go pound sand, gumshoe,' he said. 'I ain't sayin' nothin'.' He crossed his arms and tried to look tough.

In the army we had a specific set of procedures for dealing with people who wouldn't talk. We were told the methods were legal, but that was based on an opinion no one had the security clearance to read. If a professional was there, he'd strap them to a wooden board, put a rag in their mouths and pour water in until their bodies convinced them they were drowning. Sometimes it was as simple as a buck private losing it and beating someone half to death. I was one of the people who were supposed to follow up on the intelligence from these interrogations, but it was hard to investigate screams.

'It's time to break the habit of a lifetime, George, and act smart for a change.'

He didn't say anything.

I opened my phone and dialled three digits.

'Okay, okay,' George said.

As I closed my phone, I turned on the little digital recorder I had in my pocket. Something useful might come out of George's mouth for a change.

'I got a record already,' he said. 'They send me back, it's for the long haul.'

'Who told you to follow me?'

He hesitated.

I opened the phone again.

'We call him Mr Pyke. I don't know his first name. We ain't pals.'

Pyke. I couldn't think of anything I'd done to deserve such attention from him.

'Ernie and I were at this soup kitchen run by the Office of Mercy. This Pyke guy, he came over, asked if we wanted a job, good pay no questions asked. This frickin' economy, who wouldn't say yes?'

'Did he say what he wanted with me?'

'He told us to grab you, that's it. When you fucked up Ernie's face, he said to hang back and keep an eye on you.'

So George had thought it would be a great idea to camp out in front of my building in the same stolen car he'd used the first time. 'Where did he tell you to take me?'

'He never said. We were supposed to call when we had you.'

'Did he tell you why he wanted me grabbed?'

George shook his head. 'I got no idea. Maybe it had something to do with this piece of work he wanted us to do.' A 'piece of work' was an underworld euphemism you never wanted to hear. 'He didn't tell us who we were going to whack. Pyke had Ernie practise with this rifle, an old thirty-aught-six, and he kept me driving all over Manhattan. It was the same thing every day until he told us to grab you.'

'Where is Pyke now?'

'I don't know. Honest,' he said when he saw the look on my face. 'Most of the time he'd just call us and tell us what to do. We met at restaurants sometimes, never the same one twice. I don't call him, he calls me, you know?'

Maybe he was telling the truth. The eyes I saw in the rearview mirror were frightened enough. I didn't have the time to try to sweat more out of him. I had what I needed, on tape.

'You believe me, right?'

'Relax, George, I believe you,' I said, and brought the gun down on the back of his head. He slumped over, out cold. I took his Crusade ID with me in case it came in handy, and reached over him to get the keys out of the ignition. I left George in his natural environment, among greasy wrappers and cheap porn. The keys went down the nearest storm drain.

I went back up to the office to get my black bag. It was a doctor's bag I'd found at a yard sale, and along with the hat it gave me an official air. It contained the tools of the less than legal part of my trade: a set of lockpicks concealed in a radio, a chisel, crowbar, small hammer, binoculars and a directional microphone. The last belonged to a friend of mine. My conscience had stopped me from pawning it, but I never seemed to get around to giving it back. I only pulled it out of the closet for dirty work, and I had a feeling I would need it.

My phone rang. 'Benny,' I said.

'I got some test results from your bloody napkin. The good news is that the lab boys turned it around in record time.'

'I'm preparing for disappointment.'

'No hits, my friend.'

'How is that possible?' DNA, in addition to finger and retina prints, was part of the identity card all US citizens were required to carry.

'He could be a foreigner. Most countries don't include DNA as part of their passports, and that's all he'd need.'

'Thanks, Benny.'

'You can thank me by staying out of trouble,' he said, and hung up.

Both men had looked home-grown to me. It would take a lot of pull to make their records disappear, more than Pyke had. The two men may not have been too bright, but compared to Ernest and George they were geniuses. Add in that sniper with a laser sight, set up long before I got there, and Jack had been right after all. It was him they'd been after, and I was nearly a victim of death by coincidence. I'd have to leave that angle alone for the moment. Pyke had succeeded in gaining my undivided attention.

I called White. He was not happy. 'Where the hell have you been, Strange?'

'I told you I was following a lead.'

There was a pause that would have been filled with curses if White had less self-control. 'I told you to keep me informed,' he said, when the moment of temptation had passed. 'Things are spinning out of control, Strange. The Elders have convinced themselves that this murder is the opening shot in a business coup.' White was still afraid to use Brother Isaiah's name over the phone. 'I've used all the influence I have to calm them down, but it hasn't worked. We don't have much time.'

I resisted the urge to remind him about reaping and whirlwinds. 'Did they mention any fat cat in particular?'

'The names of the conspirators change every time I talk to them,' White said, without giving me any examples.

I wanted to throw Thorpe's name at him to see what would happen, but then he might figure out what I'd been up to. I changed the subject. 'I don't see how throwing someone to the wolves now is going to make everyone play nice.'

'It will draw a line under the whole sorry mess and give moderates on both sides a chance to negotiate.' White included himself in the moderate camp, as a religious man bought and paid for. 'What about your lead?'

'Do you remember that Crusade big wheel I asked you about, called Pyke? He set two amateurs on me,' I said. 'One of them used a Taser to try to persuade me to take a ride, and the other has been sitting on my office.' I left out the 'piece of work' George had told me about and Ernest's part in it. Pyke had him practising with the same type of rifle that Jack had said he favoured in his letter to the Crusade. The 30.06

was a common rifle, but I had stopped believing in coincidences right after I lost faith in the Easter Bunny. I needed to find out if it was actually relevant before I gave White the chance to railroad them and shut down the investigation.

'What does he want with you?'

'I don't know. I leaned on the driver, but the yegg didn't know anything. I need you to tell me what Pyke's been up to.'

'I have no idea.' The lightness of White's tone was undercut by a touch of defensiveness. He knew exactly what I was getting at.

'I know you have members of the Crusade under surveillance,' I said. 'A man of Pyke's senior position probably rates a tail as well as phone taps.' I waited while White decided whether he would bother to deny it. 'We need to find out if Pyke was involved, and like you said, we don't have much time. Just prefix every sentence with 'hypothetically'.'

There was another pause. 'Give me a minute.' The possibility that the assassination was an inside job had been too tempting to resist. 'He's been a very busy man this week. I need something to narrow down the search.'

'Tell me where he lives and I'll take it from there.'

'The Crusade rents a townhouse in Brooklyn. He seems to be the only one who uses it. I'll send you the address. I shouldn't ask you this, but are you going to break in?'

'Hypothetically, yes.'

I checked that George was still tucked in, and headed for the subway.

★ ★ ★

The townhouse was a rectangle of dull red stone. From the outside it looked the same as its neighbours; rows of cereal boxes stacked up the hill on each side of the street. The only difference was that every other building had been broken into apartments, while Pyke still had the whole house to himself. I did a quick walk around the block. A fence stood between me and the building's back entrance. All the windows were barred. They'd be alarmed just like the door.

The subway ride over hadn't given me enough time to think of a way of breaking inside in broad daylight. The street was full of upstanding citizens going about their legitimate business. Retirees shuffled towards appointments, a postman did his rounds, and young mothers or their nanny substitutes pushed children along. Any one of them would make an unimpeachable prosecution witness.

I had no choice but to knock on the front door. If a servant answered I'd use George's Crusade ID as part of a song-and-dance. If Pyke came to the door, I'd punch him in the mouth and then think of something. No one answered.

The building across the street would have a good view of what was going on inside the townhouse. There was a middle-aged man in faded overalls sweeping the stoop, and he watched my approach with suspicion. I tried to ignore him and hoped he would do the same.

'What can I do for you?' he said, the sentence coming out like a single word as my foot was about to touch the first step. He moved between me and the door, blocking my view of the names on the mailboxes.

I gave him my best false smile. 'Do you mind if I go up on your roof?'

He gave me peculiar look. When he saw the suit and the black bag, he must have assumed I was selling something. God knows what he thought of me now. 'What are you, some kind of pervert?'

I laughed, more than was probably necessary. 'I'm just a tourist. I love these old townhouses, but I can't get the right shot from down here.' I saw my words floating behind his eyes, 'tourist' and 'shot' picking up some of the free-floating paranoia twenty-four-hour news had been pumping into the atmosphere for years. The super started to remember all those scaremongering reports about terrorists posing as tourists to case targets. I didn't know what he thought was worth blowing up around here, but I should have chosen my words more carefully. The only reason he hadn't pulled a gun or called the police was the colour of my skin.

'Buddy, you'd better — '

'Wait,' I said. Against my better judgement, I showed him my licence. 'I'm a private investigator, see?'

He held the broom tight, trying to decide whether he should swing it at whatever part of me was nearest.

'The guy across the way has got a lady friend. Her husband isn't too happy about it.'

'What's that got to do with me, Shamus?'

'That townhouse is their romper room. I need some candid shots so the divorce court will know how much of a Jezebel she is.'

He didn't move.

I could see he believed my story; he was just waiting for the right kind of push. 'You know what they say about good deeds, don't you? They will be returned tenfold.'

That got his attention. 'Just how much tenfold are we talkin' about?'

The building he managed was as ritzy as Pyke's. I had to be generous.

He watched Benjamin Franklin disappear into his greasy breast pocket. 'Anybody asks . . . '

'I'm a pervert who broke in.'

He stepped aside.

The roof was flat, empty and covered in pigeon shit. I had an unobstructed view of the townhouse's front door, but the angle made it difficult to see into the lower windows facing the street. I got comfortable.

A few hours later, George appeared on the corner and stayed there. Through the binoculars I saw a worried face sweating in the cold autumn air. He stamped his feet, chain-smoked and watched the townhouse. When he first appeared I'd assumed George had been summoned for a spanking. Now I wasn't so sure. George might be hoping to give Pyke his side of the story before his boss heard about the tune he'd sung for me.

Half an hour later a black Mercedes stopped in front of the townhouse. A Stillwater man playing a secret service agent got out of the passenger side. He opened the back door for

Pyke, who got out with another bodyguard. He paused on the sidewalk but didn't look in George's direction. Pyke went inside, his Stillwater dogs standing on either side of the front door. George finished his cigarette and walked to the town-house. The bodyguards let him inside.

I panned the directional microphone across the front windows, and got lucky on the first floor. I could hear papers shuffling, and then a knock at the door. I started recording.

'Did anyone follow you?'

'I was careful, just like you said.'

'You've come to explain yourself.'

I could hear George's voice crack. 'Boss, listen — '

'I'm not interested in your excuses, George. Has anyone come to his office?'

'Nobody.'

'Have you ever seen him with this man, or heard the name Ezekiel White?' Pyke said.

George's head shook.

'Think hard.'

George tried, and the way he breathed the effort was painful. 'I never seen him with anyone.'

'He's a private investigator, George, a tool. Only an enemy of Jesus would use such a corrupt, ungodly man.'

I was almost flattered.

'Tools can be thrown away. It's his master we want.'

'But this guy White, he runs the committee of something-or-other. Don't that put him on our side?'

'He's on our side as much as Judas was on the Lord's. White is one of these men who love to stand in the street and pray, so we can all see his righteousness. When he is at home, who do you think he prays to, God or Mammon?'

'I don't know, boss,' George said, not realizing the question was rhetorical.

'Hypocrites like White are easily dealt with. It's the weak and pious men I worry about. No one doubts their faith, but they lack the will to do what is necessary. God has a plan for His son's return, and it is the duty of every Christian to bring it about. Those who cannot do what the Lord commands must be pushed aside. Jesus needs soldiers. Do you understand, George?'

'You know I'm a God-fearing man, boss.'

'I hope so.'

Neither man spoke. I heard more papers being shuffled. A phone rang and was quickly turned off. 'I'm worried about Ernest,' George said.

Pyke took his time answering. 'Why is that?'

'Strange was asking about him, and he ain't been answering his phone lately.'

'He's in a safe place.'

'Then why are you so worried, boss? Strange doesn't know nothing.'

'He knows my name, George. Thanks to you.'

'But you're in the clear. That piece of work we're gonna do — '

'No more of that.'

'But we ain't even done nothing yet, so — '

'Shut up.'

George did as he was told.

'We have been overtaken by providence.

Nothing has been done and nothing will be done. You will never speak of that again.'

There was another long silence, broken only by a drink being poured; a tall one, by the sound of it.

'I'm sorry, boss. He had me over a barrel.'

'I forgive you,' Pyke said. I heard him swallow a large shot of his drink. 'It's important that you know that.'

Relief nearly drowned out his words. 'Thank you, boss. I'll never fail you again.'

'I know, George.'

To the indifferent ear it sounded like a single, sharp cough. George groaned, and then I heard the sound of his body hitting the carpet.

The Stillwater goons were still standing guard. I didn't like my chances of running down four flights of stairs and overpowering two trained killers to make a citizen's arrest. In my condition, walking was enough of a trial.

I heard dialling. 'A mess needs to be cleaned up.' Pyke gave the townhouse address and then hung up.

When he came out the front door a minute later, Pyke's face was the colour of ash. His Mercedes returned, but the Stillwater men remained by the door. I took a photograph of Pyke as he got in the car. The man on the right looked up in my direction as the car drove off. I hid the camera. He kept staring at the roof, but didn't say anything to his partner. My camera lens might have caught the sunlight, or maybe there was a funny-shaped cloud behind my head. I wasn't going to bet my life on the latter.

I crawled away from the edge and then tried to sprint down the stairs. The four flights wouldn't have been a problem under normal circumstances, but my body had received so little nourishment in the past few days that my legs were shaking by the time I reached the ground floor. There was a back way out and I took it.

No one was waiting for me. I wanted to get a look inside that townhouse, but I wasn't going to try while those apes were in residence. Pyke's cleaning service would arrive before I got a chance to look at the body. The recording was good leverage, but it wouldn't be enough on its own if Pyke wanted to go to the mattresses. I'd have to settle for the better part of valour for now.

★ ★ ★

Washington Square Park was quiet, even for a weekday afternoon. Toad sat on a bench by himself in front of the Holley bust, twiddling his manicured thumbs.

'Afternoon, Strange. You look like hell.'

I joined my chemical supplier on the bench. Through the trees I could see the chess tables, less than half full. There were no musicians or buskers by the fountain, and the winos had been moved on from their park bench homes. Behind us columned archways led to the homes of the once and future rich.

'What's with the weather, huh?' Toad said.

A desire to make small talk wasn't the only reason Toad was an atypical drug dealer. With his bleached hair, deep tan and a grey suit showing beneath his overcoat, Toad was the mirror image of the pharmaceutical companies' own sales reps. I didn't know how he got his nickname and didn't want to ask.

'How's business?' I asked.

'Reliable.'

A large group had gathered near the fountain. Teenagers held babies so that their parents could brandish placards. An old woman in a cardigan and tennis shoes waved a sign reading: 'The wages of sin is death' in bright green letters. Their leader was a tall, doughy man in his forties. His face was burning scarlet from informing passers-by of his favourite scripture passages via megaphone. A band of men in army surplus fatigues ringed the group. They sneered at anyone nearby and hid behind their aviator sunglasses.

The group had made a small mountain of reading material in the dry fountain. A torch burned in their leader's hand.

'Who's having the cookout?' I said.

'The usual suspects.'

The group's name was American Families for Christ. Religious groups had multiplied and grown strong under federal patronage. The competition for souls and government money was often bitter and broke down along denominational lines. A more cynical man would think that it was designed that way. The support always came with a sheen of legitimacy, using vague terms like urban renewal, life counselling and family planning. The grant money they were using to fund this party had probably been awarded for community outreach.

The toy soldiers were the second type of group that had done well since Houston. Most did nothing more than let citizens dress up on weekends and parade around. The few that got government money were tame. They organized civil defence-style projects like standing guard outside chemical plants and informing citizens how much duct tape they'd need in case of a nuclear attack. Other militias were so extreme that the government didn't want to be seen supporting them directly. They attached themselves to Christian groups, who paid them with tax dollars to protect the flock against Satanists lurking in the bushes.

'They don't look like they're from around here.'

'Groups have been flying in from all over the country,' Toad said. 'I saw it on the foreign news.'

'They say why?'

'Nobody's commenting. They had footage of all these chartered 747s coming in, and coaches lined up near JFK. There must have been hundreds of people, maybe thousands.'

A line of young men pushing large wheelbarrows full of books and magazines went past us towards the fountain.

'That's some vintage tail there,' Toad said, craning his neck to get a better look at the contents. His smile cracked his face around the eyes, wrinkles standing out against orange skin.

The men scowled in return and pushed on.

'What a loss to civilization.'

It wasn't just dirty pictures. There were novels that had been deemed unpatriotic and science textbooks that were too accurate, plus boy wizards, ghost stories and anything miraculous not sanctioned by God. When all the wheelbarrows were emptied, the mountain was doused in gasoline.

'Aren't you worried about doing business with them around?'

'Naw. Everyone in that crowd does business with a guy like me, or is related to someone who does.'

The way Toad dressed made it easier for his clientele. If they'd ever bought street drugs, it was in a distant past they'd tricked themselves into forgetting. Now they were God-fearing people with yellow ribbons on their minivans, the kind who voted for politicians who promised to get tough on crime. They weren't like those degenerates lurking in the shadows to buy smack. Instead it was medication for hypertension, heart disease and arthritis, illegally imported from generics factories overseas. Even with a hefty mark-up Toad could sell the pills for a third of what the pharmaceutical companies charged, and justify the margin because the law made no distinction between him and a crack dealer.

'Is there something you need?'

'Reds.' I needed Delectra and Evalacet as well, but couldn't afford all three. Reds were the one drug I couldn't live without.

Toad sighed. I'd never heard him do that

before, and it worried me. 'I got nothing for you.'

'You always have something, Toad.'

'Last night some Jersey boys hit a delivery truck before it got to the city.'

'So they lost a truck.'

'It had the whole shipment of reds in it, among other things. It's not exactly a club drug, you know. Demand for it is never high, legitimate or otherwise. Are you dry?' he said when he saw the look on my face.

I nodded.

'Why didn't you come to me sooner?'

'You're a cash and carry operation, Toad.'

He acknowledged that fact with another accordion smile. 'I'll call a guy I know in Jersey,' he said. 'Unloading a boutique medication like that ain't easy, and they'll probably want to make a deal. Can you meet me here tomorrow morning?'

'You'd get out of bed before noon for me?' I said. 'Thanks, Toad.'

He shrugged. 'I am in the service business.'

With great ceremony the American Families for Christ's leader put the mountain to the torch, behind the backs of the two Washingtons — general and president — who watched over Fifth Avenue from the Arch. The fire blossomed, feeding on oiled glossy paper and spitting black smoke into the air. It stayed in place for a moment — a dark stain spreading across the sky towards the silhouette of Bobst Library hiding behind the trees — before the wind took hold. Poetry and smut, their still flaming pages borne aloft by the heat, were scattered on to the lawn in a single rain of ash. The group began to sing 'Amazing Grace', the guards mumbling along under their breath. Toad looked at the flames and then, like everyone else, he averted his eyes.

★　★　★

Iris and I sat in the Starlight's main restaurant area. The bar was to my right, the raised booths where I should have been sitting on my left. There were two exits — the diner's front entrance, and a door to the kitchen at the back near the bar — and I couldn't watch both of them. Even worse, our table was completely visible from the street through the diner's wall-to-wall front windows.

'Is something wrong?' Iris said, picking at the garden salad in front of her. She wore a white cashmere turtleneck and her dark hair was up. Her ruby knee-length skirt matched her shoes. The only jewellery she wore was a small gold cross around her neck. The ensemble reminded me of a restless convent student. 'You keep looking around.'

'This isn't my usual table.' A waiter had met us at the door and explained why half the booths had been cordoned off. Two tables of drunken men from different militias had started a fight over words no one remembered. The police were called in to throw them out, but by then they'd done a number on the upholstery.

'I never figured you for the obsessive-compulsive type.'

'It isn't that,' I said. I sat at the booths for a

217

reason. Down here I felt exposed. Knowing every place that bullets could come from was an instinct I'd had to develop, and now it was impossible to turn it off. It was difficult to explain, so I changed the subject. 'Did you have any luck today?'

'I'm not sure,' she said. 'I looked up all Junior's friends in the city to see if I could trace his last movements before he disappeared. Half have left town with their parents. The rest hadn't seen him lately.'

'So what's the confusion?'

'I ran into a friend of his near Park Avenue. Her family was packing up so I didn't have much time to talk to her. She told me the last time she'd seen Junior was a week ago, and he'd been blind drunk.'

I was still waiting to be impressed.

'He started complaining to her, in this histrionic way he has at the slightest inconvenience, that he was going to miss some big date on Saturday.'

'Who was the date?'

'She didn't know, some girl he'd met the week before. What's important is that he said he'd be gone all weekend.'

'Did he say why he had to leave?'

'No, but she got the impression it had to do with his father. He's the only one who can get Junior to do something he doesn't want to.'

'Maybe he lied to her about coming back. I'm sure Brother Isaiah's memory was longer than forty-eight hours.'

'She said he was completely trashed, and

Junior isn't that cagey to begin with.' Through force of will she had gone back to referring to him in the present tense.

'Maybe we're not giving Thorpe enough credit,' I said. 'Moving Junior out of the city might have been too risky, so Thorpe stashed him somewhere. Whether he knows about Brother Isaiah or not, it would make sense to keep the boy wonder under wraps.'

The TV in the corner had been showing footage of the anchored ships on a loop. 'Going overseas is a smart move on the parents' part,' I said. 'The others won't be far behind.'

'They're overreacting. Whatever the disagreement is, lawyers will sort it out.'

'We'll see,' I said. The Starlight was packed with the tail end of the dinner rush. There were a few regulars that I was on nodding terms with, salarymen, and a few out-of-towners with large cameras and comfortable shoes. A pair of men sitting at a table just past the bar piqued my interest with their contradictions. They were both dressed well enough to pass for Holy Rollers. One was a white man in his mid-twenties with a tangle of dirty-blond hair and a week of growth on his cheeks. The other was a black man about the same age, with short hair and a thick goatee. Their faces were completely slack, as if both men had only a finite number of expressions and didn't want them to go to waste. Both had eyes that had seen the inside of solitary confinement. If they had come to Jesus, it had been at the end of a long, dark road.

'If Thorpe does have Junior somewhere, he

wouldn't be stupid enough to visit him right now. I may have another lead though.' Pyke's words kept coming back to me: 'Those who cannot do what the Lord commands must be pushed aside.' Someone specific had been in Pyke's mind when he said that. 'You said Brother Isaiah wasn't too hot on the idea of building the temple,' I said. 'Did he tell you why?'

'The answer is long and theological,' she said.

'Give me the short version.'

'He believed it was interfering with God's plan, and that it was prideful and arrogant. The scripture is clear: the Jews rebuild the temple, not us.'

'He never went public with his feelings?'

'No.'

Brother Isaiah's last sermon, the one White had given me, was still in my phone. 'Listen to this for me,' I said, putting its speaker close to her ear. I drank my coffee and watched her face. The sound of Brother Isaiah's voice made Iris remember his kindness and feel his loss at the same time, a tug of war that played out on her face. Her tears were on a hair trigger, even as she looked happier than I'd ever seen her.

'I've never heard this before,' she said, when it was done.

'It's his last sermon,' I said. 'They found it on his body. Is there some hidden meaning that I'm not getting?'

'Maybe. Listen to this.' Iris rewound about halfway through and then put the phone to my ear. 'For as Christ said unto the apostles: of that day and hour knoweth no man, no, not the

220

angels of heaven, but my Father only. Yet it seems as if every day a silver-tongued man proclaims the day of our Lord's imminent return. They tell us this knowledge — denied to the angels and Christ himself — was revealed to them in a vision or hidden in a secret code within the Bible. These men are liars, yes, but they are guilty of a greater sin: pride. When the stricken Job questioned God's plan, our Lord answered him out of the whirlwind: 'Shall he that contendeth with the Almighty instruct him?' '

'Arrogance, pride, I got that,' I said.

'But it's a specific kind of pride,' Iris said. 'Brother Isaiah warned his flock about false prophets a number of times. There are a lot of hucksters out there trying to part the faithful from their money. But I've never heard him do it in these terms. He's talking about men who are arrogant enough to think they understand God's plan. Does that sound like anyone you know?'

'The Elders,' I said. 'You mean he was going to call them prideful liars on national radio?'

Iris nodded and pressed play. 'These men tell us the things we want to hear. I know you are eager for our Lord's return. So am I. It fills my days with the anticipation of grace. We believe that if we know the day and the hour, we can ensure that we meet Him at our most pure. Brothers and sisters, this cannot be done. For the day of the Lord will come as a thief in the night, and all our great preparations for His return will be for nought. We must live as if each day is the coming of the kingdom of God. We cannot control the hour that we are called to

221

account with the quick and the dead, only what has been written below our names in the book of life. Have I given to the poor? Have I controlled my desires? Have I glorified my saviour's name and spread His word? These are questions that must be in our minds.'

'He was finally going to come out and say it,' Iris said. 'This is a denunciation of the whole Holy Land project.'

'It is?'

'Why rebuild the temple if 'all our great preparations for His return will be for nought'? He is telling us to focus on our own souls, not on the fallen world. That is the only way to prepare for Christ's return.'

'Who would know what Brother Isaiah was talking about?'

'Not many average listeners,' Iris said, 'but anyone with a good theological education would be able to read between the lines.' That meant every important person in the Crusade would have known what he was talking about. If he had given that sermon, the whole organization would have turned against the idea of building the temple. Even if Brother Isaiah was dead, Pyke would have a hard time persuading the rank and file otherwise. No wonder White hadn't been shy in giving the sermon to me. It would have destroyed the Crusade, or at least ended any chance of it being a rival to White's Committee for Child Protection.

It was more or less what I was looking for. 'Thorpe didn't kill Isaiah.'

'I know Thorpe is involved.'

'Did you turn up any evidence today, or is that conviction still faith-based?'

'Don't you have hunches?'

'Sure, and some of them turn out to be wrong,' I said. 'We have nothing on Thorpe directly, and our motive is somewhere in thin air.'

She ate for a while instead of replying. 'You sound like you have someone else in mind.'

'I do. His name is Pyke.'

'The man you told me about earlier?'

I nodded.

'I know you'd love to blame the Crusade — '

'Hear me out,' I said. I told her about Ernest and George, and what Pyke had said to the latter before he put a bullet in him. That last part put a dent in her scepticism. 'The sermon clinches it.'

'Are you positive?'

'Mostly.' If Iris was right about the sermon, then that was the motive. Pyke knew Brother Isaiah's itinerary, so he had plenty of opportunities. It was the method that was nagging at me. A man marked for death by high-powered rifle had ended up strangled on a hotel bed. The sermon squared that circle too. If Pyke had found out about it he might have panicked and done the job himself.

'Mostly? That's all?'

'People have gotten a needle in their arm on a lot less than that,' I said. 'I have an idea. You're not going to like it, but it's our best chance to bring Pyke in.'

She didn't say anything.

'A tape and supposition aren't enough to take

on a man like Pyke. White may want a Crusade scalp, but he's got a four-lane yellow streak and won't move unless he's sure things will break his way. Thorpe will want to help if he can. The Elders think he did in Isaiah to start a war with them. Proving his innocence will be the best way to save Thorpe's business. With their shared history, the two might even like the idea.'

'What about Junior?'

'If the government is holding him then White will know where he is. It will be a straight-up trade for both parties.'

'Pyke's trial will be an embarrassment for everyone.'

'There won't be a trial. Pyke will disappear down a hole, and White will trot out whatever patsy he's had on ice since the body was found. He wouldn't trust his future to a private dick like me, brilliant or not. He's got an insurance policy somewhere.'

She was being convinced against her will.

I made the final push. 'Listen, maybe Thorpe was involved, playing Pyke behind the scenes. If he was, then going to him with this evidence might make him tip his hand.'

'If Pyke killed Isaiah to stop him from broadcasting that sermon, why did he leave it with the body?'

That was a good question. The waitress's return gave me time to think of a reply. Marta was an exception to the rule that the prettiest waitresses got the most tips. She was a short, wide Puerto Rican woman comfortably into middle age. She did well because she managed to resemble everyone's mother, regardless of ethnicity.

'Where's Mrs Rose?' I asked. Linger in the Starlight for five minutes, and you'd see her pouring coffee, working the register, or hear her yelling about something in the kitchen.

'She's visiting her sister, poor thing,' Marta said. 'Cancer.'

'Rose is always here,' I explained to Iris. 'When was the last time she wasn't at work?' I said to Marta.

'Her husband's funeral. Are you asking about Mrs Rose because you're worried about her, or worried she'll see you're not eating again?' she said to my cup of coffee. 'You look bad, Felix. Don't you feed him?' she said to Iris.

'He's not my responsibility, thank God.'

'Will you at least have dessert?'

'Why not?' I said, and held up my empty cup.

Marta scowled and turned back to Iris. 'How about you, dear?' The moment of temptation in Iris's eyes was all Marta needed. She whistled and a busboy brought the dessert cart our way. It was a serious affair: a dozen cakes and pies sheathed in glass that was cool to the touch.

Marta started to pitch the confections to Iris with the self-assurance of a carnival barker. I studied the two men while Iris prevaricated. When I'd told White to keep off my tail I'd assumed he wouldn't listen, but not even Daveys were stupid enough to sit right in front of me. The two men were also having a coffee dinner and being careful not to look too long in my direction. I stared at them for a few seconds.

225

They pretended not to notice, which wasn't the mark of a civilian. Instead, I saw their hands inching towards the pair of black gym bags at their feet.

'The apple pie looks amazing,' Iris said, 'but it would be gluttonous. What do you think, Felix?' she said, hoping to lose her weak conviction.

The two men reached into their bags. In the dark space between the zipper's teeth, gunmetal caught the light.

'Skip the pie,' I said, and threw over the table.

A blast from the shotgun in the white man's hands blew a corner off our table. His partner fired an Uzi he couldn't control, spitting bullets into a steak behind us and the stomach it was supposed to go in. I turned to Iris and started to tell her to run, but my words were drowned out by the sound of her putting rounds down range with a .380 pistol.

They took cover behind their table. I fired off a shot or two to keep their heads down while I looked for a way out. The shooters were blocking the front, so customers either trampled each other trying to get out the kitchen door or hid under their tables and prayed. If we couldn't escape, then Iris and I had to find a better position. Wood and a thin layer of chrome weren't much defence against lead travelling at high speed.

According to the New York average, about one in ten of the diners should have been armed. Most were smart enough not to draw them, but in any crowd there was always one guy who was a hero or an idiot depending on how things went. This time it was a paunchy man in one of the booths with a magnum revolver the size of his head. He became my lifelong friend by firing at the two shooters. He didn't hit anything, but it did force them to fire at him instead of us.

I used the distraction to wheel the dessert cart towards the counter. The blond noticed and put buckshot through all the cakes a few inches from my face. I sheltered my eyes away from the flying glass in the crook of my elbow, stuck my gun up in their direction and fired blind. That got me to the counter. I dived over the edge and stayed down. The man with the Uzi shattered the bottles on display and mortally wounded the clock on the wall behind me.

I couldn't see anything, and all I heard was screaming and gunfire laced with the sound of empty shells hitting the parquet floor. I peeked above the corner of the bar and saw a dumpy, fortyish woman in a Florida T-shirt firing a small pink automatic at anything that moved. The smell and concussion of all that gunpowder had snapped one of the moving parts in her head. The man who had come to our aid earlier was sprawled over the booth in a pool of his own blood.

The shotgun shredded her gun arm and took some of her torso with it. I caught the blond with a round in the shoulder, enough to make him try to take cover behind another table. Iris, despite the shredding of the table in front of her, was still firing at both of them. The man with the Uzi came to his partner's defence, ripping a few more chunks out of the counter.

In the cupboards were a few bottles of spirits that hadn't yet taken a bullet. I grabbed a bottle of vodka and a dish-rag already soaked in alcohol and broken glass. Only two guns were firing now. Iris was out of ammo, or she was dead. Both men were now pouring fire into the counter. The lovely thick oak I had always admired was now saving my life. I lit my cocktail and lobbed it over the edge.

I heard the encouraging sound of screams. Fire was eating its way up the man with the shotgun's arm. I finished what I'd started, putting a lead pill in his head. His partner was running away from the bonfire that had once been their table. His gun arm started to swing in my direction. I put three shots into his back. He hit a table at full run, turned it over with his weight, and lay very still.

I called Iris's name through the fog of burning vodka and gunsmoke. She crawled in my direction. She'd survived with a few cuts and bruises, her hair in lovely disarray. 'Are we still alive?' she said.

'I'm in a lot of pain, so we must be.'

'Who were those men?'

'I don't know, but that doesn't matter right now. You have to run. The police will be here soon.'

'What about you?'

'The staff know me here; the police will pick me up anyway. As soon as I'm arrested, someone will tell White. You don't want to be part of the collar.'

The sprinklers came on. Iris stared at me — black tears of mascara running down her face and collecting underneath her chin — eyes still not quite with the living. She looked at the bodies around her. There were four, not counting the shooters, the hero in the booths and the woman in the T-shirt. One was twelve years old. The table was still smouldering, trying to hide itself from the shower with thick dirty smoke. There wasn't a window, bottle or glass left unsmashed. Everything was quiet.

Iris leaned forward and kissed me on the cheek. 'Thank you,' she whispered, and walked unsteadily out the kitchen door. Sirens were already screaming in the distance. I put my gun down, got on my knees and knitted my fingers behind my head.

Friday

Every interrogation room looked the same. The fluorescent lighting made you look half dead before a single question had been asked. No matter how many hours you spent in one of the steel chairs that sat around a steel table, it was impossible to get comfortable. The one-way mirror kept you on edge, wondering whether there was someone on the other side watching and taking notes. I hummed something tuneless and scuffed the dirty linoleum beneath my feet. It was hard to stay entertained for four hours with only your own haggard face to look at.

A detective about my age named Park had spent a fruitless hour across the table asking me about the shooting. I'd told him that I'd never seen the men before and didn't know why they'd opened fire. After that I lawyered up, as a stall rather than a legal tactic. The public defender's office was so swamped it would take them hours to send someone. The constitution was supposed to protect me in the meantime, but that hadn't stopped Park from trying his luck. I kept my silence. Park gave up and left me in there alone.

The shooters had to be Pyke's men. With George dead and Ernest probably sharing his unmarked grave, I was another loose end to be tied up. I'd expected Pyke to take another shot at me, but I was surprised at how brazen it was. A shoot-out in midtown Manhattan was the sort of thing that sent jitters all the way to the governor's mansion. On my way through the station I'd seen a lot of SWAT members and police from other precincts. Park's lieutenant had probably been taking browbeating calls from his superiors as long as I'd been cooling my heels. It was a mystery that no one higher up had paid me a visit yet.

The door opened. White walked inside, accompanied by a woman in plainclothes I didn't recognize. 'That will be all, Lieutenant,' White said without looking at her.

She was in her forties but looked older. She was past the point where political appointees could make cracks about children, but nearing the perfect age to be forced into early retirement. They'd make her life difficult until she went, and a man like White could be a powerful ally.

'You took your time getting here.'

'Why didn't you call me?' White said.

'You promised to send me down a hole if I threw your name around.' If I'd called White, he would have used it as an excuse to put me in his pocket for ever. The pay may be lousy, but I preferred to remain an independent contractor.

'You haven't told them anything?'

'You've got the police report in front of you. See for yourself.'

White sat down opposite me and flipped through the report. I waited.

White whistled. 'That's a lot of firepower they were throwing in your direction. Any idea who they were?'

'I didn't know them from Adam. What does the file say?'

'Mike 'Ike' Lane and DeShawn 'O' Williams. Both were natives of Los Angeles. Ring any bells?'

I shook my head.

He read more of their files and frowned. 'Both men had cleaved to the dark path for some time.'

White turned the files around. They had a rap sheet as long as the proverbial arm, specializing in assault and armed robbery. They were the suspects in several unsolved homicides, but no charges had been laid.

'Assassins,' I said.

'Two men tear up a diner with a submachine gun and a shotgun trying to kill you, and you have no idea why?'

I showed White my hands. 'They weren't considerate enough to air their grievances beforehand,' I said.

White took the files back and pretended to read through them while he phrased his next question. 'Witnesses say you were eating with a woman.'

'It's happened before.'

'Perhaps she was the target.'

'I doubt that. She has nothing to do with the case.'

'You didn't tell her anything?'

'I don't talk up my work to impress or frighten anyone.'

'I'm sure that's true,' White said. The thin half-smile he managed couldn't hold back the torrent of insincerity behind it. 'Give me her name, and I'll confirm it.'

'It's a private matter. I'm not billing you for the meal.'

White took off his thick glasses and rubbed the bridge of his nose. 'That's not good enough, Strange. I need to know her name.'

'I should have known you and I would have a different definition of privacy,' I said.

'I am your client. Tell me.'

'No.'

White's hand struck the tabletop with a hollow sound. The few strands of hair on his head had slid off, leaving only a dome of sweat-drenched skin that reflected like a heat mirage. 'If I hadn't read your file, Strange, it would be easy to mistake your stubbornness for stupidity. You've had a problem with authority ever since you left the army.'

'I had no trouble following orders then,' I said. 'If you've read the file, then you know why that changed.'

White let out a phlegm-drenched sigh and pushed himself to his feet. 'I'm not here to argue about the past, Strange, and I have no more time to waste on you. If you refuse to understand your position, that's none of my concern. I will turn you over to others who will correct your problem with authority.'

There it was again: my life and freedom in the hands of a sweaty, unelected mental midget. 'You're going to have me tortured?'

'The United States does not torture people, and our allies only use enhanced interrogation techniques on Americans if we let them.'

It was a bluff. White couldn't afford to have me wasting time shackled naked to a floor in a foreign country. They'd confiscated my painkillers when they arrested me, and the burning in my muscles gave a sharper edge to my usual sunny disposition.

'Tell me about the Free Enterprise Foundation.'

White's eyes jumped at the sudden change of subject. It was more of a reaction than I expected.

'I'm a fellow there,' he said. 'What has that got to do with anything?'

'I did a little reading. In addition to the stipend you receive from the position, it got you speaking engagements, book deals and even cruise appearances. A Thorpe newspaper published your column before you ran the Committee for Child Protection, and that made you a regular guest on the Sunday morning shows. You were practically an employee.'

A vein on the side of White's forehead traced itself with pressurized blood. 'You'd better have a point to these insinuations, Strange.'

'I've been following the news,' I said. 'Thorpe's gambit with the container ships must be driving the Council of Elders up a wall. That's where you've been,' I said, leaning back in my chair with an idiotically beatific look, as if I'd just received these facts by divine revelation. 'They've been raking your ass over the coals, asking why you haven't brought in your buddy Thorpe for what they think he's guilty of.'

'They're mistaken.'

'For your sake I hope so,' I said. 'How long will it be before someone calls Thorpe's fit treason? Having a traitor for a patron would be a tough break for your career.'

'I'm comforted by your concern.'

'You are my meal ticket,' I said. 'How would you like to clear Thorpe's name, and put him and the Elders in your fan club?'

White's mouth narrowed to a wry line, but my hook was already inside.

'I have a theory. It's related to something that happened this morning.'

'Don't say his name,' White said. His eyes flicked in the direction of the mirror. 'Do you have any evidence?'

'I have evidence of something else that he'd kill to keep quiet. He already has, in fact.' I could see White salivating. I really wished I could leave the room.

'We can't discuss the matter here,' he said. 'Too many interested ears.'

'Then spring me.'

White formed his mottled sausage fingers into a steeple and stared at me over them. 'How do I know you're not lying?'

'You can always turn me over to the others if I am.'

'Tell me her name,' White said, 'as a sign of good faith.'

I rolled my eyes to the ceiling. I wanted off this merry-go-round.

The sound of something plastic arriving on the table brought my eyes back to his level. Between us was a small bottle of red pills. I had a hell of a time pretending they weren't there.

'Tell me her name and they're yours.'

'Did my file say I was susceptible to bribery?'

'Your psychometric profile suggests the opposite. But these are hardly in the same class as an envelope of unmarked bills,' White said. He gave the bottle a gentle shake so I could hear the pills rattle inside.

The army had given me a lot of bad reasons when they cut me loose, but this scenario was the only one I couldn't disagree with. If I was ever captured by the enemy, all they had to do was take away my medication and wait. If I didn't tell them what they wanted to know during a seizure, they could make me lucid long enough to crack.

'I'm no doctor,' White said, 'but I don't think you have a lot of time left.'

I'd stopped listening to White. All I could see were the pills in his hand.

A man in a deputy chief's uniform charged into the room. He was short, bald and built to the design of a brick shithouse. He looked White and me over, his nostrils flaring wide. I was disappointed he didn't have a ring through his nose. He was followed by Pyke, who stopped just over the threshold. This precinct must be on a party line.

'This interview is over,' the deputy chief said.

'On whose authority?' White said, rising.

'The United States' District Attorney for Manhattan,' Pyke said.

'Sir, this man is an eye witness to multiple homicides,' White's lieutenant started to say as she came into the room, but the gold eagle on the deputy chief's lapel stared her into silence.

A balding, saturnine man that I assumed was her captain followed her in, and stayed just as quiet.

'This is now a terrorism case,' the deputy chief said. 'Members of several Christian groups were eating at the Starlight Diner at the time of the shooting. The US Attorney believes this attack was a hate crime by secular nihilists.'

'I killed the terrorists,' I said. 'When do I get my medal?'

'Stay out of this, Strange,' White barked.

It was only my neck, after all. If Pyke and his pet took me into custody, my life would last precisely as long as it took to get from this precinct to a deserted area. 'If the Attorney is so interested in me,' I said, 'why isn't he here?'

'He sent us,' Pyke said. 'Call him if you don't believe me.'

'That man is a civilian,' White said to the police. 'He shouldn't even be here.'

Pyke squared up to White. 'Those Beltway perverts you have files on may be scared of you, Ezekiel, but I'm not.'

White showed Pyke all his expensive dental work. 'When the Attorney General finds out you've disturbed his vacation by playing chicken with me, you might change your mind.'

The lieutenant and her captain butted in, and pretty soon I was deafened by the sound of five large egos crashing head-on. The interrogation room was starting to look like the monkey cage at the zoo. I had to do something before they started throwing their filth around.

'I want to make a phone call.' That stopped the room.

'Shut your mouth,' Pyke said. He leaned over the table until he was only a few inches from my face. He enjoyed the novelty of having a height advantage, so I stood up and took it away from him.

'Arrest me, or let me make a phone call.' I looked at each person in turn.

Nobody moved. The lieutenant called in Detective Park, who escorted me to his desk. I dialled Benny's home number.

He answered with a groan. 'Who the hell is this?'

'It's Felix.'

'Do you know what time it is?'

'I'm at the sixth precinct. I need you to come down here.'

'I'm not going to fish you out of the drunk tank, Felix.'

'This is a precinct phone,' I said. 'I can't tell you why, but if you don't get down here within the hour, this might be the last conversation we have.'

The tone in my voice woke him up quick. 'Fuck,' he whispered, Miriam probably asleep beside him. 'I'll haul ass. Can you stall them?'

'I'll think of something,' I said, and hung up. 'Has anything been removed from my bag?' I said to Detective Park.

'No. It's evidence, so I can't give it back to you.'

'Just keep it handy. I'll need it soon.'

'Who bought your fairytale?' Park said.

I didn't answer.

'Come on, 'this might be the last conversation we have'? You're in an NYPD precinct. It's not like you're going to disappear.'

'I won't insult you by believing that you're as naive as you say you are, Detective.'

He didn't say anything, nor did the other detectives who were pretending not to listen. Instead he pointed in the direction of the interrogation room.

White and Pyke were at opposite ends of the room screaming into their cell phones. The police had decided to let their puppet masters fight it out, and leaned against the mirror making small talk. They eyed me warily, but without malice. Cops didn't have much love for private investigators, but I was being fought over by people they liked even less. I sat in one of the uncomfortable chairs and waited.

Good to his word, Benny burst in half an hour later wearing a rumpled suit and an expression that was more disgusted than usual. He took one look at me, and it got worse. 'What have you animals done to him?'

'It's okay, Benny. I arrived like this.'

'Are you his lawyer?' Pyke said.

'Another crack like that and we'll take it outside,' Benny said, showing them his identification.

'Who sent you?' White asked. 'I was told the director was unavailable.'

Benny cleared his throat.

I saved him the trouble of making something

242

up. 'He's here to take Mr Pyke and me into protective custody,' I said, 'as a suspect and material witness, respectively.' It was a nice change to be the only one in the room not surprised.

Benny's eyebrows tried to touch the ceiling. 'Yeah, that's why I'm here.'

'On what charge?' Pyke said.

'Two murders and a conspiracy. May I have my bag?' I said to Detective Park.

He hesitated.

'Get this man out of here,' Pyke said to the deputy chief.

He didn't jump. Instead, he looked at Benny and me in turn. He hadn't seen any paper to back up my accusation, but he didn't have any to ground his own story. The appearance of the FBI had spooked him a little, and he looked inclined to let things play out until he understood the angles better.

'Get him his goddamn bag,' Benny said. 'I'm sure everyone would like to know what the hell is going on.'

Park fetched my bag and gave it to me. I found the recorder and put it on the table. 'Early yesterday morning, I confronted a man watching my office. He'd been the getaway driver for a plot to kidnap me on Tuesday.'

George's earnest whine filled the room. He told everyone about the kidnapping and Ernest. When George mentioned Pyke's name, he exploded.

'Whoever that man was, he's lying.'

'Was?' I said.

The police looked at Pyke out of the corners of their eyes.

'The next conversation was recorded yesterday afternoon. It was inside a townhouse owned by the Crusade. The voices should be familiar.' I could hear Pyke gnashing his teeth as his voice came over loud and clear on the recording. He closed his eyes just before the gunshot. 'If you want to find George and his partner Ernest, I'd start trawling the East River.'

'What piece of work were they talking about?' Benny said. In the mirror I saw White connecting the dots.

'Pyke pulled these two shitbirds out of the gutter and made them into assassins. Ernest was the shooter. George was the driver. Once the job was done, they were a liability. I'm surprised he let them live so long.' Pyke was an amateur, but he wasn't that stupid. I added it to the other loose ends that bothered me, but I kept it to myself. Now was not the time to play Devil's advocate.

'I'm not going to listen to this slander any more,' Pyke said. 'When he's done spouting conspiracy theories, take him into custody.'

The deputy chief no longer seemed so eager to carry out his orders.

Pyke took a step towards the door, and found Benny in front of him. 'Get out of my way. Do you know what organization I represent?'

'Listen, shortpants,' Benny said, leaning in a little to make the most of their height difference. 'The only thing airing other people's dirty laundry in public makes you is a TV producer. I

244

am a federal agent. When I tell you to stand there and shut up, you do it.'

Pyke glared at Benny, but did as he was told. 'Is that enough?' I asked.

'It might be worth a chat at the office,' Benny said, 'depending on who the target was.'

I looked at White. Flop sweat dripped from his nose and his eyes had lost some of their focus. For a man used to getting exactly what he wanted, receiving both more and less than he expected was a new experience. 'The answer to that question is classified.'

'Then they can discuss it with the director,' Benny said.

White barely heard. All his attention was focused on me, and none of it was friendly. 'We'll see each other soon, Strange.'

'Sure we will,' I said. 'If I'm right about Pyke, then you owe me some money.'

Benny pushed me out the door, and sent Pyke after.

Pyke complained and threatened all the way down to the parking garage. Benny locked Pyke in the back of his car. We stayed outside so Pyke couldn't hear Benny chew me out.

'Have you got a paddle in that bag?' he asked. 'Because I am up shit creek past the horizon over here.'

'I'm not asking you to arrest him,' I said. 'Just lose us in the bureaucracy for a while. White is going to be looking for me, and I need to keep Pyke on ice until I'm finished tightening the noose around his neck. Is there somewhere we can stash him for a while?'

'Make a big Crusade muckety-fucking-muck disappear. Is that all you want? Listen to this guy.' Benny kicked his car and grimaced with regret. 'The ADIC is going to parboil my nutsack if he hears about this.'

'That's a fatted calf you've got in the back of your car,' I said. 'When he gets hauled in front of the cameras, the director and the ADIC will be grateful you gave them a way to shoehorn the Bureau into the spotlight.'

'I don't give a fuck about all that,' he said. He got the wrong idea, and was a little hurt.

'I know you didn't come down here to further your career.'

'That's for fucking sure.'

Benny rested his head against the car. I started to have second thoughts about dragging him into this mess. I didn't want to threaten my friend's livelihood when his wife had a bun in the oven. 'Listen, Benny, I was wrong to ask, especially with Miriam — '

'Forget it,' he said, straightening up his beanstalk frame. 'They had my number as soon as I walked into that room; I might as well do something to deserve it. There's a safe house in Queens we use to hide squealers and threatened families. We can put him there.'

'Who else knows about it?'

'Only a few other people in my department. We compartmentalize their locations.' The Assistant Director in Charge would know as well, but once he was involved it was over anyway.

'Thanks, Benny.'

Benny shrugged. 'I tell you to keep out of trouble, and twenty-four hours later look where we are. If I'd told you to get involved in a wild-west shoot-out, you'd probably be home knitting right now.'

We drove up the Avenue of the Americas, on our way to the Midtown Tunnel. Pyke was still threatening us both from the back seat, but he quietened down after Benny mentioned a gag. The street was full, as it was in Manhattan at all times. Most of our companions on the road were yellow cabs. Around the time the street became Sixth Avenue again, I noticed a blue sedan that had been with us since at least Tenth Street.

'We've grown a tail,' I said. 'One of the brand-new Chinese Fords, about a block behind us.'

Benny looked in his rear-view and frowned. We zigzagged around a bit, going east on Twenty-sixth, up Fifth, and then Twenty-eighth Street to Lexington. The blue sedan stayed with us.

'Don't look so delighted,' Benny said to Pyke. We turned on to Thirty-fourth Street.

Benny kept one hand on the wheel and felt beneath his seat with the other. 'Let's see if their brand-new car came with a siren.' Benny slammed the wailing blue light on the hood, and charged into the traffic of Second Avenue like a knight of old.

A chorus of horns joined our siren. Other motorists speculated about our intelligence and parentage. The blue sedan hit the chaos we left behind and added its horn to the discussion. All that accomplished was bringing it to the attention of the genealogy experts in the other cars.

We blazed into the tunnel at the same speed. The other motorists tried to get out of the way, but Benny was in no mood to wait. He weaved through the yielding and confused traffic, the brake forgotten, leaning on the horn when he felt the siren wasn't enough. I looked behind us to see if the sedan was still there, but all I saw was Pyke with his eyes closed, praying.

We left the tunnel with the siren off, travelling at the speed of a solid citizen. Benny took us on a tour of Queens to make sure the tail was gone.

'Pull over,' I said, when we passed a mini-mart with a pay-phone out front. 'I have to make a call.'

'Got a sick mother?' Pyke said from the back.

Benny caught my arm without taking his eyes off the road. 'Don't take it personally; he doesn't know.'

'The fucking bastard does know. He's read my file.'

'Normally I'd let him sock you one on principle, but I want to return you in good condition,' Benny said to Pyke. 'But if I hear another word out of you, I'm going to find a phonebook and give you a little sensitivity training.'

I got out, went to the payphone and dialled the number Iris had given me. She picked up on the fourth ring. 'Did you have any trouble with the cops?'

'No. I have a lot of previous experience

dodging the police. How did you get out?'

I gave her the short version of what had happened at the precinct. 'I'm still with Benny and Pyke. We're going to take him somewhere safe and see what he has to say for himself.'

'You still think it's Pyke?'

'Unless you got a signed confession from Thorpe recently.'

'What's our next move?'

'Do you have somewhere safe you can lie low for a while?'

'Felix, I'm not going to run away,' she said.

'Doesn't your religion say to submit to male authority?'

'We aren't married.'

'The way you're ignoring what I'm saying, it's starting to feel like it.'

Benny told me to hurry things up with his hands.

'White knows a woman was eating with me, and he might get enough out of the other diners to get a description of you. Just stay out of sight for a while. I've got enough things to worry about right now.'

Pyke gave me the evil eye from the back of the car.

'If anything happens, you'll call me?' she said.

'You'll be the first.'

Benny was getting frantic.

'I have to go. I'll call you in the afternoon,' I said, and hung up. I got back in the car. Pyke was wise enough to keep his mouth shut.

* * *

249

Benny drove to a street full of undistinguished frame houses. 'We're going for a little walk. Are you going to behave, or do I have to gag you?'

Pyke looked at the floor. 'Does it matter?'

Benny laughed. 'If I was going to whack you, why would I bring you to a street like this?'

Pyke left the car quietly. We walked down the street for two blocks and stopped at a house that was once just like the others. Decades of neglect had peeled the green paint on its two storeys, and time had put its finger on the centre of the porch and pushed it towards the ground. The lawn and the flowerbeds had become a single nature preserve. On the other hand, the chain-link fence that bordered the property was strong and new, as were the security cameras hidden in the eaves and the bars on all the windows. On first impression I would have assumed that it was a drug dealer's stash house.

Benny led us to the kitchen. He chained Pyke to a bracket set into the floor. 'Some of our witnesses are more reluctant than others.'

'You have no right to hold me here,' Pyke said.

'That's where you're wrong, sport,' Benny said. 'You're accused of planning and supporting a political assassination. Pursuant to the new PATRIOT Act, the Homeland Security Defense Initiative, the SAFE Act — what does that one stand for again?'

'Strategy Against Foreign Enemies.'

'Really?' Benny's nose wrinkled up. 'Well, pursuant to the aforementioned and a bunch of other acronyms our lawmakers passed in the middle of the night without reading, we can hold you without charge for as long as it takes to clear this matter up.'

'Those laws are meant for terrorists.'

Benny got in his face with a smile. 'That's what you look like to me pal,' Benny said. 'Of course I'm just a working stiff. All this national security bunk, it's above my pay grade. I can't evaluate whether you're an upstanding citizen or not, so we'll have to wait until someone with the proper clearance wakes up. Better safe than sorry. Isn't that what the posters say?'

Pyke didn't reply. I wondered if he'd ever imagined looking down the barrel of those laws. Even now, he probably didn't think they applied to him. In his mind, Benny and I were corrupt, godless men. We were abusing our authority, instead of using the law against the people it was intended for: others.

I pulled Benny aside. 'You mind if I have some quality time with him?'

'Knock yourself out.' Benny looked at his watch and cursed. 'I'm going home to get what sleep I can. He gives you any trouble, call me.'

I poured a glass of water from the kitchen sink and took one of my painkillers. Pyke watched me and said nothing. It was the second time in as many hours that I'd faced Pyke across a table. This one was made of maple and covered in a plastic tablecloth whose yellow checked pattern had faded almost to white. A single bare bulb above us illuminated the nameless seascape that hung on the wall. Pyke raised his arms, felt the weight of the chains attached to his cuffs, and let them rest on the table.

He said nothing. Pyke's silence wasn't surprising; I'd already caught him on tape once. It wasn't easy for him though. He was a Witness who'd been taught to proclaim his faith, loudly and often. He was playing quiet, but the light in his eyes was still there. Pyke wanted to proselytize; I just had to give him the excuse.

'You aren't the sort of person to work for White, no matter what he offered you,' Pyke said.

'He didn't give me a choice,' I said, though by now he was as thrilled with the arrangement as me.

'It's not too late for you,' Pyke said. 'The Crusade can offer you its protection. Come with me,' he said, holding out his bound hands, 'repent your sins, and be set free.'

'I am a sinner,' I said. 'It's pride that compels me to find Brother Isaiah's killer. That puts us on opposite sides of the coin, doesn't it? Besides, once the Crusade finds out what you've been up to, the only thing it'll offer you is a noose.'

'I didn't kill Brother Isaiah, I idolized him,' Pyke said. 'Do you know where I was before I took Jesus into my life?' The question was a rhetorical opening to what felt like a familiar spiel. 'I was born in a trailer in Appalachia. My father put a shotgun in his mouth when I was six. My mother was a drunk. We lived on welfare and a little money my mother brought in cooking methamphetamines on our kitchen stove. Everyone I knew was drunk, high or pregnant. When I finished high school, I could look forward to pushing a mop or stacking shelves for the rest of my life. That's what the secular world offered me.'

'One day a missionary from the Crusade of Love came to our little town. He set up in the Baptist church and put up signs for a meeting on Thursday night. The degenerates all laughed at him, but there was never much in the way of entertainment around there, so they came. The missionary's name was Brother Michael. On the outside he was a big, bald man in his forties. You wouldn't have looked twice at him. But as soon as we were in the room, we could feel this presence.' He drew out the last word, focused it, gave it weight. 'Just being there with him parted the cloud of despair a little.'

'Then he began to speak. Of course we'd heard the good news before; you could turn on the TV and hear it twenty-four hours a day. I'd never believed it, but Brother Michael was different. He was filled with' — he paused for effect — 'purpose. He told us God had a plan for each and every one of us. I began to understand that we had been destroying ourselves because the secular world offered nothing but material-ism and fear. I saw drug addicts and single mothers, welfare bums who beat their wives, all of them down on their knees crying. I got down on my knees and cried with them.'

'When the meeting was over I approached Brother Michael. I told him that I was ready to dedicate my life to Christ, and that I wanted to help the Crusade any way I could. He looked into my heart and saw the truth of my words, so

Brother Michael took me under his wing. I have served the Lord ever since.'

'And the Crusade made you the rich, successful man you are today.'

'Yes, I stay in nice hotels, I eat good food, and I have the use of a fancy car. I live well. Why shouldn't I? Who is more worthy of the Lord's blessings than those who work for His kingdom night and day?'

Even at this late hour, Pyke still believed he was on the clock for Jesus. 'If wealth is a sign of God's favour, then Marcus Thorpe must be one of His most beloved sons.'

'Money and grace are not the same thing.'

'And yet God favours the corrupt.'

'God allows the corrupt to choose the manner of their downfall.' Righteous indignation was forcing blood into his face, his nostrils flaring with the heat of his own boiling blood. 'Thorpe has set himself against the whole nation, and why? Because of pride, the oldest and greatest of the sins. He and his degenerate son will not escape judgement.'

The mention of Junior nearly pricked my ears up to the ceiling. 'The son is just as bad as the father?'

'The Crusade's file on him ran into hundreds of pages. He will be at the top of our list when the sinners are named.'

'You may not have the chance, unless you want to speak ill of the dead. Word on the street is that the Thorpe heir has disappeared.'

There was neither guilt nor Christian charity in Pyke's cut-glass eyes. 'He probably overdosed in some high-priced brothel, and his father is covering it up.'

'What did the Crusade have planned for the Thorpes?'

'Judgement,' Pyke said. 'Only Brother Isaiah knew the manner of their temporal punishment. If you want to know their ultimate end, find a Bible.' Pyke assumed that there was some prime beachfront property waiting for Thorpe and his son by the lake of fire. It was the first thing he'd ever said that I agreed with.

Pyke's hatred of sin was about to carry away the conversation, so I tried a different tack. I put my phone on the table and played Brother Isaiah's last sermon. Pyke put his hands together and lowered his head on instinct. I watched his face. There was sadness, anger when Brother Isaiah spoke of arrogance, but no signs of guilt or remorse.

'But do not lose heart, brothers and sisters. Remember that God has a plan for all of us. That is enough; we do not need to know His grand design. Remember the words of Isaiah: 'But they that wait upon the Lord shall renew their strength; they shall mount up with wings as eagles; they shall run, and not be weary; and they shall walk, and not faint.' Good night, brothers and sisters. You are in my prayers.' The sermon finished, and Pyke stared into the silence it left.

'Have you heard it before?' I said.

'No.'

'But you know what he's getting at.'

'Of course I do.'

'So would the Crusade, and the Elders. If that

sermon had gone to air, no one in the Crusade would have followed your mad ideas about the Holy Land. It wouldn't have mattered, because the Elders would have moved in and shut down the whole outfit as soon as Brother Isaiah defied them. Your holy mission and the organization you've devoted your life to would disappear, along with your address on easy street. When it comes to motive, that's an embarrassment of riches.'

'I didn't kill Brother Isaiah. He was a great man,' Pyke said.

'You pulled two men off the soup line, trained one how to kill, and planned his assassination. Is that how you honour great men?'

Pyke gave me nothing but burning conviction from every pore. 'Brother Isaiah was a great man,' Pyke said again, 'but he was wrong.'

'And that was why he had to die, didn't he? 'Those who cannot do what the Lord commands must be pushed aside.' Your words. Brother Isaiah lacked the stomach to do what the Lord commanded, so he became an obstacle that had to be removed. I found out about it, so I became an obstacle too. You sent those goons after me, and they killed six innocent people. One of them was a little girl.'

'I had nothing to do with yesterday's atrocity.' He stood up a little, before the threat in my eyes pushed him back into his seat. 'I've already prayed for the dead, including that unfortunate girl,' Pyke said, as if that was enough to consider the matter closed. 'Why would I send two thugs to kill you?'

'You sent two amateurs to kidnap me,' I said. 'Murderous thugs are just one rung up on the ladder of evil.'

'You don't have enough evidence to charge me.'

'You and I both know that's not the point. Brother Ezekiel and the Elders have never been that big on due process.'

The vice I had him in hit the hard core of his faith, the belief that had grown in him since that day in Appalachia that said he walked with the angels no matter what the circumstances. The tension and fear eased out of his body, leaving a film of patient resignation in his slackened face. Pyke had resolved to play the martyr, whether he'd been cast in the role or not.

'An atheist like you will never believe a word I say. Shoot me now or hand me over to White, it doesn't matter,' Pyke said. 'I know where I'm going after I die. What do I have to fear from you and White? You are just men.' Pyke looked down at his bound hands, and refused to say another word.

I led Pyke into the master bedroom and chained him to a radiator near the bed. I lay in an easy chair but sleep wouldn't come. All the bits and pieces of this case were bothering the hell out of me. It felt like I was trying to make something out of two different jigsaw puzzles with my eyes closed. Every time I had a complete picture, there were pieces left over.

Pyke was a fanatic. He didn't deny Ernest and George, but proclaimed his innocence when it came to Isaiah's murder. Sooner or later zeal should have overcome caution and intelligence. I couldn't dislodge him from his story, and I didn't think it was because my game was slipping. If he had truly believed that killing Brother Isaiah was necessary to carrying out God's work, Pyke wouldn't have hesitated to cop to it, no matter the consequences. The more I thought about it, the less sense it made.

I hadn't gotten around to listening to that Brother Isaiah lecture that Iris had recommended. I had nothing better to do, and it seemed stupid to break a promise to Iris over something so trivial. I went to the Crusade website on my phone. What she wanted me to listen to was part of a much longer lecture.

'We have come to the part of my story that is also a confession. Many years ago, I despaired of the people of this nation. Atheism, feminism and sexual licence ran rampant through the nation's streets and airwaves, and neither the Church nor the state seemed able to stop them. I saw women who behaved like men, men who acted like children, and children who dressed like whores. I held up my arms to the ocean of sin drowning this country, but the waves would not recede.'

'So I abandoned the country of my birth. It still pains me to say it. At the time, I believed that the African people were less spoiled by the modern world. They had not suffered through our godless schools or been assaulted by our media. The continent had grave problems, but most were material, not spiritual. I believed I could make a difference in this world and the next.'

'We chose to begin our work in Ghana, at a small village on the Black Volta. We had many successes there. We built schools, drilled wells, and gave the people a place to pray. The villagers were healthier, happier and coming to the Lord in increasing numbers. The hand of providence seemed to be guiding our labours.'

'Yet there was still a shadow that hung over this village, and all the others we visited. I'm speaking of course of Aids. Husbands slept with women of low character, and gave the disease to their wives. The wife would become pregnant, and an innocent life would come into this world marked for an early death. I spoke against these sins every Sunday. The people came and listened, but every week more sick people arrived at our free clinic. The wages of sin weren't arriving in the next life but all around them, and yet they persisted in their dangerous ways.'

'I began to despair. If I could not convince these souls of the evils of sin when it was such a clear and present danger, then what was the point of me being there? Every day my doubt grew stronger. I preached the word less and less, and focused on humanitarian efforts I knew were doing some good. I began to question my reason for living, and even the existence of God Himself.'

'The Lord works in mysterious ways. It is one of my favourite sayings. The atheist sneers at the words, sees them as our excuse for all the evil things in this world. They do not understand that those words are the only way to explain how good things can spring from a seed of evil. The seed I speak of is the tragedy of Houston. An entire city reduced to ashes, the way our Lord's vengeance fell upon Sodom and Gomorrah. When the word reached us in Ghana, we wept for the dead. We had become an ungodly people, but even in our fallen state I could not understand why we deserved such wrath.'

'Then I heard Adamson speak. I will not repeat his words here, for you should know them. Of all our leaders, he alone understood that this atrocity was our chance to begin again as a nation. There was to be a new city on the hill, free of the vice that sapped our strength and destroyed our families. That sad day was not a punishment from God, but a flood of tears to wash away our wickedness. I had left my brothers and sisters to their fate, and it took that horrible day to open my eyes. I fell on my knees and beseeched God to forgive me for the terrible sin I had committed: the sin of doubt.'

'My brothers and sisters in America asked for my help, and I answered the call. I left our work in Ghana in the hands of capable men and returned home to a changed nation. The desire for renewal was palpable, brothers and sisters, in every house and on every corner. People returned to the faith by the millions, and our government was finally making laws that were good for its people.'

'If there is one thing I want you to remember from what I have said here today, it is this: all of us are children of God, regardless of what we have done. Every soul is the gift of our Creator, no matter what container it is in. If your brother is in peril you must offer him your hand. If he falls, you must pick him up. We must do more than love the sinner; we must save his soul from his nature. Brothers and sisters, I have abandoned the souls of this nation once. With God as my witness, I will never do it again.'

I took off the headphones to get away from the deafening applause. Iris had wanted me to understand Brother Isaiah, to hear his conviction and compassion. That had come through loud and clear. I wondered if she'd also heard a man in deep denial, unable to reconcile his vision of human nature with the suffering around him. Instead of facing his doubts head-on, Brother Isaiah had retreated into despair and his work, just like most human beings. Houston wasn't the opportunity for renewal that he had claimed it to be; it was an excuse to forget. Maybe to him that had been the same thing.

★ ★ ★

I was asleep in the easy chair when Benny kicked me awake and offered me a bagel. 'Where's Pyke?' he asked.

'He's asleep in the master bedroom, chained to a radiator.' I took the coffee Benny offered me and tried to get my head working. The pain was creeping back into my joints. I tried to stretch and had to stifle a scream. Benny eyed the bottle of painkillers I took from my coat pocket.

'Are you taking the medication you're supposed to, Felix?'

'I'm taking the medication I have,' I said, and

washed down the pills with some coffee.

'I have to go to the office,' he said.

'They'll grab you if you do.'

'Not if I get there early enough. By the time someone arrives with a subpoena, I'll be in a parking garage where phone signals and GPS can't reach. You want a ride back into the city?'

I nodded.

'Then wear this,' he said, handing me a fresh shirt. 'You don't look so good in the daylight.'

I changed without looking in the mirror. I didn't want to know how accurate Benny was. 'I want to take another run at Pyke.'

'Save it. We have to get on the road now.'

It wasn't Benny's usual flavour of impatience. 'Is something going on?'

'I'll tell you in the car,' he said, and threw me my hat.

'What about Pyke?' I said.

'My cousin will look in on him in a few hours.'

'He won't think Pyke's situation is a little odd?'

'He was a marine,' Benny said. 'He's seen a lot worse.'

Benny waited until we were stuck in the tunnel before he started to fill me in. 'A friend of mine in the mayor's office called this morning. Have you heard about the Revivalist and militia groups coming into the city?'

'I ran into some of them burning books in Washington Square Park yesterday.'

'Well, the crazy brigade got reinforcements this morning, and they're getting restless. They've surrounded Thorpe Industries and a dozen other companies. The mayor has called out all the SWAT teams and pulled in every off-duty officer still in the city, as well as asking for help from the county PDs. He was trying to persuade the governor to call up the National Guard, but the oily bastard is sitting on his hands.'

'The governor can't figure out which way the wind is blowing, and doesn't want to risk pissing into it,' I said. 'What do the Elders say?'

'The mayor's office put out feelers, but they say it has nothing to do with them. 'Spontaneous demonstrations by patriotic, God-fearing citizens' are what they're saying, in between bringing up the first amendment.'

'They brought up the first amendment? That's serious chutzpah,' I said. Of course they were pulling the strings. 'They're trying to force Thorpe to get those container ships moving again, by any means necessary.'

'I thought they were smarter than that,' Benny said, 'until I called a colleague on my way back to the safe house.'

'It gets worse?'

Benny's first attempt at an answer was drowned out by the horn of the car behind us. He moved us a foot forward and stuck his finger where the other driver could see it. 'Dozens of material witness warrants arrived by courier from the Department of Justice. The targets are a who's who of the filthy rich. He got on the horn to DC to try to find out what the hell is going on, and he heard even worse was coming. Warrants have been issued under the Sanctuary laws.'

I heard myself exhale. The Sanctuary bill had criminalized any actions that aided and abetted the destabilization of Israel, or reasonably led to violent actions against our troops stationed there. The definition of reasonable had been left deliberately vague. Penalties included the forfeiture of all assets, and even imprisonment. 'I thought they just waved that law in front of peace activists to shut them up. It's never been used before, has it?'

'There's a first time for everything.'

So our two ruling classes had finally decided to see who ran the country. The republic's history placed heavy odds on the merchants, but it was the holy men who had troops on the ground. I wondered what the Elders planned to do with the plutocrats once they were under federal bond.

Between the war with Iran and the occupation of Israel, our adventures in the Middle East had bled the treasury white. The nation's super-rich were worth billions but the money was scattered in banks and sunk into property all over the world. Even if the Elders could get at it all, the total would fund the Holy Land occupation for less than a year. Besides, there were still more than enough people willing to lend the administration money. When the emperor was your biggest creditor, it wasn't smart to point out that he hadn't been wearing pants for years.

However, a forfeiture order would tie up the oligarchs' assets in the courts for a long time. The Elders didn't even have to go through with it; the possibility would be enough to restrain any further desire to question their policies.

'Will the director go along with it?'

'He doesn't write the laws. What I need to hear from you,' Benny said, 'is that your case has nothing to do with this approaching clusterfuck.'

I stayed silent.

I expected a torrent of curses, but Benny stared at the car in front. 'I think it's time I knew what your case is.'

'Since I got it I've been shot at, Tasered, smacked around, and had a gun put in my face more times than I'd like to remember,' I said. 'You may want to reconsider your curiosity.'

'I'm up to my asshole in it now anyway,' Benny said. 'I might as well know why.'

'Someone killed Brother Isaiah on Sunday.'

Benny blinked, and blinked again. 'Why are you investigating it?'

'Ezekiel White wanted a layer of plausible deniability. I'm that unlucky sucker.'

'So you think Pyke whacked him? That's who the assassination plot you talked about was aimed at?'

I nodded. 'The Elders believe otherwise. I've heard they blame Marcus Thorpe, but I don't know why.' I hated lying to Benny, especially since he was the only man I trusted, but I had promised to keep Iris's existence a secret. I gave him some time to absorb what I'd said.

'That explains the Wall Street Seven. I was baffled why the Elders picked a fight with their meal ticket.'

'The rest snowballed from there.'

Benny was staring even harder at the car in

front, almost hypnotized by the tail lights. I could see all the different calamitous scenarios for the future running through his head. 'We're fucked,' he said, his voice barely above a whisper. It was his final thought on the matter.

We waded through the traffic down to southern Manhattan. Benny let me out a block from Federal Plaza, the grey slab of the federal building his destination. I could almost read the inscription on the New York Supreme Court building across the street: 'The true administration of justice is the firmest pillar of good government'. It grew more ironic every year.

'Can I leave my bag in your trunk?' I asked.

'Sure, knowing you it's probably just evidence of a crime,' Benny said. 'So what are you going to do now?'

'I thought if I brought them Pyke's scalp, I'd get paid and things would be smoothed over. Now I haven't got a clue.' My first priority was to get to Washington Square Park and meet Toad. Unless I got more of my real medication, I'd be just another paralysed spectator.

Benny looked at me in a careful way, maybe memorizing the details in case missing persons would need them. 'You know, Felix, some day you're going to get tired of thinking up ways to get yourself killed, and then what will you do with your life?' He sped off before I had a chance to answer. The son of a bitch always had to have the last word.

I was walking north on Lafayette towards Washington Square Park when I noticed a stretch limousine moving slowly behind me. It was midnight black with tinted windows, the sort of vehicle favoured by the rich and private: CEOs, politicians and gangsters. None of my friends fitted into those categories, but more than a few enemies did. The back window on the driver's side began to slide down. I reached for my gun.

'Wait!' Thorpe barked. The limo pulled up beside the kerb. Mr Lim, sitting opposite his master, opened the door. 'Get in quick, before someone sees me,' Thorpe said.

I obliged. The limo began to move south.

'The FBI is looking for you,' I said.

'That's why I was at Federal Plaza. The Assistant Director in Charge is a friend of mine. He's given me a forty-eight-hour head start to get my affairs here in order.' Thorpe didn't appear worried; he must pay someone to do that for him.

'Are you going to run?'

Thorpe snorted. 'This bullshit will be over in forty-eight hours.'

The Canyon of Heroes was a stretch of lower Broadway that got its name from the ticker-tape parades held between its skyscrapers. I usually avoided going that way, but I wasn't driving. My unit had marched there, part of a large parade celebrating a self-declared victory after Tehran became Ghost Town. I was just out of hospital and my syndrome hadn't shown itself yet. We marched beneath a cloud of confetti, the cheering from the crowds echoing off the steel and glass gorge. Benny punched out one of the President's advance men for trying to pin a cross to his lapel. Security tried to remove him, but our line linked arms and shouted them away. It was a happy memory, and I wanted to protect it from the dull reality of the street where it had taken place.

We got just within sight of Thorpe Industries. All the streets near the Stock Exchange had been blocked off by the police. 'I heard you had visitors,' I said.

Three preachers competed against the crowd and each other to be heard. Half of a destroyed Israeli bus had been towed into the road in front of the building. A large sign on top read: 'Israeli children killed by Thorpe Industries', even though the bus was at least a decade old. On the sidewalk, a row of militiamen in army surplus glory faced a phalanx of Stillwater men guarding Thorpe Industries' front door. A line of police in riot gear surrounded the area, but they didn't look inclined to intervene on either side.

'The Elders think they can frighten me with their trailer trash,' Thorpe said. 'If it weren't for the damn press, I'd tell my boys to open fire.' Out of the corner of my eye, I saw Lim's eyes roll.

'I have a message for White,' Thorpe said. 'Don't play dumb,' he said, when I didn't respond. 'I know who you work for.' I wondered which one of White's trustworthy Daveys had sold me out. The smart money was on the one I'd punched in the nuts. 'It took Mr Lim longer than usual to find out, but he always does.'

Lim didn't react to the compliment. He knew about the gun under my left arm but hadn't taken it from me when I got in the car. He also didn't seem bothered by the fact that my hands were two feet from his master's neck. Lim lay against the black leather and watched my shoulders and hands with the half-open eyes of a sunbathing cat. It was a level of confidence I found insulting.

'If you want to give White a message, pick up the phone.'

'He's forgotten how to answer it.' Anger made Thorpe's eyes phosphorescent in the tinted dusk. 'Tell him he'd better convince the Elders to cut this shit out if they want the country to go to work on Monday.'

'That sounds like a threat.'

'It's a prophecy. They love those.' He looked out at his headquarters under siege, its façade still imposing and indifferent. 'When my grandma dragged me to church every Sunday, what I heard from the pulpit was snake oil and promises. All that prayer didn't create one new job or stop a single crack dealer's bullet. I realized then that you could depend on no one — not the government, God or your own people — for help. I've seen the will of the world, and the meek ain't in it.'

Thorpe's reverie was over as suddenly as it had begun, and he was looking at me again. 'Just tell him our patience is almost up.'

'It might help if I knew who the plural was.'

'He'll know. In the meantime, I expect you to let me know what White is up to.'

'You expect me to betray a man like White?'

'I pay far better than he does.'

'I was thinking more about his capacity to retaliate.'

'Don't worry about that. When it hits the fan, you and I know who really runs this country.' His voice had its typical gruff bravado, but Thorpe's two-day stubble and bloodshot eyes told me he needed reassurance.

'I used to think so.'

It wasn't the answer he was looking for, but he let it pass. 'I'll leave Mr Lim here to sort out the details. He has some work to do.'

Lim opened the door and I took the hint.

When we were both out, Thorpe threw a small wad of bills at me. 'Consider that a retainer. I don't know what you've been doing, but get yourself cleaned up. You look like hell.'

I saw Thorpe reach for the mini-bar, my existence already forgotten before his fingertips touched the whisky. Lim closed the door.

The limousine reversed and went down a side street, leaving Lim and me looking at the money on the pavement between us. After a moment he bent and picked it up. 'Consider it compensation for being in his company,' he said, and offered it to me.

I couldn't refuse. 'Your boss seems pretty confident, considering.'

'He thinks he's seen worse,' Lim said. 'Mr Thorpe prides himself on never running from a fight. It's a rule that's served him well in business and life. He sees no reason to change.'

'And you think differently?'

Lim smiled. It made me uneasy. 'I'm not paid to think.' He gave me a card, blank except for seven digits. 'We'd prefer it if White contacted us directly. If he insists on using you as a go-between, leave his reply at this number. If you think there's something we should know, leave a message there as well. The line is secure.'

The phalanx of Stillwater men hadn't moved from their position. The militia facing them didn't have the same discipline: they squinted, shifted and looked around. A few were already pining for a warm place to drink, though the number was less than I would have expected. The mercenaries stood completely still, oblivious to the hymns, prayers and shouts directed at them. The only proof that they were alive was their breath in the cold air, a ghost that danced in front of their faces for a moment before it disappeared.

'Would you really take a bullet for that man?' I asked Lim.

His reply came so fast I could tell he'd already thought about the question. 'Every man has to feel he is part of something greater; it takes some of the sting out of being just one among billions. The price you pay is realizing that you're expendable.'

I didn't think Marcus Thorpe believed there was anything greater than himself, but I saw his point. He knew I would, and was already walking away.

'Take my employer's advice and get your medicine,' he said, his voice somehow cutting through the noise of the crowd. 'We still have an appointment to keep.'

I didn't need that arrogant fool or his creature

to tell me what I needed. Thorpe had cost me time I didn't have and told me nothing. I had to get to Washington Square Park immediately. Without the red pills, I had only an even chance of making it through the afternoon, and those odds dwindled and disappeared with the sun.

I got the One train and headed uptown. The demonstrations had filled the subway with more rowdy out-of-towners than usual. It was only a few stops and then a short walk to the park, so I wouldn't have to put up with them for long. Two militia members sat next to me on the orange curved plastic. One was in his forties. The other was barely out of high school.

'A guy from Amarillo told me this one: when the Antichrist takes over the United Nations, where's he gonna move the headquarters?' the older man asked.

'I don't know.'

'Nowhere. It's already in Babylon.' The older man began to kill himself with laughter. His young companion took his time to respond.

'I don't get it.'

A middle-aged militiaman with captain's silver bars on his collar stopped near me. He was middle-aged, unshaven and still wearing his mirrored aviators. 'Fred' was stitched on his shirt above the breast pocket. He belonged in a Wal-Mart hardware department, nursing an old dream to manage the whole store one day. Behind his head, an ad posed the question: 'Does the person next to you look like a terrorist?' Below it was a toll-free number. There was no Spanish translation.

The jokers next to me shut up as soon as he appeared. He looked me over, gears in his head grinding louder than the subway on the rails. He was trying to match me to a type he had in his head, a phrenological outline of something he feared or didn't understand. I'd seen the look before, but it was the first time it had been directed at me.

'You a Jew?' he said.

I decided not to pay attention. New York made you immune to all sorts of unpleasant things, and I had bigger worries. There was a tingling on the back of my neck. It would begin to spread down my nerves and through my body. The storm was coming.

'I asked you a question.'

If I hadn't been so run down, I would have noticed earlier just how many militia members were in the car with me. They sat in small groups but didn't talk. At their feet were army surplus canvas kitbags, as if the subway was taking them to a deployment. Only a few were actual vets, eyes ground down to nubs by the sands of the Holy Land.

'What if I am?' I said. I wasn't inclined to explain my family history to anyone, but if he was looking to start his own pogrom it was better he tried it with someone who could settle his hash.

'You aren't in the Holy Land.'

'No shit.'

The captain looked surprised. If he was expecting me to apologize or justify myself, he obviously hadn't been in New York long. 'Well, why the hell not?' His voice was pitched somewhere between accusation and grievance.

I became aware of all the other militiamen in the car watching me, and the few civilians doing their best not to.

'That's where you people are supposed to be.'

I was resisting the urge to show him where my fist would be when the driver's voice came through the PA: 'Due to an incident this train will terminate at the next stop, Houston Street. We apologize for any inconvenience to your journey.' The train stopped, the doors opened, and I left before the captain said something that would force me to knock him down.

The Village was dead. The streets weren't this quiet at four in the morning, let alone the start of a work day. Down Seventh Avenue I could see crowds gathered in Christopher Park. They sounded more numerous and less peaceful than the mob gathered in front of Thorpe Industries. It looked like Benny's contact at City Hall hadn't been blowing smoke: whatever the Elders had started was spreading. Captain Fred formed his troops up on Houston, shouting at anyone who stepped out of line and obviously enjoying himself. I stayed away from the marshalling forces, not wanting to be the focus of any renewed attention.

A row of mounted police held the line at Houston Street. They were in full riot gear: Kevlar, leather and plexiglass obliterating all traces of the man inside. They were immobile and silent, a ghostly cavalry waiting for the call to war. Like the police outside Thorpe Industries they were not there to intervene, just stop whatever was happening near Christopher Park from spreading. I wondered if they were still taking their orders from City Hall. Steam rose from the sewer grates and made their black and brown horses pale before my eyes.

The only civilian around was an old, stooped man just big enough to fill out the news-stand he ran on the corner. He didn't seem surprised at what was going on in front of him, or bothered by the lack of customers.

'Hey, pal,' I said, 'do you know what's going on?'

'No idea,' the old man said. 'But I don't need the late edition to know it's the frickin' apocalypse.' The militiamen began to march. Against my better judgement, I followed.

Discarded signs littered Seventh Avenue, a trail of hateful breadcrumbs. Most were scriptural: 'You shall not lie with a male as with a woman. It is an abomination', and 'And turning the cities of Sodom and Gomorrah into ashes condemned them with an overthrow, making them an example unto those that after should live ungodly'. Others were simply vicious, the worst a large banner that reproduced a section of the Aids quilt, with the words written over: 'Killed by Aids, God's punishment'.

A famous gay club called the Stonewall had stood just around the corner on Christopher Street. It had been the scene of a seminal moment in the gay rights movement at the end of the sixties. Tired of constant harassment by the police, the club patrons fought back during a raid, and the riots lasted for several days. Gays refused to be invisible any longer; not a small thing, when the American Psychiatric Association still classified homosexuality as a mental disorder. The unrest forced the rest of the country to accept their existence, and helped to create hundreds of gay rights groups.

For the Revivalists it was a terrifying fairy tale, like pretty much everything else that had happened during the sixties. The government would have loved to level the whole area (and most of the Village) but they settled for removing its status as a National Historic Landmark. In its place they added a small, much defaced plaque in Christopher Park commemorating 'Victims of Gay Terrorism'. It was no coincidence that the Revivalists had chosen this place to tell gays and lesbians to get back in the closet.

The area around Christopher Park looked like the epicentre of a gang war. The demonstration that Captain Fred and his men had joined had been met by a counter-demonstration, and the result was predictably violent. Preachers shouted very little about peace or brotherhood. The flocks were the usual mix of young and old, well-meaning and hateful — the type of people that shouldn't be in the middle of an urban melee. They'd lost some of the courage of their convictions along with their signs on the way to the square. Now they sang hymns and clustered around their pastors for safety. None of the side-parted young Daveys looked eager to join the fray.

The faithful were protected by the Holy Sons of American Liberty, according to the gold-fringed standards carried by boys no older than thirteen. An eagle carried a cross towards Mount Rushmore. Beneath the cross were the names of the broken and forgotten cities of the interior: Cleveland, Flint, Raleigh and Cincinnati. The men who marched under the banners (there were no women) wore green camouflage on the grey streets. They used nightsticks, bottles, bricks and bats to beat their enemies. Almost every man had a sidearm strapped to his thigh, but they hadn't yet been drawn.

Their enemies wore no uniform. They were in jeans, track suits, chinos and even pyjamas. They could have been any random crowd, except for the rainbow flags they wore and waved to rally one another. The residents of Chelsea had come out to defend their homes. Women fought side by side with men, using whatever came to hand.

Captain Fred had noticed me while I was taking in the scene. In his mind I was already an uppity Jew who wouldn't do what the Bible commanded. Now he suspected me of homosexual tendencies. I could see him talking to some of his soldiers, and decided it was time to disappear. I ducked inside the nearest door, a gay bar called Sardinia.

It was empty and depressing, like all nightspots during the day. The coloured lights and large sound system were off. A mop stood in a bucket in the middle of the dance floor without a partner. The back wall was taken up by the bar, the Christmas lights that hung above the mirror behind the only illumination. I called out, and a man in his forties with a fake tan popped up from behind the bar with a shotgun aimed at my teeth. In the mirror I saw my reflection raise his hands.

'Do I look like a toy soldier to you?' I said.

The man looked me up and down, taking in the rumpled suit, fedora, pale skin and darkened eyes. He lowered his weapon. 'What y'all doing here?'

'I'm trying to get to Washington Square Park,' I said. 'I have an appointment to keep.'

His laugh was a long drawl. 'You picked a fine day to feed the fucking pigeons. The police have closed the park and all the subway stations near the Village, but haven't lifted a finger to help us. God forbid they should actually do their fucking job.'

'My name's Felix.'

'Walt.'

We shook hands across the bar. It was a subtle test of my politics: any bigot in disguise would have hesitated.

'What the hell is going on?'

'A big ol' state-sponsored gay bash is what. They came marching in half an hour ago, singing hymns and praying for our hellbound souls at the top of their lungs.' Walt rolled his eyes. 'They might as well have pissed on our rugs and jabbed their fingers in our eyes.'

Chelsea was the natural place to start a purge. As government persecution got worse, most gays who could afford it had moved abroad, taking their skills and capital with them. Those without the desire or the means to emigrate had fled to the few remaining cities where they could expect to be left alone. The newcomers had settled in traditionally gay areas for extra safety, making Chelsea the largest homosexual ghetto in the country.

'So who's giving it back to them out there?'

Walt smiled. 'Gay and Lesbian Self-Defense League.' Even the Elders had balked at a Senate bill requiring religious and sexual preference to be displayed on all passports and driving licences (children, terrorism, et cetera, et cetera) so there was no way the government could prevent gay groups from arming themselves. The groups had become popular not just because of government harassment. The police seemed to lose interest in a case of assault if the wrong orientation came to light.

'I don't think the weekend warriors expected this kind of reception,' I said.

Walt smiled. 'It does warm my heart to see all those rainbow flags come out of the closet again.' New York was the last American city to have a gay pride parade. The state had found it so embarrassing that Albany finally shut it down by threatening the city with the same financial starvation that had broken San Francisco.

A brick came through one of the blackened front windows. 'Fuck you too, snake charmer,' Walt yelled as he sent a load of buckshot back outside.

I helped Walt turn over one of the tables and push it in front of the broken window. We put another one in front of the door. Through the

279

broken window we saw Molotovs sailing through the air, and then heard the sound of breaking glass and hungry fire.

'Jesus Christ,' Walt said. 'They're firebombing everything.' As bad as it had been, today was new and darker territory. Other than in a few big cities, displaying a rainbow triangle attracted an audit or a brick, depending on how bad the job market was in the area. New York was an exception, and that rare display of pride was now being used by the Holy Sons to pick their targets.

Walt noticed the bulge beneath my left shoulder. 'Is that just for show?'

I wasn't sure any more. The tingling had spread to my hands. I made fists until the nails dug into my palms to stop the shaking. If things got ugly, I wasn't sure how good I was going to be. 'If someone comes through that door, we'll find out.'

A young woman leapt through the window on the other side of the door. She fell hard and didn't get up. The girl was tall, thin and no more than sixteen. Her hair was as golden as the cross around her neck, except where the gash in her forehead had darkened it with blood. We lifted her away from the front door, and Walt poured half a shot of rye down her throat. She coughed and opened her brown eyes.

Almost immediately they focused into horror as she realized where she was. She sat up, her whole body tense with the desire to run. Any stories she'd been told about gay bars had been neither pleasant nor accurate. I'd heard one radio pastor speak of writhing gay orgies with young boys, while another had talked about a black-robed priest invoking Satan while violating men with a cross. The imaginations of demagogic pastors were unusually fertile when it came to acts of depravity.

'We're not going to hurt you,' I said. 'Do you have a first-aid kit?' I asked Walt.

He nodded and reached behind the bar.

'Watch the front.'

Walt grumbled something about not taking orders in his own place, but went to the barricades.

She had glass in her skin and a dozen scrapes, but it was the wound on her head that worried me. I reached out to inspect it and she flinched away. 'If it makes you feel any better, I'm just an atheist. It isn't contagious.'

She grimaced when I touched her forehead, but didn't move away this time.

'What's your name?' I asked, taking a sterile bandage out of its packet.

'Harmony.'

'I'm Felix, he's Walt.'

'We didn't want violence,' Harmony said to herself, like a prayer, while I wrapped some gauze around her head to hold the bandage in place.

'Then maybe you shouldn't have attacked us in our homes,' Walt drawled.

'You attacked us,' Harmony yelled back, a dangerous note of hysteria in her voice.

'That's enough,' I said, before it got any worse. 'Walt, what's going on out there?'

281

'I can't see a damn thing,' he said. A muffled explosion made the liquor bottles behind the bar dance. 'What was that?'

It had sounded like a pipe bomb, but I didn't want to panic the others unless I was sure. 'Have you got a compact in there?' I said to Harmony, pointing to the handbag that had come through the window in her arms.

She fished it out for me while I grabbed a broom that rested against the bar. I opened the compact and tied it to the end of the broom with gauze. I crawled over to Walt, and eased my contraption out the window.

The compact showed me urban warfare framed in pink. Christopher Park had become a triangular death trap, the Self-Defense League using their home advantage to fire down at the Holy Sons from the upper floors. The town-houses were ideal sniper nests, with rows of tall windows and flat roofs only three or four storeys up. Anyone who tried to leave the low foliage of the park had little hope of crossing the two lanes of Grove Street alive.

The militias had responded by taking whatever cover they could find in the square and returning fire. Assault rifles and a few M-60 light machine guns came out of the kitbags I'd seen on the subway. A small group of fighters had clustered around to defend two men whom I recognized from Captain Fred's unit. I'd tagged them as veterans in the subway, but it would have been obvious as soon as I saw what they were pulling from their bags.

Each had a rocket-propelled grenade. Every

soldier in the Big Sandbox had learned to dread its distinctive outline: the long shaft and pistol grip of the launchers that ended in the bulbous tip of the grenade. The men mounted the RPGs on their shoulders and took aim. My brain was thinking they must be souvenirs from the Holy Land, while my body was diving to the ground and telling Harmony and Walt to do the same.

For a heartbeat I saw the hot white lines of the grenades' rocket exhaust. The explosion knocked the broom from my hand and drowned out the sound of gunfire. Harmony wailed until Walt put a hand over her mouth. I picked up the broom and angled the mirror back into position. The grenades had hit two of the buildings facing the square. They'd gone through the windows and sent a rain of shrapnel and body parts back out. All glass near the two burning storeys had rained down on anyone nearby. A few silhouettes stumbled around on the buildings' other storeys, but were cut down before they could take human form.

I pulled the compact back in before it attracted attention. 'Is there a back way out of here?' I asked.

Walt shook his head, and then something occurred to him. 'There's a delivery elevator that goes from the cellar to the street. It's made for moving booze, but it should be big enough.'

Harmony had calmed down enough for Walt to take away his hand. I looked at her and she hesitated. 'Do you want to get out of here with two sinners, or wait for one of your

283

co-religionists to throw a bomb through that window?'

She followed me towards the back. We were behind the bar before I noticed that Walt wasn't following.

'A man's got to defend his property against all comers,' he said. 'Don't worry about me; I got enough shells to last until doomsday.'

We saluted with nods, and I led Harmony into the gloom.

The basement was tiny and the elevator easy to find. It would be just big enough for the two of us. I grappled with the controls while Harmony cried and stared at the floor.

'Listen to me,' I said, and gave her a shake when she didn't respond. 'If you want to live, you will stay quiet, follow me and do exactly as I say. Do you understand?'

I gave her another shake and she nodded.

'Why are you helping me?' she asked.

'Ignorance isn't a good enough reason to leave someone to die.' I opened the top hatch, and the elevator carried us up under protest.

The world above was shrouded in thick white smoke. I thought it was fallout from the bombing, until the smoke stung my eyes and burned its way down my throat. The police had finally decided to step in and do their jobs. I tried to tell Harmony that it was tear gas, but only coughing came from my throat. I put my hat over my mouth and nose and Harmony got the message. She put one arm across her face and grabbed on to my hand with the other.

I listened for the sound of gunfire and headed

in the opposite direction. Harmony stumbled after me. I looked at the world through slitted eyes, the gas making my tear ducts work overtime. Silhouettes of streetlamps faded in and out of the mist, the masts of lost ships passing each other in the fog. We got maybe a block before the girl had to stop. There was no time to be understanding. I gave her arm a sharp tug, but she still refused to move. I turned around and saw her lying on the ground. I knelt and felt for a pulse, unwilling to believe the dark stain I saw spreading across her chest. There was nothing I could do. I had to leave her lying there in the street. I crawled away from the sound of explosions I hoped weren't coming from the Sardinia, and tried to navigate through the sea of my tears.

There wasn't any chance of me meeting Toad now. Even if they hadn't closed the park down, he would have disappeared at the first sign of all those police, let alone the beginnings of an urban war. I doubted anyone else on the island would have what I needed. My only hope was to get to Pyke's townhouse before he found his way out of the bureaucratic maze I'd thrown him in. If I found something incriminating, and convinced White to share my view, he might give me that bottle of reds he'd flashed as a down payment on my fee. I'd think about the consequences later.

After a while the smoke formed into the shape of a yellow cab. It was occupied by a young Sikh man reading the paper. Hallucinations had never been a symptom of my condition, but who knows what gas and sleep deprivation had done to my brain. I knocked on the front window, as much to make sure the vehicle was real.

When he turned to see a man with a fedora on his face knocking on his window, the cabbie nearly jumped out of his seat. We regarded each other with mutual disbelief. I motioned for him to open the back door and he gave me the finger. I raised my arm and threatened to smash the glass. The engine was off, and he'd have a cab full of tear gas before he could get it started. With a rag over his mouth, the cabbie opened the door with great reluctance.

'Are you out of your mind?' the cabbie said as I threw myself in the back seat and closed the door quick. The air in the taxi was clear enough to breathe almost normally.

'I could ask you the same question,' I said. 'You're reading the sports pages in the middle of a war zone.'

'I don't have a choice,' he said. 'Some crazy guys in fatigues have set up checkpoints all over the Village. They see brown skin and they'll shoot.'

'The police are finally involved,' I said. 'The militia will be too busy trying to stay alive to bother with us.'

The cabbie wasn't convinced. He looked out the window and tried to see through the gas. The ID card on the back of his seat said his name was Sanjiv.

'Sanjiv, do you really want to stay put?'

His fingers played over the meter for a while, then pushed it down.

We crawled down the side streets. The police's

assault on Christopher Park had metastasized the riot. The gas showed me only silhouettes: lonely, wandering figures and groups of fighting shadows. My eyes found the list of charges stuck to the back of the front seat. There were surcharges for rush hour and late at night, but no agreed price to drive through a civil war.

The police had set up roadblocks at Eighth Avenue. As soon as Sanjiv saw them he started to slow down. I grabbed his shoulder. 'Keep going. Stopping now will be suspicious. You're taking me to St Vincent's.'

When we got within fifty yards a young officer wearing a gasmask signalled for us to slow down. He eyed Sanjiv as we rolled towards him, and tried to get a good look at me. The air was clear enough that Sanjiv could roll down his window as the officer approached.

'I have to take him to the hospital,' Sanjiv said.

The officer gave me another once-over. I looked the part. He waved us on without a word.

The trouble looked confined to the west and south of the island. We did a wide arc, up almost to Union Square before we went south-east towards the Brooklyn Bridge. Any other day we would have been stuck in gridlock for hours trying to go through the centre of the city, but most vehicles had been chased off the streets. Sanjiv flipped through the radio stations looking for word of the riots, but all it could offer us was prayer.

'Are you going to answer that?' Sanjiv said.

My phone was ringing. It was Benny. 'Where are you?' he asked.

'I just got out of the free-fire zone formerly known as Greenwich Village.'

'The whole city's lost its fucking mind. I'm going out on assignment any second, but there's something you need to know: Pyke is a free man.'

That was very bad news. 'What happened?'

'I'm not as good at evading my colleagues as I thought. Bigwigs from the Crusade, the city and Albany got to Federal Plaza before me and raised ten kinds of holy hell. I'm sorry.'

'It was only a matter of time. When did they spring him?'

'An hour ago.'

'Jesus Christ, Benny, why didn't you tell me then?'

'Because the ADC has been digesting my ass for the last hour, that's why. They wanted to know what compelled me to put Pyke in irons. Don't worry, I didn't say a thing, but I'm in the fucking dog-house right now. I can't even leave the building without the Assistant Director's say-so. If you need my help — '

'You've put your ass on the line enough for me today, Benny,' I said. 'Don't worry. If I call again, I'll have something to trade.'

'Good luck, you meshugener bastard,' Benny said, and hung up.

By the time we got across the bridge I was getting worse. My legs were starting to shake and I was sweating. There was something bright in my brain, and it was heating up my insides.

Sanjiv's eyes in the rear-view mirror were grim. 'You okay back there?'

'Gas,' I said, and coughed for effect.

'Are you going to die on me?'

I shook my head, but I could see he was panicking. 'I'm fine, just get me there.' I was choking on every word and only scaring him more.

He stopped the car. 'Get out of my cab. No charge.'

I mumbled something about a large tip.

'Get out of my cab,' he yelled.

When I didn't move, he did. I heard the front door slam, and the one near my head open. Hands grasped my shoulders and pulled me to the pavement. There was the sound of an engine and screeching tyres. I was looking at the sky.

I had to move. The thought entered my head but it didn't have any immediate effect. It was an irritant, a fly I couldn't see. The proof I needed was only a few blocks from here. Now was my only chance. My hands searched out and found a trashcan. I held on tight and pulled myself to my feet.

I dragged myself along using lamp posts, fences, signs and whatever else I could stumble into. I was climbing the street more than walking it. Even with the news blackout, word had travelled fast. Most people were smart enough to stay in their homes. A few caught sight of me clinging to their gates and watched my progress with horror. They looked at my pale face and strange walk and saw an angry spirit called out on to the streets by the smell of blood.

I saw Pyke's townhouse. I don't know how long I'd been walking. The buildings were taller and more crooked than I remembered. They were leaning forward to watch, betting on how far I'd get. The townhouse's front door had grown with the rest of the building, imposing as the gates of hell. All the witnesses had left the street. I was getting inside one way or another. I didn't have time for games, and my black bag was gone anyway. I squared my shoulder, threw myself at the door, and fell right through.

I was so relieved to be lying down it took me a moment to realize that the open front door was a bad sign. The house was empty, or at least no one had screamed or taken a shot at me yet. Through doorways I could see teak and bone china, but it didn't interest me. Upstairs was an office where George had met his end. I pulled myself upright with the banister and crept upstairs, pistol in hand.

The office was the first door on the left, half open. I listened at the threshold for a moment, and then pushed it open the rest of the way with my gun. I didn't believe what I saw at first: it was a figment of my misfiring brain, a side effect of the tear gas. Pyke lay on his stomach behind the desk, his face turned towards the window. A safe that had been hidden behind a seascape was open on the wall behind him. Across the wall, written in Pyke's blood, were the words: 'WE'RE HERE'. I lurched forward and held on to the desk. The sun in my head was pushing all my thoughts out my ears. I couldn't think, couldn't understand how he'd gotten here all the way from Queens just in time to die.

Pyke or his killer had left papers strewn over the desk. I picked up what looked like an itinerary for Brother Isaiah. There were prayer breakfasts, sermons and meetings with frightened and sycophantic politicians, appointments he would never make. Another folder I didn't need to read. It was a copy of the Crusade's file on Jack Small. There were other pages but I couldn't read them. The characters kept jumping out of place, refusing to stay in their lines on the page.

A single shot to the head had killed Pyke. There wasn't much blood and his skull was mostly intact, so it must have been a small calibre. I tried to look in his pockets but my fingers weren't working. Any instructions I gave to my body were filtered through the kaleidoscope of my malfunctioning brain, and what came out was a constant surprise.

I couldn't think, but I didn't care any more. Everything was a thousand times brighter, lit by the sun inside my head. The case and its questions seemed impossibly remote, the day-to-day worries of an ant colony. I was in the centre of a great, warm silence. I wanted nothing and was happy with everything. Out the window, I saw a sparrow across the raging sun. I thought it would be burned — the sun was so close I could almost touch it — but it flew past, unconcerned. I reached out to them both.

I was on the floor. My arm was looking for my phone, annoying me as it searched my pockets. I tried to tell it to stop but it wouldn't listen. It found the phone, dialled, then dialled again. I heard Iris's voice, beautiful and wary like a feral cat.

Words came out of my mouth. I heard the address, in between some pleas. Then I repeated the names of my drugs, over and over, like a magic spell. I told my mouth to stop, but it wouldn't listen. Somewhere, she was replying. I caught Pyke's dead glass eye, tried to ask him a question, but it was too late.

The storm had come.

Saturday

The windowless room I saw when I opened my eyes wasn't in Pyke's townhouse. I was tied to a queen-size bed, wearing only an undershirt and a pair of pyjamas I didn't recognize. One of my enemies had finally caught up with me. I wondered what unmarked place was beyond the walls: a military base maybe, or an airstrip that had no name. There was a form somewhere with my name on it, a big red stamp declaring me an enemy combatant. It would disappear into a cabinet the way I'd disappeared into this dark place, the only record of my existence hidden behind walls of fear and privilege.

My head was pounding and I ached all over. I felt like I'd drunk a bathtub of home-made gin and then run a marathon. It could have been a lot worse. I'd cut myself badly and broken bones during convulsions before. Considering I'd collapsed alone, I was lucky I hadn't bitten off my own tongue.

I tested my bonds and looked for an escape route, until I realized that the abyss shouldn't smell like cinnamon. Abstract paintings were on the wall, and a framed photograph of Angkor Wat. There was a television near the door, which was slightly ajar. If it was a cell, it was the strangest one I'd ever been in.

On my left was a small night table inhabited by a fat, smiling Buddha. In front of him were three familiar prescription bottles and a syringe. The only way to bring someone out of an episode was to wait for one of the calm periods and mainline the drug they needed. When I was at the VA hospital, a doctor had shown me a tape of one of my attacks. He had half joked that before they discovered the off-label use of the reds they'd considered calling in an exorcist. I didn't blame him; there was something infernal in my contorted, flushed face, its eyes wide open but focused on demons only they could see. In another time, I probably would have ended up tied to a stake.

I hesitated to call out. I still didn't know who was holding me, and the only advantage I had right now was that they didn't know I was awake. The rope that tied me to the bed was too thick to break. If I strained I could get my teeth on the rope that bound my arm. I tugged at the knot with my mouth with no success, until I heard Iris's distant voice.

'O Lord my God, in Thee do I put my trust: save me from all them that persecute me, and deliver me, lest he tear my soul like a lion, rending it in pieces, while there is none to deliver.' I could have called out but I didn't. She was praying, and for some reason I couldn't disturb her. 'O Lord my God, if I have done this; if there be iniquity in my hands; if I have rewarded evil unto him that was at peace with me; yea, I have delivered him that without cause is mine enemy: let the enemy persecute my soul, and take it; yea, let him tread down my life upon the earth, and lay mine honour in the dust.'

I waited, but she did not speak again, and neither did I. I told myself it was out of fear that she'd been captured as well. It was really a desire to hear her speak another verse. Under those circumstances I could stand a little more time in confinement.

Iris solved my dilemma by sticking her head inside the room. 'You're awake,' she said, as if we were in this situation every morning.

'What time is it?'

'Late Saturday. You've been asleep for a day and a half.'

'Are we safe?'

'We're in my apartment,' she said. 'No one saw you come here. I hid you in my car, a cute red electric MG. It's part of my cover.' She answered my question before I had a chance to ask it by stroking a large bump on the back of my head. She let her hand linger there. 'Sorry about that. I couldn't get you into the car in your condition. While I was waiting for the medication I was afraid you'd wake up and hurt yourself. That's why I had to tie you up.'

I didn't want to think about how she'd found me: broken, convulsing, trying to scream through foaming lips. It was a small mercy that I never remembered the episodes. 'Forget about it; I'm a bigger danger to myself in that state anyway. Is this place part of your cover?' I said, indicating the room with my chin.

Iris picked up the Buddha. 'I'm a very spiritual broad but not, you know, religious. Men think they have a chance that way.' It wasn't fair for her to smile like that. There was nowhere for me to hide.

The ropes that bound me to the bed were tied with something resembling a sailor's knot. 'I see you've had some experience in this department.'

She fingered her work on my left arm. 'Girl Scouts summer camp for underprivileged kids. All that fresh air didn't improve my morals, but I did learn how to tie a knot.'

'The seizures won't come back, as long as I take my medication.'

'That's good,' Iris said.

'You can untie me.'

'Right,' Iris said, with a little laugh. She leaned over me and struggled with the rope around my arms, her hair a dark curtain that fell over half the room. Annoyed with the skill of her own work, she used a penknife on my legs.

I picked up the medicine bottles. 'Where did you find these? I couldn't get them for love or money yesterday.'

'I called in a favour,' she said. 'My smart set has a lot of powerful sons. It turned out there were a few boxes sitting in a warehouse outside Bayonne. It took me a while to understand what you'd said. Imagine my surprise, picking up the phone and hearing Felix Strange speaking in tongues.'

The bottles were full, enough medication to keep me going for a month. I picked each one up and felt its reassuring weight, but I shied away from the needle. Too many bad memories.

'Thank you,' I said, 'for bringing me here, for

the medicine, for everything. I had no right to call you for help.'

'We strays have to look after one another.' She started to ask something and then stopped. 'You were screaming,' Iris said, 'in your sleep.'

Of course I didn't remember. 'Did I say anything?'

'I couldn't understand most of it. You did repeat a name: Athena. You said it over and over. Was she an old girlfriend of yours?' Iris said with a coy smile. It vanished when she saw the look on my face.

' 'She', was an A-10 Warthog close air-support jet fighter,' I said. 'My unit prayed to her every day but, like God, she rarely answered. I never did meet the lady behind the call sign. I don't even know if she survived the war.'

'Tehran?' she said.

I nodded.

'I was a teenager during the war, and never paid much attention to it. It was easy to ignore, and I was busy screwing up my life. I do remember the parades though.' Everyone remembers the parades. 'Do you want to talk about it?'

'No.' I turned away from her. It was a lousy thing to do, but some memories had escaped the cage I had put them in, and I didn't want her to see my face while I rounded them up and stuck them where they belonged.

'Do you mind if I turn on the TV?' I asked, and found the remote before she answered. 'I need to know how badly the country has unravelled while I've been asleep.'

'Police stopped a series of violent uprisings

299

today in New York City,' an announcer said. They cut to footage of men and women being handcuffed in Chelsea and thrown into vans. Too many embarrassing questions guaranteed they'd never get a fair trial. 'Sources within the government believe that the attacks were organized by homosexual terrorist groups, bent on gaining rights for their deviant lifestyle through violence.' Footage of the riots themselves was telling in its absence.

I flipped to another domestic news channel, but that was just choosing a different stenographer in the same typing pool. They were showing a news conference with the Secretary of the Department of Homeland Security holding forth from a podium. Behind him was the mayor of New York, director of the FBI, and several other officials I didn't recognize. They were guarded, as all major public officials were, by a detachment of Stillwater mercenaries, one just visible on the left side of the podium. The department's slogan was tiled over the backdrop: 'vigilance, patriotism, faith'.

'Were the attacks in New York isolated incidents?' a voice said off-camera.

'There were a few minor incidents in Chicago, San Francisco and Salt Lake City, but we don't know if they are related at this time.' The mayor looked uncomfortable. He knew what had really happened yesterday, and the consequences of holding back the NYPD in front of his constituents. The Revivalists weren't able to rig local elections with the same finesse they brought to federal races.

300

'Were the attacks part of a wider agenda?' said a different journalist.

'We know foreign powers fomented this unrest for their own ends,' the Secretary said.

'Who do they mean?' Iris asked.

'This week's foreign bogeyman is China,' I said. 'I doubt they'll take the insinuation lying down.' All the questions at these news conferences were softballs or plants. The government wanted China to know who it blamed, though I'd be surprised if it had any evidence.

' . . . once again underlines the importance of a united front against terrorism,' the Secretary continued. 'Those who seek to divide America with angry rhetoric, or who through their actions undermine the godliness of the nation's character threaten its very security.'

They switched back to the studio for an analysis of just how scared we should be. The coiffed emptiness manning the anchor desk had a confused, pained look on his face: the look a child gets when he stumbles on his parents fighting and doesn't want to take sides. Even after the fatwa the Elders had laid on their corporate masters, the press was afraid to speak against the government.

'I don't suppose you can get foreign stations on this thing?' I asked.

'Of course,' she said. 'I need to keep up with all the latest godless propaganda.'

She fiddled with the back of the TV, and the BBC appeared. They were showing footage of the riot under the caption: 'The Battle of

Christopher Park'. The cameraman had been on the opposite side of Seventh Avenue, north of the square. He ran over to a trash can and knelt beside it, zooming in on the square itself. Holy Sons tried to find cover behind the benches and iron railings while exchanging gunfire with the tenements around them.

The camera caught only the first RPG hit, on a tenement on Grove Street. The camera jerked with the shockwave, then panned left to show the second building in flames. The two explosions had emboldened the militiamen to leave their cover in the square with their home-made bombs. There were more explosions nearer to the square. The cameraman jerked around but he couldn't follow all the bombs. At least four buildings had been hit, but it wasn't the burning buildings my eyes were drawn to. In the road a Holy Son lay on his back, a burning Molotov cocktail in his cold, dead hand. Bodies lay in the square itself, some trying to move, others still. Militiaman, resident and Revivalist all looked the same at this range, their lifeblood disguised as rainfall by the red brick.

'Turn it off,' I said. I'd already seen enough of that day.

Iris did as I asked. 'How could something like that happen?' she said.

'They overreached,' I said. The Elders only talked to each other and the hardest core of the faithful, who if they had any doubts kept them deep down out of respect for God, or the hierarchy they'd been told to serve. They took the silence of the rest — because until now it had been easy to deny what was going on if you were the right kind of person, and fear shut you up if you weren't — as unspoken support. The Elders began to believe their own claims of divine right, and thought no one could stop them.

'They bussed in people taught to hate and fear the secular world, turned them loose in a strange city and told them to destroy the enemies of their faith,' I said. 'It was inevitable.' Those images had awakened an old anger that had been in me since Tehran. It was the sick, cold fury of watching people given as burnt offerings on the altars of the powerful. 'The rotten bastards took one look at the water and thought they could just stroll right over.'

'But the Elders didn't mean for something like that to happen.'

'Maybe they didn't want things to go so far, they aren't stupid,' I said. 'It doesn't matter; they've shown the world their true face. Things will only get worse now.'

'Why do you hate Christians so much?'

I tried counting to ten. I didn't want to have this discussion right now, especially with my host/nurse.

'If you told me, maybe I'd understand.'

Maybe she would. I wasn't very good at refusing her anyway. 'I grew up in a suburb upstate, among the last dead-enders of the vanishing middle class. I had main street dreams and a typical life, until my mother got sick. Cancer. She had insurance but they weaselled out of paying for the treatment somehow. Our savings disappeared into the pockets of lawyers, doctors and drug companies. I quit school and went to work, but it wasn't enough to afford the chemotherapy.'

'My father was a lapsed Baptist, my mother a theoretical Jew. When she became ill, my parents found their respective Gods. It brought peace to them both, in the beginning. My father prayed every day, and when his prayers went unanswered he didn't lose his faith. Instead he began to believe in miracles. He watched Brian Binn all day.'

'Brian Binn is a fraud.'

'You'd think that would be self-evident when a man claims to heal the sick through the television, but my father wanted to believe. He gorged himself on a twenty-four-hour diet of miraculous healing and prayers fulfilled. He scraped together the last of our money and gave it all to Binn's ministry. They dispatched one of their Prayer Warriors to pray over my mother for a few days. I was glad she was too out of it on the illegal generics I'd bought for her to know what was happening.'

'She passed away at home, at peace. The Prayer Warrior blamed his failure on the fact that my mother was a Jew. Funny how he'd never raised that objection before the cheque cleared. I broke his jaw. All that did was add an assault conviction to my list of mistakes. My father blamed himself — for being taken in or not believing hard enough, I could never tell. I swear he was relieved when he had a heart attack six months later.' I'd held my father's hand as he lay on the gurney on the front lawn of our

304

foreclosed house. He'd pleaded with his eyes for me to tell him he was forgiven, while a whisper at my elbow asked me if my father had insurance.

'It shouldn't have happened that way.'

'It shouldn't have,' I said, 'but it did.'

'Things are different now,' Iris said. There was a note in her voice that I couldn't put my finger on but didn't like. 'The Office of Mercy provides free emergency care, runs clinics, and even buys cancer drugs.'

'That would have been great for my father, but my mother wasn't a Christian.'

'The Office of Mercy doesn't care what religion you are.'

'You know that's a lie,' I said. 'The doctors and nurses may not care, but where do you think the Revivalist administrator is going to put my mother on the waiting list? What about Buddhists, or atheists like me?' The word seemed to hurt her, though I hadn't meant it that way. 'Under your benevolent system we're pretty much fucked. When I joined the army I swore to defend this country and its citizens, not its Christians or its Wiccans.'

'Binn isn't a real Christian,' Iris said. 'He's a huckster and a liar who gives real Christians a bad name, that's what Brother Isaiah always said. You can't hold him against us.'

'I can and I will. Brother Isaiah may have opposed him, but that didn't stop the other Elders from going on his show or standing with him on a podium. The man's legion of gullible viewers are too many votes to pass up. They gave

305

him the fucking Presidential Medal of Freedom for 'increasing the nation's faith'!' I pushed past her out of the room.

The other room in her apartment had a television and a designer sofa with a small kitchenette at the back. There was more abstract art on the walls, and bronze Bodhisattvas guarded her spare bookshelf. It felt more like a set for a show about a single girl in Manhattan than a place where somebody actually lived.

'Where are you going?' Iris asked.

'I don't know.' I'd had some ideas about leaving in a rage, but couldn't seem to put my hand on the front door.

'Eat something before you go,' she said. 'You must be starving. Cooking isn't part of my cover, but I do know a good Indian takeout around the corner.'

I was ravenous, and I couldn't go out in public like this anyway. 'What did you do with my suit?' I said.

'It needed dry cleaning, and so did your shirt. They're in that bag hanging on the door.'

I wasn't going anywhere, so I might as well make myself presentable.

★ ★ ★

I took a shower to wash off all the delirium sweat. By the time I got dressed the food had arrived. The first half of the meal we ate in a good silence, the reconciling kind.

'I'm sorry I yelled at you,' I finally said. 'But

that's as far as I'll apologize.'

'The Elders shouldn't associate with a false prophet like Brian Binn,' Iris said. 'Since you were at least a little right, I guess I'll accept what I can get.'

'I don't know why you put up with me,' I said.

'You're a good man. That's such a novelty I want to keep you around.' Something occurred to her, and Iris went to the tiny closet near the front door and brought back my hat. 'I nearly forgot about this,' she said, and put it on my head.

'Thanks.' It was still in good condition, considering. I'd been threatened, lied to, shot at and gassed, but at least I still had my hat on. That had to count for something.

'I found it behind the desk,' Iris said, which would have put it right next to Pyke's body.

'You saw Pyke?' I asked. I wanted to make sure he hadn't been a hallucination.

Iris nodded. 'I was afraid to bring it up before. You didn't . . . '

'I'm not a fan of vigilante justice.'

'Do you know who killed him?'

'I know who I'm supposed to think killed him.'

'That writing on the wall,' Iris said, 'I've seen it before.'

'It's part of an old gay rights chant: 'We're here, we're queer, get used to us.' ' The slogan had come back into fashion as graffiti. It was a reminder for the Revivalists that gay people could be forced back into the closet, but not out of existence. 'Someone wants people to believe gay activists killed Pyke in retaliation for what

307

happened yesterday, and it will work.' They might as well have nailed Pyke to a cross to drive the message home.

'I know you think religious people are gullible — '

'That has nothing to do with it. There are a lot of people whose bread and butter is outrage and conspiracy. Someone in the police will leak the story to the press, and the opportunities for hysterical grandstanding will be too good to pass up: senators can table pointless bills, cable can scream about the fags, and everyone gets to feel good about themselves. Anyone who questions the gravy train will be the target of insinuation or worse.'

Iris believed me, but she didn't want to. 'So many people will know it isn't the truth.'

I shrugged. 'We've been ignoring the truth for years; it's a tough habit to break. Whoever killed Pyke knows how to tell people what they want to hear.' That fact didn't narrow the list of suspects: the country was drowning in quislings, sycophants and ad men. 'I don't really care who killed him. I'm more worried about how his death will affect White's desire to pay up.' I still had the recording of George and Pyke's last conversation. White would need it to eliminate any doubts about Pyke's hand in Brother Isaiah's death. The problem was that he would still want to know Iris's identity, and White didn't take rejection well.

'You still think he killed Brother Isaiah?' She looked disappointed in me.

'He didn't deny planning it, but wouldn't

admit to going all the way. Maybe he was just a pawn.' It would explain why Pyke had been released just in time to meet his maker. 'That's good enough for me. I'm sorry it wasn't a liberal or a terrorist, but you'll have to accept it.'

'That's not why I don't believe you. I just . . . '

I could see in her eyes that it was a question of faith, and she thought I wouldn't understand. She still didn't believe me, and she wouldn't find some peace until she did.

'What can I do to convince you?' I had to find some piece of evidence that would put her mind at rest. I owed her that much.

Iris went into the bathroom and opened the top of the toilet. She pulled a package from the tank, sealed in a plastic bag, and handed it to me.

'What's this?' I asked.

'Everything I have on Thorpe and his son.'

Inside the bag was a memory stick and several folders. They were copies of the Crusade's files on the Thorpe family. 'Why didn't you show me this before?'

'I didn't trust you before. Find something in there that proves Thorpe's innocence.'

From the thickness, the Crusade had showed its usual thoroughness when digging up the secrets of others. 'It may take me a while.'

'There's no rush, and you need to rest. It's time for bed.'

I helped Iris clear things away.

'I'll take the sofa,' I said.

'I can't take a sick man away from his bed.'

There was a pregnant silence. She kissed me. I

kissed her. After that it was a team effort.

Iris drew back suddenly, just far enough to fill my eyes with her conflicted face. 'I'm sorry,' she said. 'I want — I promised Brother Isaiah that I wouldn't have sex again until my wedding night. It seems silly considering everything I've done — '

'You never have to explain yourself to me,' I said.

'I want to. My mother got pregnant when she was seventeen. I don't think she knew who the father was. She was going to have an abortion, but there was only one place in the state that would do it. While she was on the waiting list she went to a pregnancy crisis centre. They showed her pictures of foetuses, told her how the doctors would butcher me, and prayed with her. By the end she decided to have me. When I was six months old she killed herself. She didn't leave a note. Everyone assumed it was post-partum depression and left it at that. The state buried my mother, and I disappeared into the foster system.'

'I don't want to repeat my mother's mistakes, and I don't want to kill a baby that might have been me. I have to keep this promise; I've broken so many others.'

I had her hand, and I couldn't remember when I'd taken it. 'It's better this way. You don't want to get more tangled up with me than you already are,' I said. 'Bad luck follows me around.'

'Me too. If we put our luck together, maybe it will turn good,' she said, but neither of us believed it. She took her hand from mine and

310

went into the bedroom. I did not follow.

I spread the Crusade files out on her coffee table. It had catalogued the Thorpe clan's moral failings with an attention to detail exceeded only by the Book of Life. The reports started two weeks ago and went back for months. Operatives had been assigned to follow both men. Their mail had been opened and their phones tapped. Every infraction was catalogued and numbered according to the book I'd seen in the Crusade office. A month ago, Thorpe Junior had gambled on the horses, solicited a woman for pre-marital sex, and used variations of the word 'penis' ten times in conversation. There were hundreds of pages with the same level of detail. I resisted the urge to raid Iris's liquor cabinet.

After an hour of digging through Junior's adventures in the bars and fleshpots of the city, the only conclusion I'd come to was that I envied his life. I switched to the father. He must have some kind of business connection that made assassinating one of the leading Revivalists in the country an act of economic suicide. Most of the files were open financial records I'd already seen the first time I stuck my nose into his life. Here they were laid out together and cross-referenced, and I began to get a sense of the sheer scale of Marcus Thorpe's wealth. Leaving out the hundreds of millions stashed in a Byzantine collection of numbered overseas bank accounts, Thorpe had two houses in the city, two private jets, a fleet of luxury cars, four other homes in Europe, three in Asia, and that palatial cabin in the Adirondacks.

The file had the same picture I'd seen before of Thorpe and White standing in front of the cabin with the other members of the Free Enterprise Foundation. Something about the photo bothered me, and it wasn't just the shit-eating grins on display. I looked closer at what they were wearing, what was in their hands, anything that might be the source of my irritation. Everything was what you'd expect: expensive cigars, ancient whisky and toxic levels of entitlement. I was surprised the trees could stand to be in the same picture as them.

I stifled a yell and then a stream of curses. The trees that surrounded Thorpe's cabin were pine trees, maybe the same kind as the pine needles that had been found on Brother Isaiah's body. A quick search on the Internet confirmed they were both white pine. It was circumstantial, but the odds of it being a coincidence were non-existent.

The other odds and ends I'd picked up along the way started to fall into place. Brother Isaiah's driver had been found in his car upstate, between the city and the Adirondacks. The stab wounds on the driver were too elegant for a street thug, and unlike anything I'd been taught in the military. They were the work of someone with deadly finesse, a martial artist like Mr Lim.

Thorpe had been involved in Brother Isaiah's murder after all. Iris was right, and if I told her, I'd probably get her killed.

The Day
of Rest

I'd driven through most of the night, taking the Interstate North into the forests of upstate New York. My driver's licence had been suspended because of my condition, so I stayed to the speed limit and drove like a nun. I couldn't afford an encounter with the highway patrol.

The Crusade files had listed the cabin's location, but it was at the end of a private road cut into the forest and difficult to find. Once I got near I asked around at a few all-night gas stations. The size of the building and the aggressiveness of Thorpe's security had made it infamous in those parts, so I had less trouble finding it than I expected. I'd parked about a mile away, but I wasn't getting out of the car.

I couldn't stop thinking about Iris. I'd slipped out not long after I put the pieces together, taking Iris's car keys with me. After all she'd done for me, I didn't feel too good about stealing her car. Hopefully she'd see it as a gesture of affection. It would be best for her if I brought things to an end before she opened her eyes. I'd meant to leave with no explanation for maximum security, but I chickened out at the last minute and wrote a note. If something happened to me Iris deserved to know the truth, and I wanted to say goodbye.

I got on the move at last, leaving the distinctive silhouette of my fedora in the car. I had my pistol, three spare clips of ammunition, a punch dagger strapped to my leg, and a pair of opera glasses I'd found in the glove compartment. It wasn't much considering I was up against a man with his own private army. I stayed low to the uneven ground and relied on the light of the half-moon to navigate. The eastern pines towered above me, watching my progress with the same indifference that they greeted the seasons.

After half a mile, I heard someone whistling. The tune sounded familiar: something sentimental that had haunted the radio for a few weeks and then disappeared. I crouched behind a tree and waited. A red-headed man came into view. From the man's nonchalance it looked like he was out for late-night stroll with his favourite shotgun. I let him saunter past me, and then brought the butt of my gun down on his head. He fell badly, hitting his head on a rock hidden by the undergrowth. I checked his pulse. He was still alive, and he wouldn't need that shotgun any time soon.

Thorpe's cabin was as grotesque as the pictures had suggested. It had two floors and maybe twelve bedrooms. It was made to look like it was built of interlocking pine logs, but it was the first cabin I'd seen whose front porch was held up by Ionic columns. There were two hundred yards of tended grass between the house and the trees, and a large gravel area in front for cars. The whole compound was lit by floodlights that someone had stolen from Yankee Stadium.

I circled the perimeter, staying well behind the tree line. The opera glasses showed me Thorpe sitting in the large front area by a fire. There was a Scotch in his hand and he wasn't doing much of anything. No one else was visible. There should have been more sentries guarding such a besieged and paranoid man. I wished for the thousandth time that I hadn't been forced to leave my black bag with Benny; the microphone would have come in handy to find out who else was here. Thorpe's shadow Mr Lim would be around somewhere, and I had to get the drop on him. Surprise was the only thing I had going for me.

There was a tool shed around the back. It would get me within a hundred yards of a set of windows that led to an anteroom. I watched the room for a quarter of an hour. No one passed through. It was my best way in, but the ground in between was a perfect killing field. The war had made me distrust quiet, open spaces. Crossing an empty square always looked like a cakewalk, until you heard the first crack of a sniper's rifle. However, that knowledge hadn't stopped me from stepping out of cover when I didn't have a choice, and I didn't have one now.

I ran low across the lawn, eyes fixed on the house. No one appeared or shot at me. I took another look at the anteroom through the opera glasses, but it was still empty. The windows were hinged on the outside, which gave me an idea. I slipped inside the unlocked shed and groped around for what I needed. There was a chisel and hammer that would do the trick. I ran up to the side of the house, still unseen.

The only furniture in the anteroom was a single table. Some frontier Americana hung on the walls: colonial hunting parties, men in coonskin caps standing tall on mountains and looking into the distance. Two electric sconces provided more light than I would have liked. The floor was bare hardwood, and probably creaked like hell for the sake of authenticity. There was a corridor on the left side of the room, right next to a staircase leading up. The far right corner opened into another corridor. None of the entrances had doors to shield me from view, but I'd have to take my chances.

I slipped the chisel in between the hinge and the bolt of the window nearest me. I eased the bolt out with taps from the hammer, each strike a boom to my ears in the pre-dawn forest silence. It took for ever to ease the bolt out but no one came to investigate. The hinge came apart. With a final glance inside I pulled open the window. A klaxon loud enough to signal the second coming went off inside the house.

Not my finest hour.

I dived inside the room. I could hear rushed and uneven steps coming from the corridor next to the stairs. I stood flat against the wall near the doorway. The footsteps came closer. I waited until they were almost on me and swung out into the doorway, shotgun braced high. A young man in his Sunday best hit the stock goatee-first. His torso kept running but his face stayed put. The momentum pivoted his body on the stock until it was almost parallel to the floor. There was a moment where it looked like he was floating above the ground in a trance, and then he fell to the floor, out cold or worse. I was quite pleased with myself, until I saw Lim standing in the other doorway, twin revolvers in his hands.

There was no chance I could bring the shotgun to bear before he gave me a new set of air holes. I dropped it and put up my hands. Lim holstered one of his pistols and walked towards me, casual as ever. I wondered if I was going to die now, and then thought about the number of times I'd had to consider the possibility before. It didn't say much for my choice of career or my life in general. Before I had a chance to follow that line of reasoning, everything went black.

★　★　★

A slap in the face woke me up. 'Why are you here?' Thorpe said.

I'd been tied up twice in the last twenty-four hours. The circumstances this time were less favourable. I was in the cabin's foyer, where I'd seen Thorpe nursing a whisky. His breath told me there'd been more than one. Through the big front windows I could see the empty driveway and one side of the neo-classical porch. The large stone fireplace was on my right, a fire burning in its hearth. On the walls were the heads of a menagerie of dead animals.

'Why are you here?' Thorpe asked again.

'I'm too curious for my own good,' I said. 'I want to know why you had Brother Isaiah killed.'

The punch hit hard on my right cheek. Thorpe

might have been a greying man, but there was still a lot of meat behind his hands. My cheek was already starting to swell. Thorpe wound up and made my face symmetrical again.

'We need him alive, sir,' Lim said. 'When White arrives we'll confront him with Strange. It should make him reconsider doing anything stupid.'

Thorpe snorted, swore and hit me again. I got the feeling it was more for the therapeutic value than the chance I'd give something up.

'If White doesn't do as he's told, I'll put him in the ground. There ain't nothing but places to hide a body around here.'

When I ceased to be useful leverage against White, they'd put me in one of Thorpe's convenient forest graves.

He went to the sideboard near the fireplace and made himself a tall drink. Lim took the opportunity to check my bonds. The rope that tied me to the chair was so soft it was almost luxurious.

'Comfortable, isn't it?' he said, near my ear. 'I know the rope is loose, so don't get any ideas. I don't want ligature marks to spoil my narrative.'

The ropes were tied with knots more intricate than Iris's, but the chair I was tied to was a frontier antique. My arms were bound to the three thin spokes that connected the headpiece to the seat. Time had not been kind to the glue that held the joints together.

'You've damaged my property, Strange,' Thorpe said. 'If it wasn't for my employee's cooler head, you wouldn't be alive right now.

Did Ezekiel send you here?'

'I wandered in on my own.'

'Bullshit. Are you here to kill me?'

'Like I said, I came here to find out why you murdered Brother Isaiah. White hired me to find the killer.'

'He knows what happened,' Thorpe said.

'That's news to me. White never let me in on the joke.' I now had no idea why White had bought my services. I'd have to ask him when he showed up.

'What do you know about my son?'

'Just that he was taken by professionals.' That wouldn't be enough to placate Thorpe, but if I lied it would only make things worse once White showed up.

'My son may not be the best person in the world, but he's mine,' Thorpe said. 'It was hard enough keeping him out of trouble before that preacher and his army of snitches came to town. When Brother Isaiah stuck that video in my face, I thought he was after money. I'd paid to have my son's problems go away before, and Isaiah wasn't the first holy man to come to me with his hand out. All he did at first was quote scripture: 'The wages of sin are death', 'I am the way and the life' ' — Thorpe waved the good book away with his drink — 'like I hadn't heard that bullshit all my goddamn life. I told him to stop preaching and name his price.'

'But Brother Isaiah didn't play ball,' I said.

'He didn't want money. The son of a bitch was after my son's soul. Junior's baptized, just like I am, but Methodism wasn't good enough for him. Too soft and weak, Isaiah said, not willing to stand up for the truth of God's mission. The only way my boy could repent was to be baptized into his congregation. I'm not a religious man, but my father marched against segregation as a Methodist. If it was good enough for him, it's good enough for me and my fucking son.' Thorpe upended his glass.

'Do you know the word vendetta?' Thorpe asked.

'I've run into it once or twice.'

'I admire the word. It sounds exactly like what it means.' Thorpe started towards the whisky but then thought better of it. 'I've broken men financially. Ruined them. I've fought and clawed and made grown men cry, and I'm not ashamed of any of it. It's just business. But in all my years I've never messed with someone's family. It's a line you just don't cross. Once you do, the rules change.'

So that was the story he told himself, the reason he could feel justified. 'You had no choice.'

'You're goddamn right I didn't. He refused to negotiate, and the Elders wouldn't or couldn't rein him in. I think they saw it as the perfect opportunity to get rid of me. Mr Lim objected, but he didn't understand what was at stake.'

Lim's face was impassive; the mask that hid his contempt for his employer had been screwed back into place.

'Killing a man like Brother Isaiah was harder than you'd think,' Thorpe continued. 'He may have put his faith in God, but his organization sure didn't. Two cars full of security followed him everywhere. They'd set up a perimeter before they let the old man leave his car. The people he visited were even more paranoid: cringing bureaucrats, businessmen pissing themselves with fear. Their security details were as elaborate as mine.'

'So who came up with the idea to kill him here?' I asked, looking at Lim.

He didn't acknowledge my eyes.

'White, by accident,' Thorpe said. Alcohol had loosened his tongue, but it was triumph that had set it wagging. He needed no encouragement to tell me exactly how clever he'd been. 'He came to me swinging his dick, saying he could solve all my problems, get Brother Isaiah to see reason. Well, that's what I kept leeches like him on the payroll for. He said he'd talked to Brother Isaiah, and he'd agreed to have a private heart-to-heart with my son. The arrogant old bastard thought my boy would fall to his knees and praise Jesus the minute he heard his voice. Of course I had no intention of letting him within a mile of my son.'

'Why didn't you smuggle him out of the country?'

Thorpe's face darkened. I thought he had taken my question personally, and braced myself for another hit. It never came.

'The Crusade had pulled strings to ground my jet, and they had spies everywhere. I thought it would be safer to hide him in the city, where I still had friends.'

That explained what Junior had told his

friend: he was going to miss his hot date because he had to appear to be on his way north. If he was out spending his father's money, the Crusade would hear about it.

'So how did the Elders find him?' I asked.

'I don't know. I took every precaution.' Thought of his son's kidnapping had brought back the rage I'd first seen, burning away his smugness. 'It's all that goddamn preacher's fault. My son is God-knows-where, there's panic on the streets, and the FBI is coming after my black ass in a few hours; all because that damn preacher didn't understand how the world works.' He threw the empty glass in the fireplace, cursed under his breath and lurched out of the room, mumbling something about the kitchen.

'He was off his rag about the damage to his little cabin, but I didn't hear anything about your two men,' I said, when Thorpe had gone. 'Either of them awake yet?'

'One is driving the other to the hospital,' Lim said. 'May I offer you a drink?'

'That's very kind of you,' I said, 'but I don't see how I'm going to drink it.'

Lim poured two fingers of single malt into a glass and made room for it on the table beside me. He stuck in a flexible straw and pointed it towards my face.

'Much obliged.' I took a sip. The whisky was even better than what I'd had at Thorpe's office.

Lim poured one for himself and pulled up a chair.

'I have to admit, you've had me going the wrong way all along,' I said. 'Pyke was the perfect scapegoat.' Pyke in turn had groomed a patsy of his own: Jack Small. It was a Matryoshka set-up; one frame nested inside another.

Lim took his time answering; he seemed locked in a staring contest with the stag's head behind me. 'There's a perverse aspect to my profession,' he said, which was quite an understatement. 'The better I do my work, the fewer traces of myself I leave in the world. Like an atom, people will see only the effect of my actions, not the person doing them. If I do my job perfectly, then no record of me will exist. I thought perhaps you would understand.'

'I'm not an assassin,' I said, without judgement. I wanted to see where he was going.

'You were a soldier. Both professions require the killing of perfect strangers for reasons known only to your superiors.'

'My enemies tended to be armed and fighting back.'

'I'm sure that gave the victims of your air strikes comfort.'

'You're changing the subject,' I said.

He didn't answer, but I could tell he was dying to talk shop.

'What's it going to hurt to satisfy the curiosity of a dead man?'

Lim sipped his drink and watched me with detached amusement. 'Pyke wasn't exactly a scapegoat,' Lim said. 'He fully intended to kill Brother Isaiah; he was just too incompetent to do it properly.'

'So you gave him some professional help,' I

said. Once enough suspicion had been heaped on Pyke, Lim had made it stick. It was hard for a man to defend his good name when he was dead. 'Did you kill Brother Isaiah?' I asked.

'I had no choice. Thorpe was afraid to use me or any of his other professionals, so he brought in those idiots from Los Angeles. I took one look at them and knew they'd botch the job. I would have to do it myself.'

'You're quite a control freak when it comes to murder,' I said. 'Didn't your employer object?'

'He threw a tantrum and accused me of insubordination, but he had to acknowledge I had made the right decision. Brother Isaiah wouldn't have left that car until he saw someone he knew. What did he expect those two idiots to do: blow up his car like some gangland assassination?' Lim's nose wrinkled a little. 'Even if it had worked, it would have been a mess.' He was disgusted at the amateurishness of it all.

'You were there to greet them, Thorpe's right-hand man. I saw the body of Isaiah's driver, Krenz. Why did you kill him with a knife and not one of those revolvers?'

'I showed him my empty holsters as I approached the car. I thought it would reassure them, and it did. Besides, I'm attached to those guns. I wouldn't want them showing up on a police report.'

I had noticed one of his holsters was empty now as well. I couldn't see the other.

'Imagine the driver is about here,' Lim said, tracing a figure in the air. 'He has just finished helping Brother Isaiah out of the car. He's turning back to me, and beginning to realize that something is wrong. He wore a shoulder holster, so he reached across his body for his weapon. I pinned his arm against his chest with my left hand, and then . . . ' Lim cut the air with a phantom knife in his right hand. In one undulating movement, he stabbed the temple, dragged the blade down the driver's face, and thrust into the imaginary neck.

It was the same movement I'd first seen in his walk at Thorpe's office. The motion began at the hips, two quick turns — left-right-left-right — was all the time Lim needed to take a man's life.

'Effective.'

Lim took that remark as the high compliment it was. 'Thank you.'

'And Brother Isaiah?'

'He didn't put up much of a fight. The real challenge was leaving no signs of a struggle,' Lim said. 'Once I had control of him, I strangled Isaiah with an electrical cord. It leaves no fibres behind, and it's easy to dispose of. The only thing left was the men Thorpe had hired. Normally I would have killed them just for peace of mind — '

'But you sent them after me instead.'

'I didn't want their trip to be wasted,' Lim replied. His thrift when it came to the time of two criminals had cost a lot of people in the Starlight their lives.

'You killed him here, rolled his body in one of the carpets' — I saw that the area around the front door was suspiciously bare — 'and drove him all the way to midtown. Why not just get rid of the body?'

'I had orders to follow.'

'Were the drugs and porn you left behind part of it?'

Lim nodded.

After all Thorpe's raging, it didn't take a genius to see that it had been personal.

'I was against the whole idea,' Lim said. If there was any apology in his voice, it was only to distance himself from a bad operation. 'It was irrational.'

'So why stick with him?' I asked. 'Your dental plan can't be that good. His days are numbered from where I'm sitting.'

Lim smiled. 'It's the bargain all foot soldiers make,' he said. 'We are relieved of responsibility for making the big decisions, but must carry them out even when they are obviously insane. Besides, if I left they'd hunt me down.'

I didn't get a chance to ask who they were. A black luxury sedan crunched the gravel outside and came to a stop. White got out, alone. Lim met him at the door.

'Where's Marcus?' White asked, giving Lim his Russian fur hat. 'I haven't got much time — ' The colour in his face fled along with his voice as soon as he saw me. 'What's he doing here?'

'That's what I want to know,' Thorpe said, coming into the room. 'Just why did you hire a private dick to spy on me?'

White's voice didn't seem to want to answer. He took a step back and his eyes showed his body the way to the door.

Lim closed it behind him. 'Perhaps you should sit down, Mr White.' Lim guided White to the chair he had only recently occupied.

'Why did you hire me?' I said. 'You already knew the answer you wanted me to find. It wasn't to look for a scapegoat; I'm sure you've got a dozen of them stashed somewhere, suitable for any occasion. What was I looking for?'

'Not another word from you,' White hissed at me. 'I wanted reassurances that no one else knew,' he said to Thorpe.

He laughed in White's face. 'Do you really expect me to believe that?'

'He wanted reassurances all right,' I said, 'reassurances that you wouldn't turn on him later.' The whole rotten picture was becoming clear. 'It was evidence against you he had me looking for,' I said to Thorpe. 'He couldn't use one of his Daveys; you'd clock him immediately. What hole were you going to throw me in when I got what you wanted, Ezekiel?' I strained against the ropes in a little play-act, pretending I was trying to get my hands on White's throat. It was a good excuse to weaken the glue that held my chair together.

Lim put his hands on me. 'Be still.'

I did as I was told, for now.

'I don't appreciate this kind of welcome,' White said. 'I'm here to get you out of trouble.'

'Get me out of trouble, just like you did the last time?' Thorpe said. 'We wouldn't be here in the first place if you could do your job.'

'We wouldn't be here if you hadn't overreacted,' White said.

'He threatened my son!'

All week long people had talked about Jesus, but I hadn't seen Him around lately. What I did see were assholes fighting among themselves for money and power in His name. They were children playing white hat black hat, and you'd think it was funny until you realized all the guns were loaded.

'I don't think you understand what you've done,' White said. 'If you didn't have so many friends in the Pentagon, you'd be dead already.'

I had been wondering why, if the Elders really fingered him for the deed, Thorpe was still free and breathing. There were a lot of men with stars on their shoulders depending on him for their retirement.

'That hasn't stopped the Elders from trying to lynch me,' Thorpe said. 'What the hell do they think they're doing?'

'They think they're fighting a civil war. What did you expect?' White said to Thorpe's disbelieving face. 'You assassinated one of them.'

'It was personal.'

'I've finally managed to convince them of that. The Pentagon is adamant that Thorpe Industries continue supplying the troops. In order to avoid a conflict with the Joint Chiefs that really could become a civil war, I have been authorized to make you an offer.'

Now that White had the upper hand, he took some time making himself comfortable. 'The terms are these: you sell the Elders a controlling stake in Thorpe Industries, and leave the country in twenty-four hours. In return, they will let you live.'

'What about my son?'

'Junior will meet you at the airport. He'll be there to see you sign the paperwork.'

Thorpe's hands clenched and released a few times. For a second I thought he was going to hit White, but he was thinking about his options, not violence.

'How much will the Elders buy at?' Thorpe asked.

'Current market value,' White said.

Something wasn't right. If White handled it well this deal could be a stepping stone to filling the vacancy left by Brother Isaiah on the Council of Elders. This negotiation should be the most important of White's life, but he was talking like a bored schoolboy reciting the Declaration of Independence. In a cannier operator it would have been a pose adopted for the sake of negotiation, but White's poker face wasn't that good.

'I'd talk to the Elders directly if I were you,' I said to Thorpe.

'What do you know about business?' Thorpe shot back.

'I know it thrives on finding the cheapest, easiest option. If you die, all your shares go to your son, don't they?' Thorpe didn't have to say anything to tell me I was right. 'They already have control of your son, and there are thousands of MBAs eager to fill your shoes.'

White wanted to rise and shut me up, but a

look from Thorpe kept him in his place.

'White has been betting against you all along. Who do you think has been shorting your stock all week?'

White cast an anxious glance at Lim that I couldn't read. Maybe he was afraid Thorpe would turn him loose.

'The Pentagon would never allow it,' Thorpe said, but he doubted his own words.

'All the Elders have to do is assure them the new guy will honour whatever promises you've made. The Elders couldn't risk someone finding out that you got away with killing one of them. There's no reason to let you live; all the incentives go the other way.'

Marcus Thorpe hadn't built a business empire out of nothing through dumb luck. His instincts had been muddled with alcohol and fury, but they were still functioning. He knew I was right, and that knowledge was eating away at the composure he'd fought hard to regain.

He leaned over White. 'You've forgotten where you came from, brother. Ezekiel White was a shitkicker at a no-name hick university before I made you into something. You think that tin star in your pocket makes you better than me? I can still put you down any time I want, and nobody will even notice. There's a dozen other chumps just waiting to take your place. Now tell me where my son is, if you want to leave this fucking room alive.'

Instead of intimidating White, Thorpe's vitriol had the opposite effect. White's face was a cool mask, a smug curl on his plump lips.

'You're still keeping it real, brother,' White said, playing up his accent. 'I guess what my pa used to say was right: 'You can take the monkey out of the jungle . . . ' '

Thorpe straightened up. His face had a terrible calm I recognized. 'Mr Lim,' he said.

White looked to Lim, but the curl in his lips remained. Mr Lim drew my pistol — newly adorned with a silencer — and blew off half of Marcus Thorpe's skull.

For a moment nobody moved.

'What took you so long?' White said to Lim, rising out of his chair. 'I had to make all that up on the spot.'

'I wanted to see how much Mr Strange could figure out.'

'You have misplaced priorities,' White said, and inspected the body with distaste. 'This unfortunate incident never would have happened if you'd done your job,' he said to me.

'I'm sorry to disappoint you,' I said. The parts of the chair felt loose enough to give if I gave them a big push. I'd weakened them further when I jerked in surprise at what Mr Lim had just done. That hadn't been an act.

'The terms of our agreement haven't changed,' Lim said to White.

'Drop the gun and we can get down to business.'

I looked at the way Lim was watching White, and counted the minutes that the latter had to live. White didn't know the type of wolf he'd invited into the parlour. Lim unscrewed the silencer and dropped my automatic beside Thorpe's body.

'I'll wire the money to your account as soon as I've heard the recording,' White said.

'You still need it?' Lim said.

'Of course I do. How else can I prove to the Council that I was right?'

I could see the highlight reel in White's head: he would tell them that a confidential informant had given him whatever this incriminating recording was. He came to the Adirondacks to question Thorpe but found him dead by my hand, killed in a dispute over money. I would be named as Brother Isaiah's assassin, maybe even Pyke's as well. A nationwide manhunt would be declared, and my body would be left somewhere where White and his Daveys could find it, showing up the FBI. It wouldn't be hard for White to parlay all that glory into a seat on the Council.

White was looking at me, and so was Lim. 'Feel free to shoot him any time,' the latter said. 'We have things to do.'

White shook his head. 'There's a loose end,' he said. 'He had dinner with a woman on Thursday. He might have told her something.'

'He couldn't have told her anything useful, and there will be no evidence in any case.' Lim sighed. 'I know what you're suggesting, but torture is a long and extremely tedious business.'

'My men know how to get answers without leaving any marks,' White said. 'I'll shoot him just before he's scheduled to be arrested. Leave it to me; I'll take care of both of them.'

Lim looked at White and then at me. He was still considering his options when someone took a shot at him through the front window.

Both men dived to the ground. The floodlights and everything in the cabin went dark. I wrapped my legs around those of the chair and pushed down hard while I pulled up on the seat. They separated. I kicked away what was left and broke the back with my arms. I was mostly free.

White had crawled out of the room, but Lim was flat against the wall watching the tree line. No more shots came. He seemed bemused by my escapology. 'I didn't think you could do that.'

'I found my spinach.'

'I'm glad,' Mr Lim said, and it seemed he genuinely was. 'Our appointment is long overdue.'

'I'm not comfortable hitting a man who wears glasses.'

'They're cosmetic,' he said, and began to take them off.

'I know,' I replied, and threw a lamp at his head.

Lim dodged easily out of the way, his smile wider by several degrees. A switchblade appeared in his hand by an act of prestidigitation.

When facing an attacker with a knife, the best option is to shoot him. If a gun isn't handy, the next best choice is to skedaddle in the opposite direction as fast as possible. After that, all the other likely possibilities involved internal bleeding. The remains of the chair were still tied to my arms. It was time to get creative.

I swung the chair spoke in my right hand. Lim

stayed out of the way, but it forced him to keep his distance. He ducked one of my swings and pulled at the carpet I was standing on. I stumbled back a step, and the rope got caught in a table. I was now tethered to a Victorian monstrosity that would have taken three men to lift.

Lim found my predicament hilarious. We circled the end table. I kept him at bay with the stick in my other hand, but that wasn't going to work for ever. Lim slashed at my face and I stopped it with the rope. His force cut it clean. Lim threw the switchblade at me with a casual flick. I dodged out of the way, but didn't see both his feet coming in.

The kick sent me through the window and rolling on to the gravel outside. Lim stepped through the window frame, switchblade back in his hand.

'You're holding back,' I said in between gasps.

'That doesn't sound like a thank you.'

'Why should I thank you?' I said. 'You only want to draw things out. What's the matter, did you get tired of killing defenceless people?'

'Pyke tried to have you killed,' Lim said. 'I would expect a little gratitude.'

'The fruit basket is in the mail.'

Lim surveyed the grounds, barely paying attention to me. 'I'd love to continue this conversation, Mr Strange,' he said, 'but there's an unknown gunman on the premises, and I have to find White before he crawls too far.'

'He's a loose end now too, isn't he?'

'Everyone is a loose end,' Lim said. 'I haven't

forgotten about your mystery woman. I promise it will be painless; I pride myself on that where women are concerned.'

I decided not to compliment Lim on his sense of chivalry. 'Can you at least tell me the ending you have planned?'

'I'm afraid not. You've wasted too much of my time defending yourself.' Lim showed me an open palm, and it beckoned me forward.

I came at him with the stick in my left hand. My weapon was slower than his, and Lim was already much faster. He sidestepped away from my swing and cut my hand, severing tendons and nerves. The stick dropped from my dead hand. Lim thrust in and I twisted out of the way, slapping his arm. It disrupted Lim's balance for less than a second, but it was enough time to encircle his knife arm with mine. I pulled with my left and pushed with my right, and Lim's arm snapped. He didn't make a sound. Lim turned a little and elbowed me in the head with his good arm. I got my face out of the way of most of it, but the force that was left still sent me stumbling to the ground three feet away.

Lim left his switchblade on the ground. He didn't seem to be in much pain from his broken arm, nor did he seem angry at me for breaking it. Nothing was as important as killing me with the one he could still use. He advanced towards me with deliberate steps, a hunter in no rush to finish off the kill. I coughed and twisted on the ground to disguise the hand in my sock. When he got close I reared up, my punch dagger in my right hand.

Lim caught me on the way in with his good arm. The punch was all the power of his body focused into a single point. I felt the energy go inside me, damaging nerves and bursting blood vessels. It nearly killed me, but it was too late. My dagger had found a home in Lim's heart.

We fell to the ground, locked together. I coughed up blood and anything left in my stomach. Mr Lim was still. I pulled myself up enough so that I could look in his eyes. He was still here, but not for much longer.

'Who are they?' I asked. 'Who do you really work for?'

All that intelligence, humour and menace faded from his eyes. I shook him and asked the same question over and over again. Lim said nothing. He was loyal until the end, and I understood why. I might have been the same way, if the army hadn't betrayed me first.

Lim and White had been haggling over some kind of recording. I searched his pockets and found a little digital recorder like mine inside his coat. I pressed play. Instead of the sound of Thorpe's voice, White's negotiations with Lim filled the darkness. That clever son of a bitch had suckered White with a story about a fake recording in order to make a real one.

'I had nothing to do with it.' The voice was White's, and it was coming from the house. My gun was still in there. I crept up to the window I'd recently exited from and looked inside, but it was too dark. I climbed in just as White marched into the room. Behind him was someone I would have given everything not to see here.

Iris was wearing the same tan raincoat she'd worn when I first saw her in Chinatown. I don't know why I noticed it, or the jade clip that held her hair back as it had before. They felt more important than the gun she was pointing at White.

'Hello, Felix.'

'What are you doing here?' I didn't know what else to say.

'I had to be here. Brother Ezekiel is about to testify.'

The confidence Lim's betrayal had given White was gone, leaving a frightened carrion animal in a cheap suit. 'Who is this woman?'

'My dinner date, and Junior's buyer,' I said. 'She was quite fond of the man you helped to kill.'

'I had nothing to do with it,' White said, his eyes ping-ponging between us.

'Then why are you here?' Iris said.

I thought for a moment she was going to hit him with the gun, but she kept her temper.

Against the wall, White began to speak his native language. 'There's still twenty thousand dollars coming your way, Strange.'

'It looks like I'll have to collect it from your estate.'

'I'll pay you double — ten times,' he said, when I showed no desire to move, 'anything you want, just get this crazy bitch away from me.'

The pay-day White promised could keep me in medicine for a decade, with a little left over for the first vacation I'd ever had. Best of all, it would get me away from all the married

Casanovas and insurance chisellers I had to deal with to make a living. Money was capable of a lot of things, but it couldn't have picked me off the floor while I was foaming at the mouth, or taken care of me until the seizures passed. 'If I were you, I'd throw yourself on her Christian mercy while there's still some left.'

White mopped his brow. 'May I have a drink please?'

I mixed him a large gin and tonic. He took it with the first look of gratitude I'd ever seen on his face, and drank half of it in one gulp. He coughed, swallowed hard, and began to speak.

'The dispute between Thorpe and Brother Isaiah was getting worse. If it wasn't resolved, the whole Holy Land project was in danger. I offered my services as mediator.'

'I'll bet you did,' I said.

'Why would Brother Isaiah trust you?' Iris said.

'We may not have liked each other, but he trusted my position as one of the country's pre-eminent law enforcement officers.' White tried to raise himself up enough to be worthy of the embellishment, but he failed and only made Iris more angry. 'I may have insinuated that I spoke for the other Elders.'

'You led him into a trap,' Iris said. It was a statement, like a line on a tax return, no emotion.

'That's crazy,' White said, smart enough to say it like a plea and not an accusation. 'I thought Thorpe would tell the boy what to say to satisfy the old man, and everything would be smoothed over. I swear on my soul I didn't know what he had planned.' White reached out his hands in supplication.

Iris stepped back and tightened her grip on the gun. 'You're as guilty as the rest. You tried to make an exception for Junior. You knew who killed Brother Isaiah and you did nothing.'

'I was trying to save our holy project in the Middle East.' The gin had started a small fire in White's cavernous belly. He didn't think he had anything left to lose. 'Brother Isaiah was going to ruin everything because he refused to see the bigger picture. What is the soul of one young degenerate compared to the return of the Kingdom of God on Earth?'

'All that time spent studying the Bible, and you don't understand a single word our Lord said. What we do to the least of us, we do to Him. When men like you talk about the 'big picture' or the 'real world', you're just looking for an excuse to appease sin. Junior cried out for help in the battle for his soul and you gave him cheap indulgence, not true forgiveness. Brother Isaiah went to Africa to escape people like you.' Iris cocked the hammer on her gun.

Tears began to form at the corners of White's eyes. I remembered all the times White had appeared on television, demanding an eye for an eye from whomever America's enemy was that day. Now it looked like he was about to experience Old Testament justice first-hand.

'He's not worth it, Iris,' I said.

'The Elders will never allow him to be tried.

They'll force him to retire and then hide him in a university.'

'Then we go to the foreign press.' I pressed play on Lim's recorder. White reacted to his own voice with a stolid indifference, as broken and afraid as he could possibly be already.

'It won't be enough,' Iris said.

'You've never killed a man in cold blood,' I said. 'You haven't seen the scars it leaves.'

She tried to smile at me, but Iris couldn't get all the tiny muscles in her face to do their job. What came out was broken and painful to see. 'I'm sorry, Felix. My cheek will not turn.' She shot White twice in the chest.

He stared at her in amazement. White tried to open his mouth to say something, but all that came out was blood. We watched him die.

'It's over, Iris,' I said. 'Put down the gun.'

She turned it on me instead. My pistol was still on the ground by Thorpe's body. 'Are you going to turn me in, Felix?'

'Are you going to shoot me?'

We both knew the answers to our questions. Iris dropped the gun.

'What do we do now?' she asked.

'You are going to run,' I said. 'You just put two bullets in a sworn officer of the law. Whatever they may have thought of the man, the FBI won't take that sort of behaviour lightly.'

'By the time they arrive, we could both be gone.'

I thought of the Crusade's second-favourite word after sin: temptation. I hadn't been tempted by anything in a long while; the last time I had followed its siren call was in Tehran. It had cost me. 'Everyone who knows about you is dead. It's the perfect opportunity to start over. Too many people know who I am. Sooner or later they'd come looking. You're safer without me.'

'Besides,' I said, before she could protest, because I wasn't sure if I could stand it, 'people need to see this, whether they want to or not.' Maybe it would make a difference. More likely it would get swept under the rug. I wasn't going to get paid either way, so I might as well do something right for a change.

She didn't know what to say.

'How did you get here?' I said.

'I stole a car,' she said. 'I left it a mile or so down the road.'

'Leave it there. You'll need these,' I said, and threw her the MG's keys. 'It's got nearly a full charge. White wasn't brave enough to come completely alone. There'll be Daveys waiting somewhere for his signal.' I couldn't help but look at White's body. 'They'll get restless sooner or later. You'd better get going.'

'Thanks,' Iris said.

We didn't know what else to say. We never did.

Iris started towards me and then stopped. Somehow it would be easier if she left now, if we didn't touch. That way we could pretend that we'd already said goodbye some time before, that the pain was already over, and we were now in each other's dreams.

'Take care of yourself, Felix.'

'I'll see what I can do.'

Before she went out the front door, Iris set her phone on the sideboard. She didn't look back. I watched her walk into the forest. The back of her head disappeared first, hair the same colour as the night. For a moment all I saw was the outline of her body in its tan shell, before the darkness took the rest of her from me.

I looked around Thorpe's cabin. There was a lot of my blood on the floor, a lot of blood in general, but I was still alive. I opened my phone. It took four rings for Benny to answer. Nothing coherent came out of his mouth.

'Benny, I'm in the Adirondacks.'

'Fuck you.'

'Listen to me for a second and I'll save your career. Marcus Thorpe is dead and Ezekiel White is lying two feet away from him. It's a long story and I haven't got time to explain, just get down here and bring your ADIC. When he sees this, he'll want to kiss you on the mouth. And call an ambulance; I think I might need one.' I gave him the address and then hung up before he could yell at me. If he wasn't awake enough to remember it they could use my phone to find me.

The dance with Lim had left a lot of marks. Some ribs were broken. I was probably bleeding internally. The world was spinning a little off its axis and I needed to sit down. I found a chair and set it near the window. The forest was impossibly quiet and dark, now that humans and their machines had fallen silent.

That Isaiah would be made into a martyr was a foregone conclusion; I just didn't know what the official reason would be. Revivalist vultures would circle his corpse, trying to tear off a bit of his flesh for their own good cause. A hundred other men would trample each other underfoot in a race to take up his mantle and the millions of faithful souls that came with it. They wouldn't have time to covet the Crusade; the Elders would crush it before the week was out. The whole spectacle would be unseemly and routine.

Three people had died this morning. In the last week, Pyke, Ernest, George and those people in the Starlight had all gone underground. Now that he was no longer useful, Thorpe Junior's days were numbered. They were still cleaning up Christopher Park, the stack of body-bags that held the true believers and the queers on ice somewhere far from public view. It was one hell of a butcher's bill, and I couldn't tell you what we had gotten in return.

Iris's phone squawked to life. 'Good evening and welcome to a special Brother Isaiah's Hour of Deliverance,' said an announcer. 'Our dear brother could not be with us this evening, but he sent a message he earnestly wants you to hear.'

'Brothers and sisters, in the last few years I have travelled all over this great country spreading the news of our Lord's love and forgiveness.' Brother Isaiah's voice filled the cabin, resonating off the tacky surfaces and making them almost majestic. 'There is a question I know many of you would like answered, because it is the one I hear most often.

It is a question that the disciples asked of Jesus Himself: 'What shall be the sign of Thy coming, and of the end of the world?' '

The moon passed behind a cloud. I thought about Iris, and watched the towering pines fade to jagged-edged silhouettes.

Acknowledgements

This book never would have seen the light of day if it wasn't for my agent Rob Dinsdale and my editor Kate Parkin. Both made a considerable leap of faith.

Kingdom Coming by Michelle Goldberg and *American Fascists* by Chris Hedges provided inspiration for how American bureaucracy could be used to serve ideological ends, as well as the blogs talkingpointsmemo, Glen Greenwald's Unclaimed Territory and many more. The website biblegateway.com was the source of scripture cited in the novel, and an indispensable reference.

For advice on more elevated matters, I turned to my mother, Reverend Sharyn Hall, and Rabbi Sidney Brichto. My thanks to you both.

The Kung Fu and Tai Chi in this book is based on the teachings of Sifu Andrew Sofos and Sifu Mark Green, respectively. All mistakes and exaggerations are the fault of the student, not the master.

Finally, my greatest thanks to Alice. She knows why.

We do hope that you have enjoyed reading this large print book.

Did you know that all of our titles are available for purchase?

We publish a wide range of high quality large print books including:
Romances, Mysteries, Classics
General Fiction
Non Fiction and Westerns

Special interest titles available in large print are:
The Little Oxford Dictionary
Music Book
Song Book
Hymn Book
Service Book

Also available from us courtesy of Oxford University Press:
Young Readers' Dictionary
(large print edition)
Young Readers' Thesaurus
(large print edition)

For further information or a free brochure, please contact us at:
Ulverscroft Large Print Books Ltd.,
The Green, Bradgate Road, Anstey,
Leicester, LE7 7FU, England.
Tel: (00 44) 0116 236 4325
Fax: (00 44) 0116 234 0205

Other titles published by
The House of Ulverscroft:

IF IT BLEEDS

Duncan Campbell

Infamous gangster Charlie Hook wants someone to write his biography. He chooses crime reporter Laurie Lane as ghost writer. But the next day Hook is dead, his blood and hair on the walls of his north London mansion. Who killed the last of the London Godfathers? Laurie needs to find the killer to keep his job. There are several possible suspects: the Russian businessman with something dodgy in his Hampstead garden, Hook's two sinister public schoolboy sons, and the relatives of men whom Hook had killed decades ago. And what secrets lurk in Hook's empire? Laurie's search for the killer takes him to the bars of Thailand, and the bowels of the Old Bailey — as bizarre and hair-raising a journey as it is potentially lethal . . .

JUSTICE DENIED

J. A. Jance

The investigation of LaShawn Tompkins'
murder seems straightforward. Just another
ex-drug dealer caught up in turf warfare.
Seattle investigator J.P. Beaumont is handed
the assignment under the strictest confidence. But as Beau starts digging the
situation becomes more complicated. It
appears that LaShawn really had turned over
a new leaf. Someone had targeted the man
for death. Meanwhile, Beau's lover and fellow
cop, Mel Soames, is given her own hush-hush
investigation. A routine check on registered
sex offenders has revealed a disturbing
pattern of death by unnatural causes. The
latest suggests an inside job and Mel isn't
letting go. As Mel's investigation becomes
entangled with Beau's, the two begin to
uncover a nightmarish conspiracy involving
people in high places — which could include
their own.